Caffeine Night

C000240555

The Crooked Beat

Nick Quantrill

Nick Quantrill

When Joe Geraghty's brother finds himself in financial trouble, it's only natural that he turns to the Private Investigator for help. But when it relates to a missing consignment of smuggled cigarettes, it's not so easily sorted. Drawn into the murky world of local and international criminals around the busy port of Hull, Geraghty knows the only way to save his brother is to take on the debt himself. As he attempts to find a way out of the situation, the secrets and conspiracies he uncovers are so deeply buried in the past, he knows he's facing people willing to do whatever it takes to keep them that way.

The Crooked Beat

Fiction aimed at the heart and the head...

Published by Caffeine Nights Publishing 2013

Published in Great Britain by Caffeine Nights Publishing

www.caffeine-nights.com

British Library Cataloguing in Publication Data.
A CIP catalogue record for this book is available from the British Library

ISBN: 978-1-907565-56-4

Cover design by
Mark (Wills) Williams

Everything else by
Default, Luck and Accident

Also by Nick Quantrill

Joe Geraghty Novels

Broken Dreams
The Late Greats

Novellas

Bang Bang You're Dead

Dedication:

For my mum, Sylvia Quantrill.

Acknowledgments:

With thanks to…

Darren Laws, Sandra Mangan and Mark Williams at Caffeine Nights. Writing some words down is the easy bit. Turning them into a book is much harder.

Ian Ayris, Paul Brazill and Luca Veste for gamely reading the early drafts and offering help and advice without complaint. Fine writers one and all.

Andy Rivers at Byker Books for indulging me with the novella and short stories. Top man.

Nick Triplow for his entertaining and wise company on the motorways of Northern England. "The Humber Beat" is always available for bookings at libraries, bookshops, and pretty much anywhere you can hold a function.

Jason Goodwin remains a man of great patience and impeccable character as he digs me out of one hole after another with the website.

I've been fortunate enough to meet countless readers, writers, librarians and members of the press over the last three years. There really are too many to mention, but you know who you are.

Richard Sutherland for the use of his name…

Lastly, I wouldn't be writing without the support, patience and love of my wife, Cathy, and my daughter, Alice. I'm very lucky.

Drop me a line:

www.nickquantrill.co.uk
www.twitter.com/nickquantrill

The Crooked Beat

To,
Jindy,

With best wishes

Nick Quantrill

The Crooked Beat............... Nick Quantril

Hull, December 1979

*'I'll say it again, slowly this time, so you understand,'
Andrew Bancroft said. 'I don't want to talk to you, Don. I
don't like you. I think you're a cunt.'*

*Ridley sat back in his chair. 'It's Detective Constable
Ridley to you. Not Don.' He paused for a moment. 'And
watch your mouth.'*

'I want to talk to Holborn.'

*'You're talking to me. Detective Inspector Holborn isn't
available.'*

*'Out doing proper work is he?' Bancroft took a drag on
his cigarette. 'Not wasting his time talking to me in this
shitty interview room of yours?'*

'I told you to watch your mouth.'

*Bancroft repeated his request. 'I want to speak to
Holborn.'*

'Tell me about the money I found on you.'

*Ridley waved the question away. 'Won it on the horses,
didn't I?'*

*'Right.' Ridley placed the money he'd taken off Bancroft
on the table. A mixture of notes - ones, fives and tens.
'There's about £200 here. Looks like the takings out of the
pub's till to me.'*

*Bancroft finished his cigarette, stubbed it out and stared at
Ridley. 'I like a bet, don't I?'*

*'You won it on a bet with the landlord? Is that what you're
telling me?'*

*'When did it become illegal to have some money in your
pocket?'*

*'Depends how you got that money. Did the landlord just
hand it over to you?'*

'Like I said, I like a bet.'

'And you were collecting your winnings?'

Bancroft smiled and nodded.

'We'll see what the landlord has to say.'

Bancroft laughed. 'You think he'll speak to you?'

'I saw you with my own eyes. You were taking protection money off the man.'

'You saw fuck all, Don.' Bancroft leaned back. 'You can to do better than that, surely?'

Ridley rattled off a long list of convictions. 'It doesn't look good, does it?'

'It doesn't look good for me?' Bancroft said. 'What about you? You're going nowhere, hanging around pubs, accusing innocent men like me. Anyone who knows what they're doing is on Sagar's team, trying to catch whoever set that house on fire. They're not chained to the station making cups of tea for when they come back.'

Ridley lunged across the table at Bancroft and grabbed his coat. 'Don't forget who you're speaking to.'

Bancroft smiled. 'Be a good lad, Don, and take your hands off me.'

Ridley let go, sat back in his chair and took a deep breath.

'What's Sagar so wound up about, anyway?' Bancroft said. 'Everyone knows what that family are, bothering people all day and night, taking the piss.'

'That's not the point.'

'The area will sort it out. That's how it works. No one wants you lot poking their noses in where they're not wanted.' Bancroft stared at his fingernails. 'They never bothered me, though.' He smiled at Ridley. 'But they wouldn't, would they?'

Ridley banged on the table and raised his voice. 'Children died in that fire. I gave up my Christmas for it, so don't tell me what's worth bothering with and what's not. You've got no idea.'

Bancroft lit up another cigarette. 'If you're after a thank you from me you won't be getting one.'

Ridley stood up and paced the small room. He stopped at the window and stared out. Relentless rain battered against it. A few miles west of Queens Gardens Police Station, the Humber Bridge was being constructed. It was a new beginning for the city in a new decade. He turned back to face Bancroft. 'I didn't even get to see my little girl open her *presents this year because I was talking to people like you. People like you who don't give a shit about doing the right thing. People like you who don't care that kids died in that fire.' He jabbed a finger at Bancroft. 'Fucking scumbags, like you.'*

Bancroft walked across the room to stand next to Ridley. 'All that time away from home working, it sounds like your wife might be a bit lonely.'

Ridley slammed Bancroft into the wall. 'If you so much as mention my family again, I'll knock into next week. I don't care how big you are or who you think you know.'

The men stared at each before Bancroft smiled. 'You might need to watch that temper of yours.'

Ridley released his grip and walked back to the table.

Bancroft rearranged his jacket. 'Like I said, Don, if you're accusing me of something, I want to talk to Holborn, and I want to talk to him now. I think you're a cunt.'

CHAPTER ONE

Niall only called me Joseph when he was in trouble. My brother didn't need to ask me twice. I put my mobile in my pocket and picked up my car keys. I was still working out of the office space rented by Ridley & Son, Private Investigators in the Old Town of Hull. I wasn't Don Ridley's son, but it didn't make the decision to close any easier. The lease still had a month to run, so it was a base for the time being. After that, I had no idea. I was now a former Private Investigator.

Niall rented a lock-up on a housing estate. It was out to the east of the city, but I made good time by weaving through the rat-runs I knew. I parked up outside and made my way in. The lock-up was basic with four concrete walls, a bare floor and a light bulb with no shade dangling from the ceiling. My brother was making furniture for friends and family. The lock-up was effectively a small workshop. After working in the caravan industry for so many years, he had the joinery skills. It had gone unspoken, but I knew it had kept him occupied during the long days before he'd decided to go into business with some of his mates. Starting again in his mid-forties was brave, but I wasn't far behind that and had nothing. I took a step back and knocked on the door so he knew I was there.

He stopped work on the wardrobe he was putting together. 'Thanks for coming so quickly.'

'Not a problem.' I looked at what he was working on. He was a craftsman, that much was clear. It was obvious to me that he took a lot of pleasure from his work.

'Already got a buyer lined up for it,' he said, following my gaze.

My brother only spoke in his own time. He had something to say, but I would have to wait for him to get to the point. He nodded at the framed rugby league shirts and photographs in the corner. I walked over and carefully flicked through them.

'I thought we'd make a feature of Dad's stuff in the bar.'

'Good idea.' Our dad, Jimmy Geraghty, had played for Hull Kingston Rovers before retiring to become a publican. He'd been one of the club's finest ever fullbacks. It was a neat way of squaring the circle.

'We can put some of your stuff in, too, if you like?'

'I haven't got much to give you.' Injury had finished my rugby career early. Niall had always been content to watch. He never missed a game. He'd travelled all over with our dad to see them before continuing the tradition with his son, Connor, though Connor had stopped going once he'd hit his teenage years, preferring the football with his mates.

Niall threw the rag into the corner and cleared his throat. 'I've done something stupid.'

'It can't be that bad.'

'Want to bet?'

I stood alongside him. 'Nothing we can't sort out.'

'Not this time.'

'Why not?' I passed him over one of the deckchairs he stored at the back of the lock-up. We both sat down.

'Remember when I was doing the security work on the docks a couple of months ago?'

I nodded. He'd got the work through an agency.

'One of the lads there needed some storage space and I helped him out.'

'Storage space?'

'Ted's still got the lock-up next door, but he hasn't been using it, so I borrowed it off him and gave him a few quid.'

I didn't like where this was heading. 'What did you need to store?'

'Cigarettes.'

'Cigarettes?'

'I was looking after them for someone.'

'Fuck's sake.' I understood what he was saying. Smuggled cigarettes. 'How many?'

'A thousand cartons.'

'How much money are we talking about?'

Niall shrugged. 'Thousands, I suppose.'

I didn't know what to say. However much we were talking about, it was serious.

'I need to put food on the table,' he said.

'I know.' I wasn't judging my brother. I took a breath, the decision made. 'We'll tell your mate that the space is no longer available. No harm done. We'll go and see him together if that makes it easier.'

Niall shook his head. 'I can't back out of it now.'

'Why not?'

'Someone's stolen them.'

I made it clear to Niall that if I was to help him, I had to know everything. We walked across to Ted's lock-up. I stopped for a moment and glanced up at the four tower blocks which surrounded us. Maybe someone had seen what had happened, but there was no way of knowing. There were too many doors to knock on and it wouldn't change anything. Ted's lock-up was exactly the same as Niall's.

'I've replaced the lock,' Niall said. 'Same model. I don't want Ted to know what's happened. No point worrying him. He won't even notice.'

I'd met Ted. He was an old man looking to make a bit of money. He didn't need to be involved. The lock was heavy duty. I knew they weren't always effective and appearances were deceptive, but weighing it in my hand, it would have been more than enough to put off an opportunistic thief.

'Who did the cigarettes belong to?' I asked.

'I don't know.' He paused. 'My contact is Terry Gillespie, a mate from security on the docks.'

'Where does he live?'

Niall only knew the street, so we returned to his garage. He had a stack of old telephone directories. I made a note of the address we needed.

We joined the early evening traffic on the ring road heading for King George Dock. Lorry after lorry lined up to board the commercial ferries which taxied between Hull and continental Europe. To me, it was still the heartbeat of the city, our reason for existing.

I parked up outside Gillespie's house. Niall said he hadn't visited it before. It was the same as any other on the street. I knocked on the door. Gillespie wasn't thrilled to see us. I put my foot in the doorframe to stop him shutting us out. He relented and we followed him into his living room.

'Lucky to catch me,' he said. 'I'm on my days off now.'

I looked around the room. The place was a shit-hole. Aside from the dated and tatty decor, takeaway cartons and dirty plates littered the settee and chairs.

'The fuck you staring at?' Gillespie asked me.

'You might want to think about washing up once in a while.'

Gillespie spoke to Niall. 'Who is this wanker?'

'My brother,' he said. 'A Private Investigator.'

Gillespie laughed. 'Seriously?'

I told Gillespie to sit down. 'I want to know about the cigarettes.'

'It's none of your business.'

I walked over to the window and took a deep breath. I'd taken an instant dislike to the man. 'You've involved my brother in your shitty world, so it is my problem.'

'You come into my house, turn your nose up at it, and expect me to help you?'

I shrugged. 'Like I give a shit what you think.' I walked across the room to him. 'But you need to understand I'm the only person who's going to help you at the moment.'

Gillespie spoke. 'The cigs were in your lock-up, Niall. You're the one who fucked up.'

'Your problem, too,' I said. 'Do you think this is going to go away? You know how many cigarettes were in the lock-up, so you can do the sums.' I didn't want to say it in front of Niall, but Gillespie wasn't giving me a choice. 'You're not walking away from this.' The room went quiet. I couldn't look at Niall. Gillespie understood what I was saying, though. 'Tell me what happened. From the start.'

Gillespie knew what was good for him and started to speak. 'I've worked on the docks for years. These things go on.'

'I'm sure they do.'

'I was asked if I could help store these cigarettes which were coming in. That was all. The problem was that they were coming in the following day and I didn't have anywhere to store them myself.'

'So you thought you'd drag Niall into it?'

'He didn't need dragging into anything.'

'How were they were smuggled into the country?'

'No idea.'

I let it go. I wasn't too bothered about the mechanics of the situation. What was done was done. 'Who else knows?' I asked him.

'No one.'

He knew what I was working up to. 'Someone turned a blind eye at the docks? Who was it?'

'I can't tell you that.'

'You don't have a choice. If anyone comes looking for Niall, I won't hesitate to point them in your direction. And I promise whatever happens to him will be twice as bad for you.'

Gillespie took my point. 'The only one I knew about was Peter Hill.'

'Who's he?'

'Customs guy.'

'Where will I find him?'

'He lives somewhere off Sutton Road.'

I made a note of the address. That was all he had for me. I nodded to Niall that we were done here for now. I picked up a beer-mat, scribbled my mobile number down and threw it at Gillespie. 'We'll be speaking again soon.' I certainly wasn't finished with him.

We didn't speak as we drove west towards the bar. Niall wanted to put a couple of hours' work in. The opening night was only three days away. I also knew it was his way of zoning the problem out. The visit to Gillespie had left me thinking and acting like a PI again. That had been the way Niall had introduced me. I was worried I quite liked it. We drove past the new Craven Park. Building work was ongoing as the ground expanded. The club had played there for over twenty years now, but it wasn't the same to me. The old Craven Park was the place I'd made my memories, both as a player and as a supporter. Now the site housed a supermarket. Seemingly, it was progress.

'I'm not cut out for this kind of thing,' my brother eventually said. 'I'm a family man.'

I wondered if that meant I wasn't a family man? That I'd never be a family man? Was I the opposite of Niall? Were the two things mutually exclusive? All I knew was that you play the hand you're dealt. You either deal with it or you fall to pieces.

I turned onto Hedon Road. We both stared at the docks as we sped past. The last few lorries boarded the ferries with their cargo. Hull Prison stood on the other side of the road. I knew he was making the connection to the situation he was in. I got down to business. 'What do you know about Gillespie?'

'Not a lot.'

It was going to be hard work. I started with the easy question. 'Does he live alone?'

'His wife died a couple of years ago.'

'Kids?'

'Doesn't see much of them.'

'Has he always worked on the docks?'

'He used to have a proper job on them, but it went years ago.'

It sounded about right. 'Got a lot of mates on there, then?'

'He knows everyone.'

We pulled up at the traffic lights on Myton Bridge. 'Do you think he's capable of taking the cigarettes and ripping you off?'

'He wouldn't.'

I didn't need to spell it out. Someone had stolen them. 'He's top of my list.'

Niall stared out of the window. 'He took me under his wing and showed me the ropes.' He turned back to me. 'He was a mate.'

I put the car in gear and drove. We passed the marina and its moored yachts. The stupidity of one the city centre's jewels being separated from the rest of the city centre by Castle Street, a fast moving dual carriageway, never failed to amaze me. A handful of people were out walking, admiring the boats. 'People aren't always what they seem,' I said.

'We're skint,' he said. 'The redundancy is all but gone on the bar and Ruth is out working all hours.'

'How's she's doing?' I asked.

'She's solid. ' He paused for a moment. 'She's carrying us along.'

'How about Connor?'

'He's at that funny age, isn't he? Thinks he's a man, but he's really still a boy. She tells me it'll pass.'

'I thought he was helping to get the bar sorted?'

'Not really. Reckons he's out working already. All I know is that he's out all hours but I still can't actually tell you what he does.' He shrugged. 'What does a nightclub promoter do? You tell me.'

I didn't have an answer. The world had changed. Niall knew that more than most.

'I don't want him to end up like me. I've tried to speak to him, but there's no way of getting through to him. His mate, Milo, has been filling his head with all these daft ideas. He needs to think properly about his future.'

'He's still a kid.'

'He's twenty, Joe.'

'Exactly.'

We both laughed.

'It reminds me of you and dad,' Niall said. 'You drove him crazy.'

'I had no idea what I wanted to do at twenty, that's for sure.'

'Dad wanted you out there, working.'

'I did work.'

'Not a proper job, though. Not the kind of job he wanted you to have.'

Our dad hadn't foreseen the industry being slowly ripped out of the city. I drove down North Road, past what remained of Boothferry Park, the former home of Hull City. The land had been bulldozed and new houses were being built. Even the six magnificent floodlights had now gone. I turned on to Spring Bank West, heading towards Chanterlands Avenue and the bar. 'Why didn't you tell me what was going on?' We'd pulled up at the level crossing as it went down.

'You've got enough on your plate.' He looked away again, staring out of the window. 'Besides, it's not something to brag about, is it?'

'I could have helped.'

'I thought I could handle it.'

'I assume Ruth doesn't know?'

'No.'

The train passed and the level crossing went back up. I took a left onto Chanterlands Avenue and thought again about Gillespie. I didn't like the man, but more than that, he struck me as exactly the kind of person who would see my brother as an easy target. I pulled up outside the bar. Niall got out of the car and turned back to me before he closed the door. 'I'm really not cut out for this kind of thing, Joe.'

I'd taken a telephone call the previous day from Roger Millfield, a local accountant, asking for a meeting. He'd asked if I could spare him half an hour. It was the least I could do. When Don and I had the partnership, we'd done a lot of bread and butter work for professional firms. It had often been tedious, but it had kept us ticking over. It was also a chance to put the thought of Niall's problem to one side for a short while. His office was on High Street. The area had changed over time. Where once the city's wealth was built on the goods housed in the warehouses which lined the area, they now housed the innovative design companies, government funded projects and one-man start-ups which would hopefully propel the city forward. His receptionist told me to take a seat. I flicked through the local newspaper as I waited. Millfield was a self-made man who had started at the bottom of his profession and worked his way up. I respected that. He was pushing sixty and probably not too far off retirement.

He appeared and held his hand out to me. 'Nice to see you, Joe.'

I shook it before following him through to his office. He had a photograph of his daughter, Rebecca, taking pride of place on his desk. I asked after her.

'She's just finished her exams and qualified, so I want to bring her on here. One day, she'll take over. I've never known someone pass all their exams at such a young age.'

I knew she was in her mid-twenties. I was impressed. 'Can you pass on my congratulations?'

He said he would. 'I hear you and Don aren't working together now.'

'That's right.'

'Are you freelancing?'

To my mind, I was now a former Private Investigator. One chapter of my life had closed and another one was about to open. What that would be, I had no idea. But for all of my desire to start again, I had my brother's problem to think about. If I put aside the fact it was personal, it wasn't so far removed from my previous life. Millfield must have sensed my reluctance to answer.

'I've got a job I need doing,' he said.

I didn't dismiss it out of hand. I needed to earn some money, too.

'Could be matrimony.'

I'd done this kind of work for him before. He made no apologies for the fact he took care of his clients. If an important client was thinking about selling their business, they'd often want to make sure things were solid at home, that there were no surprises waiting. It was a shitty line of work, but you couldn't always pick and choose. As a consequence, he'd used his contacts with solicitors to get us work delivering warrants and court orders. I knew I owed the man. 'Which client?'

He shook his head and pointed to the photograph on his desk. His wife, Kath.

'Are you sure?' I said.

He nodded. 'I've answered several dead telephone calls now. I know something's not right.'

'What do you want me to do?'

'I was assuming you would tell me that, Joe.'

I stood up. 'I'll be in touch.' I was back in work.

CHAPTER TWO

I needed to speak to everyone who knew the cigarettes were being kept in the lock-up. It didn't seem to extend beyond Terry Gillespie and Peter Hill. They would be who I focused on. It was a starting point, but no more. I was going to need help. I headed straight to Sarah's house. She was Don's daughter, but she bore no grudge over the way things had finished, even though she had good reason to. As usual, I had to park a couple of streets away. The area was dense terracing, often two cars to every house. We'd ridden out a rough period between us, but our relationship was healing. I was pleased. Sarah was the nearest thing I had to a friend.

She let me in and we went through to her kitchen and sat down at the table. 'How's your dad doing?' I asked her.

'He's alright.'

'Still thinking about a life in the sun in Spain?'

Sarah smiled. 'Talking about it, but he'll never go. It's not him. He'll go and stay with his sister for a bit and hate it. It might be cold and wet, but Hull's in his blood. He can't leave it behind.'

'Sounds about right.' That was the Don I knew. He wasn't one for being far from home.

'Do you want to eat?'

I declined. I wasn't hungry, but it was a nice gesture. Just like the old days. I watched her eat. I was too distracted to concentrate on the television while I waited. She finished and put her plate down.

'Niall's done something stupid,' I said.

'Poor Ruth.'

I shook my head. 'Not like that.' She got on well with Niall's wife. It was easy to. My brother had chosen well. I liked her a lot. We'd had some good nights out together over the years. I knew Niall would never do anything to jeopardise that part of his life. He wasn't that stupid.

'I need your help,' I said. I'd made a mess of things with Sarah in the past, but I trusted her. I'd made a promise to Don that I wouldn't put her in danger again. I had no idea where this was going to lead us, but I knew it wasn't going to be pleasant. I felt bad, but I couldn't do this alone.

'I thought you'd never ask.' Sarah had always made it clear she made her own decisions. She was nobody's fool and no pushover. 'What do you need me to do?' she said.

I told her about the cigarettes. And the fact they were missing.

'What are we going to do about it?' she asked me.

I smiled this time. Partners. 'I want you to look into Terry Gillespie for me.' I had plans myself for Peter Hill.

I waited until the morning and set my plan into action. Peter Hill was the link to the missing cigarettes, so I needed to speak to him. I didn't want to door-step him, though. It wouldn't do anyone any good, especially when I saw two young children waving him off as he left for the day. He was driving a blue Vauxhall Astra which was easy to follow. He pulled out of his cul-de-sac on to Sutton Road, heading towards the docks. The overnight ferries from Holland and Belgium would be in, and as well as the commercial freight, tourists would be spilling off, eager to head west to places like York and Leeds, spending their money elsewhere. There was a bus between us, but I kept him in sight. The bus turned right at the Holderness Road traffic lights. I tucked in behind him. The rush hour traffic was starting to build as commuters headed for the city centre. I stayed behind Hill as we crossed the Preston Road junction. It was now or never. I flashed my headlights repeatedly at him. He got the message, indicated and pulled over. I came to a stop behind him. He was already getting out of his car. He was in his early thirties, but already had the start of a middle-aged spread around his middle.

'Is it my brake light again, mate?' he asked me.

'No.'

He looked confused. 'What's the problem, then?'

'I didn't want to knock on your front door.'

He took a step back, the colour draining from his face. 'I'm not going to hurt you. I need to talk to you about the cigarettes and Terry Gillespie.'

'I don't know what you're talking about.'

I ignored the lie. 'I need to talk to you.'

He relented, knowing he had no choice. He was probably expecting someone far worse than me to come knocking. 'I'm at due at work in ten minutes.'

'Fair enough.'

'I'll give you a call?'

I shook my head. 'What time's your lunch?'

'I usually work through it.'

'Not today.'

'One o'clock,' he eventually said.

I named the Asda on Mount Pleasant, a couple of miles away. It was the nearest place I could think of. 'I'll be in the cafe.'

He started to walk back to his car. I called after him. 'By the way, your brake light isn't working.'

Niall was hard at work when I arrived at the bar. He pointed to the corner he was earmarking for our dad's Hull KR shirts.

'Perfect,' I said.

Niall stopped working. 'I didn't sleep last night.'

I took a breath. There wasn't much I could say to help. I knew how tough it was on him. 'Where's Connor?'

'In bed somewhere.'

'Right.'

'He'll be at a mate's house or his girlfriend's place.' Niall picked up his paintbrush. 'But he's certainly not where he should be.'

'Tried ringing him?'

'He knows where I am.'

I changed the subject and asked about the cigarettes. 'Any word?'

'Nothing.'

'It makes me nervous.'

Niall smiled. 'It makes you nervous?'

'Fair point.'

'Six months ago, I had a normal job and was looking forward to booking a holiday. These days, I'm scared of my own shadow.'

I wasn't sure what to say to that. I told him I'd caught up with Peter Hill.

'What did he have to say?'

'I'm meeting him later to talk properly.'

'Do you want me to come along?'

'Don't worry about it,' I wanted to talk to Hill alone. 'What do you know about him?'

Niall stopped painting. 'Not a lot, really. I used to see him about the place. That's all.'

'Did you ever see him talking to Gillespie?'

'I don't think so.'

'I need you to think harder.'

Niall shook his head 'It wasn't for my ears. I only said Gillespie could use my lock-up because he was desperate. I didn't get involved in the details.'

I was sure Gillespie knew more about the missing cigarettes than he'd told me. He could easily have stolen them and left Niall to take the rap. Regardless, he was the best lead I had and there was still some time before my meeting with Peter Hill. I called Sarah. She was free and willing to help. If Gillespie was involved, he had to make a move. And he'd confirmed to me he wasn't working today. It was worth taking a chance. I picked up Sarah from her house and we drove across the city. I parked up away from Gillespie's house so he wouldn't see us, but close enough for us to see any movement. It was a fishing expedition, but I needed to do something.

Sarah took me through what she'd found out about him. 'He's got a record.'

'How did he end up working in security?'

She shrugged. 'It was a long time ago and he's not been in trouble since. We're talking decades ago.'

'Right.' Maybe his conviction was spent. I knew a lot of young men grew out of crime, that it was nothing more than youthful stupidity. But it didn't feel right. It said something about the man's character.

We stared at his house until Sarah took an envelope out her bag. 'I'll give him a knock.'

It was a trick we'd worked in the past. If one of us was unknown to our target, we'd knock on the door claiming to have a letter or delivery. If our target answered the door, we'd deliberately give a false name. If they didn't answer the door, we had a ready-made and plausible reason to be knocking on their neighbour's door. And that was often when we got some useful information. I watched as Sarah talked to Gillespie's neighbour before returning to the car.

'We'll find him at the shops,' she said.

'Right.' I knew the layout of the area. The square of shops also contained a bookies and a pub. It was a short drive away. We discussed a plan as we drove. The best we could do was that Sarah would walk about until she spotted him. I parked up in the centre of the shops. It didn't take her long to find him. He was watching the horse racing. Sarah went into the newsagent and got us chocolate, drinks and a newspaper.

We only had to wait thirty minutes. Gillespie came outside and lit a cigarette. Five minutes later a taxi collected him. Sarah told me to follow. It was becoming a habit. I hung back as best I could without losing sight of him. The taxi dropped Gillespie off at a pub on Hedon Road. It was set slightly back from the dual carriageway. From the outside it was run-down and in poor condition. I looked up at the shabby paintwork around the window frames and the weathered bricks. The net curtains were grey. No wonder the place was largely ignored by potential customers.

'You can't go in,' Sarah said.

I nodded. We both knew it belonged to George Sutherland. He was a name from my past.

I'd previously worked for his wife. She'd tired of his affairs over the years. It had been a simple job. I'd followed him discreetly for a couple of weeks. It had been one of my easiest jobs. He'd used a cheap chain hotel on the edge of the city centre, the woman an employee of his. It did mean I wasn't going to be welcome. On paper, Sutherland was a legitimate businessman, but the man had given off an unpleasant vibe. I recognised his black heart. I'd quickly learned he'd worked for Frank Salford in the past. Salford had been one of an exclusive group of criminals who'd exercised a grip on organised crime in the city. He'd died a couple of years ago. Cancer, rather than violence. Our paths had crossed and I wasn't upset to learn he'd suffered before dying. I hadn't dug any deeper into Sutherland than that. I'd simply passed over the photographic evidence to his wife and left it at that.

'Gillespie didn't see me at the shops,' Sarah said. 'He had his back to me.'

Before I had chance to reply, she was out of the car and walking towards the entrance. I had to wait it out. There was little to look at. The pub stood in isolation. Most of the industry which had once surrounded it was long gone. The Fenner and Humbrol factories had once employed hundreds. A new office complex was in the process of being built on the Humbrol site and a haulage firm had opened next to it. Further along, the greasy spoon was still there, a throwback to past days. I grew increasingly impatient waiting for Sarah to reappear. Nothing much happened. I saw a handful of drinkers come and go. They were all like Gillespie. It didn't appear personal hygiene was a priority for any of them. A sign in the window let me know the place was more than a pub. It offered bed and breakfast and hot meals. The £20 per night including meals meant it was definitely aiming to appeal to the less picky traveller. Sarah walked out of the pub and got back into my car.

I turned to her. 'How did it go?'

'Let's say it's not a forward-thinking kind of place. I don't think women are a regular feature in there. I feel like I need a shower.'

'Doesn't surprise me.'

Sarah changed the subject back to Gillespie. 'He was meeting people in there.'

'Friends?'

'I wouldn't say so.'

It was interesting but it didn't necessarily mean anything. It went towards building a picture, though. I started the car and pulled away.

As we drove away, I explained to Sarah that I had a meeting lined up with Peter Hill and that it needed to be alone.

'He's nervous enough as it is,' I said, explaining that he was the inside man at Customs. 'Another face might push him too far.'

'Makes sense,' she said.

I could tell she wasn't happy about it, but I also needed her to find out what she could about Roger Millfield and his wife. I needed to keep on top of things in that respect. I dropped her in the city centre at the office and agreed to head straight there once I'd spoken to Hill.

I found Peter Hill waiting for me in the corner of the supermarket cafe, well away from the shoppers. It was as close as we were going to get privacy. I went straight over to him.

'You're late,' he said. 'I've got to get back to work.'

'Did you get your brake light sorted?'

He looked at me like I was mad. 'I've been at work.'

I told him to follow me out to my car.

'Why?'

I leaned in closer to him. The place was busy with shoppers taking a break. Families, pensioners and children. 'I'm not talking to you in here.'

'I don't know who you are.'

'Niall's brother.'

He relaxed and followed me to my car and got in the passenger seat.

'We need to get a few things straight about the missing cigarettes,' I told him.

He stared out of the window. 'I'm very sorry to hear about what's happened, but this isn't my fault. It's your brother's problem to sort out.'

I put him straight and told him he was involved and every bit as liable. He was scared, but I wasn't too bothered by that. The sooner he came around to my way of thinking, the better.

I could see a tear forming in the corner of his eye. 'This wasn't supposed to happen,' he said.

'But it has, so you're going to have to deal with it.' I relented a little. 'Start at the beginning,' I told him. 'I'm the only friend you've got at the moment.'

'I was under pressure, alright? My wife worked for the council, but she lost her job. You know how it is?'

'Tell me how it is.'

'I'm skint. That's how it is. I owe money on my credit cards, I owe money on my mortgage and the kids need new things for school. This bloke approached me and suggested I could earn a bit extra if I turned a blind eye to a few things at work. Nothing serious, I was told. I needed the cash, so I didn't say no to the idea at first.'

'Terry Gillespie?'

He was surprised that I knew the name, but nodded his agreement.

'What did he want you to do?'

'I had to make sure a consignment of DVDs got through with no problems. It was only a small thing, nothing too serious. That's all it was.'

'And you did it?'

'I'm not proud of the fact. I told him it was a one-off. I wasn't prepared to do it again.'

'But he came back wanting more?'

'He passed me on to the people he was working for. Bad people. I was told if I didn't follow the instructions I was given, I'd lose my job. And that was just for starters. They wanted some cigarettes bringing through this time.'

I couldn't believe the man's naivety. 'Have you mentioned my brother to anyone?'

He shook his head. 'I wouldn't do that.'

I stared until he looked away. I was sure he'd got the message. 'What about the police? Why didn't you go to them?'

'How could I? I was stupid, but they made it very clear what would happen if I did. They sent me photos of my kids running around in the school playground.' Hill had my attention. 'If they can get to them at school, they can get to them anywhere.'

I felt bad hearing his story, but I needed the details. 'Tell me about the cigarettes.'

'They smuggled them in through big coffee tins. They're just the right size. Some of them were emptied out and the cartons were packed in with sweetcorn, so it'd feel and sound right if they were inspected. It was all catering supplies. All I know was that it was something that they'd been planning for a while. Months, probably. But things changed. I was told they were arriving and I had to deal with them. I tried to explain it wasn't my job to sort it out. My job was to look the other way, but they needed somewhere to store them. I didn't have a choice in the matter. I went back to Gillespie. He said he knew someone with a lock-up. It was the best we could do at short notice. It was only going to be for a couple of days.'

'Right.'

'You can't tell anyone about this.'

'Who do they belong to?' I asked.

He told me he didn't know. He was genuinely scared. I knew he was nothing more than a family man who was in over his head, but I couldn't afford to let him off the hook. 'Don't bullshit me,' I said. 'I need to know who they belonged to.'

'I don't know.'

I sat back in my chair. 'You've got to give me something. It's the only way I can help.' I hated the look of gratitude on his face as I spoke. I wasn't doing this for him.

'They gave me a mobile. It's pay-as-you-go, so I have to top it up. The man who's in charge calls me, but I don't know his name. He withholds his number, so I can't call him. I have to wait for him to contact me.'

I drummed my fingers on the steering wheel, unsure of my next move. 'And you've got no idea who he is?'

Hill shook his head. 'I only see his workers, Tom and Jerry. I'm sure that's not their real names.'

I tried to keep the sarcasm out of my voice as I agreed with him. I knew pay-as-you-go meant the mobile would be untraceable. It would all be cash and false addresses. Even so, I asked to see it. Hill rummaged about in his pocket and passed it over. I scrolled through the list of calls. All withheld numbers. There was nothing.

'One of the men sent me a text message,' Hill said.

I worked out how to access them and found the one I wanted. It was dated a few days before the cigarettes were stolen from the lock-up. The message told Hill that he should be ready. His guests would be arriving the following morning. Guests obviously meant the cigarettes. It made sense, but sending a text message was a basic error. I transferred the number it had come from into my mobile and told him to go back to work.

It felt strange to be back in the office we'd shared as Ridley &Son. Sarah was sitting in what had been her usual place. I found myself doing the same. We had a desk and chair each, but that was it. Don had arranged for all our case files to be held in storage. The office felt twice as large without the rest of the furniture. I stared at the carpet and could see the marks the now-removed filing cabinets had left. The walls were bare. The framed prints we'd displayed had all been bought for next to nothing in the nearby indoor market, but the room felt wrong without them there. It was like there was no trace of the company ever existing. Within a couple of weeks, another business would be in – accountants, IT support, solicitors – it could be anything. Time moved on.

'How did it go?' Sarah asked me.

'You first,' I said.

She passed me a folder full of print-outs. 'Have a look at this.'

I waved it away. 'The highlights will be fine.'

'Kath Millfield's an interesting character. Married to Roger for almost thirty years. She's now head of a charity which works with children to improve their literacy skills outside of school. It seems like she started it as something to occupy herself when her husband was working long hours and it just snowballed. She came from nothing as a child, brought up in a rough part of Hull with few opportunities. You know the drill. She worked hard to improve herself and the charity became a big success. Inspirational, you might say.'

'I wouldn't disagree.'

Sarah smiled. 'That's not what you wanted to know about her.'

'Not really.'

'It seems there are plenty of people who don't like her.' She pointed to her laptop, which was switched on and displaying a photograph of Kath Millfield. 'She's in her mid-fifties, but she's still glamorous and likes people to know it. I'm sure you don't need me to tell you that men are threatened by women with beauty and brains.'

I feigned mock outrage. Sarah slapped me on the arm before continuing. 'But seriously, you don't achieve what she has without ruffling a few feathers.'

'How so?'

'I don't think she's got many friends in the world of education.'

'No?'

'Think about it. She's more or less accusing the schools of not doing their jobs properly. She's well liked in the local media, and she knows how to play the game, but she has plenty of detractors.'

I entered Kath Millfield into Google and flicked through the photographs it brought up of her. The majority had been taken at social and charity functions. One man constantly appeared alongside the Millfields. I pointed to the man and asked Sarah if she knew him.

'Neil Farr,' she said.

'Who's he?'

'A local solicitor.'

'Right.' It was all useful background. I clicked off the Internet.

'Your turn,' Sarah said.

I repeated what Peter Hill had told me. I was beginning to feel guilty about the way I'd spoken to him.

'Heavy stuff,' she said.

I knew it was never going to be pleasant, but hearing Hill's story had brought it home to me. Niall had a serious problem, and that meant I had, too. I was dealing with organised criminals. 'I've got the telephone number of one of the people threatening Hill.'

'What are you going to do?' she asked me.

'I'm not sure.'

'You've no idea who this guy is, or who he's working for?'

'None at all.'

Sarah stood up. 'I'll tell you what you're going to do.' She picked up her bag and rummaged around inside it. She held out a SIM card to me and smiled.

CHAPTER THREE

I put the old SIM into my mobile and entered the number. A man answered.

'Who's this?' I said.

He laughed. 'Who the fuck are you?'

'I asked first.'

'Don't waste my time.'

Before he had chance to finish the call, I told him I had the cigarettes. I glanced at Sarah and waited for the man to say something. He eventually said I should give them back.

'We need to talk, then,' I said. 'Top of the path which leads to the Lord Line Building.' It was next to St Andrews Quay Retail Park which would be busy enough for our purposes. It was the best place I could think of quickly. Now derelict and long abandoned, it had once been a thriving office at the heart of the dock, sitting there proudly overseeing the fishing fleet and the River Humber.

'How will I recognise you?' he said.

'I'll recognise you.' I said he had half an hour to get there and terminated the call.

We left Sarah's house and headed for the meeting. Next to the footpath was a large car park which served a range of electrical and furniture shops. We parked between two other cars. The shops were still open for another couple of hours, so people were busy going about their business. We wouldn't be noticed. The man we were waiting for eventually appeared and stood where instructed. We watched and waited. I was pretty certain he was by himself. He wasn't nervous. He was casually waiting for me to make myself known to him. I had no intention of doing that. I waited until he relaxed and started to walk about on the spot to keep warm.

I glanced at Sarah. She was holding a small digital camera in her hand. 'Now, I reckon.'

She quickly took a couple of shots and passed me the camera.

I scrolled through the photographs. 'Perfect.' I passed the camera back, started the car and joined the steady stream of the traffic leaving the shops.

Before I headed to Niall's bar, we returned to Sarah's house and she printed me off a photograph of the man. The light at the bar was still on. Niall had been working hard. I guessed it would be opening on schedule. I walked over to the far corner and looked at the display of our dad's rugby league memorabilia. The shirts made for a great feature. Someone had sourced copies of newspaper articles and framed them. He'd played at Wembley in the mid-sixties. Hull KR's first ever appearance in the Challenge Cup Final. I was lost in thought and didn't hear Niall walk up and stand next to me.

'Alright?' he said.

I fingered the photograph in my pocket. 'You're doing a great job.'

I turned to look at him. He'd been beaten. He'd cleaned his face up, but I could see the swelling and the cuts. We stared at each other. 'What happened?' I said.

'It doesn't matter.'

'Of course it matters.'

'It was obvious someone was going to catch up with me sooner or later.'

'What did he say?'

'He wanted the money.'

I took the photograph out and showed it to him. 'Was it him?'

Niall nodded his confirmation.

I told him how I'd got it. 'Any idea who he is?'

He shook his head. 'No idea.'

I'd asked Sarah to find out what she could. He had to be known.

'Could do without this,' Niall said. 'The bar opens in a couple of nights' time. I'll look a mess.'

There was nothing I could say to that. The bruises would fade, but he'd have to wait it out.

'I'm going to call it a night,' he said.

'Do you want a lift home?'

'Wouldn't say no.'

We locked up and left. We drove across the city in silence until I pulled up outside his house.

'Do you want to come in, Joe?'

I looked at his face and thought of Ruth sitting inside, waiting. He had a lot of explaining to do. 'I'll leave you to it.'

Although I'd asked Sarah to do what she could identify the man, I couldn't let it go. I had to do something. He'd attacked my brother and I was worried my nephew was going to be next. I headed for Terry Gillespie's house. I hadn't paid much attention when I'd first visited. It was a standard council terraced house. His front garden was overgrown and in need of some work. I knocked loudly on his door. No answer. All the windows were closed and the lights were off. I knocked again and shouted through the letterbox. Eventually, one of his neighbours came out.

'What the fuck do you think you're doing?' he said.

I wasn't going to back down. 'Looking for Terry.'

'Try the pub.' He pointed down the road.

I knew where he meant. I nodded and thanked him.

I found Terry Gillespie standing by himself at the bar, watching the football on the big screen. I ordered a drink and joined him. He'd received the same treatment as Niall. His nose had been broken and his left eye had closed over. Dried blood marked his face. I stood alongside him.

'My ribs are killing me,' he said.

It was superficial damage. Enough to hurt, but not enough to do him serious damage. 'Who did it?'

'It doesn't matter.'

'How many of them?'

'What does it matter?'

'I want to know.'

He eventually answered. 'Just the one. You don't need an army to sort me out these days.'

'Who was it?'

'No idea.'

'You'd never seen him before?'

'Never.'

'What did he look like?'

He described the man. It could have been any number of men in the city. He was lying to me. He knew exactly who'd worked him over. I'd been wrong in thinking that he'd taken the cigarettes from Niall's lock-up, but something wasn't right.

Gillespie pushed his glass towards me. 'Getting them in or what? Bitter.' He gestured to his mate who had walked in. 'His is a lager.'

I told him to find a table before ordering the drinks. I left the lager for his mate on the bar and walked across the room to him. I put the drinks on the table and sat down.

'What about the cigs?' he said. 'Found them yet?'

'Not yet.'

He shrugged. 'They can keep kicking the shit out of me if they like. It won't change anything.'

I watched as he sipped at the drink I'd bought him. He was right. He had nothing to lose. Niall and Peter Hill had plenty to lose. I showed him the photograph of the man I'd seen at St Andrews Quay. 'Does he look familiar?'

He glanced at it before quickly turning away. He passed the photograph back. 'No idea.'

I held it back out to him. 'Do you want to have another look?'

'No point.'

'I don't believe you.'

He picked his drink up. 'Can't tell you what I don't know.'

He was definitely rattled. I stood up and walked back to the bar. I showed the photograph to Gillespie's mate. 'Any ideas?'

He glanced at it and nodded before shouting across to Gillespie. 'That's Alan Palmer's lad, isn't it? Carl?' He passed me the photograph back. 'Nasty piece of work, the pair of them, that's for sure.'

I thanked them. Hull really was like a large village at times.

I'd done what I could for now. I headed back to my flat. It was one of five in a converted house on Westbourne Avenue. I sat down for a moment in my living room in the hope I could make sense of what had happened during the day. My mobile vibrated. I took it out of my pocket and read the text message. Niall had told Ruth he'd been mugged. I doubted she believed him, but if that was the official line, I'd play along with it. I needed to eat, so I heated up a tin of soup. I found some bread to accompany it and sat back down. I needed to make some connections between what I knew. My concentration was broken by the noise of the buzzer to my flat. I put the soup down and walked over to the window. A car drove off, loud music escaping from its open windows. I couldn't see who was at the door, so I went into the kitchen and picked up a pan. It was the best I had to hand. I left my flat and walked down the stairs to the front door and carefully opened it.

It was Connor. 'Can I come up?' he said.

I relaxed and closed the door behind him. Back in my flat, I put the pan away and found two bottles of beer.

'Did your mate just drop you off?' I asked.

'That was Milo.'

I'd fed him bottles of milk when he was a baby. Now I was feeding him bottles of beer. And it didn't feel all that long ago. Debbie and I had regularly looked after him so Niall and Ruth could enjoy a night out. Those had been happy days. We'd played along with the situation, wondering what it'd be like to have a child of our own. Her death in a house fire had put an end to that.

'I'm worried about Dad,' Connor said, drawing me back to the present.

I swallowed a mouthful of lager. 'He's working hard. He'll have the bar ready in no time. Once it's open, he'll be fine.'

'What if nobody comes?'

'People always want a drink.' Niall was a proud man. I admired the fact he'd worked hard all his life and stuck at things. Loud factories and long hours hadn't bothered him. I knew he could make a success of anything. I asked Connor how the club promoting was going.

Connor shrugged. 'They don't take me seriously.'

'Who?'

'Mum and Dad.'

'I'm sure they do.'

'Dad doesn't.'

'He's out of his comfort zone. Don't be too hard on him.' The world had changed. Hull was changing. I knew leisure and consumerism was where it was at. Maybe green technology would be the next big thing. I certainly didn't have any of the answers.

'I'm trying to get something off the ground in a club,' he said. 'Our own night. It's not easy.'

'With Milo?'

'He's got the contacts to get us started.'

I couldn't be too hard on him. My dream had been to play for Hull KR, but like my dad, it hadn't have provided much of a living for either of us. It was never going to be a career. Not that I was given the chance to see how far I could push it. One bad tackle and it was all over. I passed Connor another beer and asked him the question that was on my mind. 'Why did you take the cigarettes?' He was peeling the sticker on the bottle, avoiding eye contact. 'That's why you've come here, isn't it?'

The tiniest nod of his head. I waited for him to speak. I stared out of the window into the darkness. There was no way someone had stumbled on to the cigarettes by accident. I'd seen the lock. Terry Gillespie just wanted the easy money. And I didn't see Peter Hill having it in him to double-cross people. He was in over his head. It didn't leave many suspects. No one else knew the cigarettes were in the lock-up. It had to be someone close. It only left Connor.

'I heard Dad on the telephone talking about them,' he eventually said. 'I told Milo about them and he said we should sell them to get the club night up and running. I didn't think it through properly.'

I swallowed a mouthful of beer. Sometimes the most stupid decisions are no more than that. Especially when you're young.

'You can't tell my dad.'

I hadn't thought that far ahead. 'What did you do with them?'

'Milo said he knew someone who'd take them off our hands.'

'Who bought them?'

'I don't know. Milo sorted it.'

'Who is Milo?' I asked, more interested in him now.

'He's a mate. I met him out clubbing a while back. He's got some great ideas about what the city's nightlife needs. Everyone thinks he's the business.'

'And you wanted to be in the mix with him?'

'Something like that.'

He didn't sound too clever to me. I was going to speak to speak to him. 'Where will I find him?'

'Don't tell my dad. Please. I'll sort it.'

I put my drink down. 'How are you going to sort it, Connor?'

He stood up. 'I shouldn't have come here. It's not your problem.'

I stood up, too. 'If it concerns my family, it is my problem.'

'I'll get the money from somewhere.' He handed me his empty beer bottle. 'It's my mess to sort out, Uncle Joe.'

Connor left. I watched him go before putting some music on low. I had to stop the police ruining Connor's life before it had even started. I stared at the wall in front of me. Things were a mess. I knew Connor wasn't a bad lad, but like most at his age, he'd gone off the rails a bit. It would break Niall's heart to know Connor had taken the cigarettes. I couldn't tell him. I tried to put it to the back of my mind and enjoy the music. My mobile vibrated. A text message from Sarah.

Could I meet her at Hull Royal Infirmary? Don had been attacked. She was in the café waiting on news. I let the news sink in before slowly easing myself up. I'd drunk three bottles of beer without even realising, and that was enough these days to knock me slightly off-kilter.

I found my coat and locked up. The cool air helped to clear my head straight as I walked to the hospital.

Hull Royal Infirmary was my least favourite building in the city. The ever-present scaffolding on its front gave the impression it was about to fall down at any moment. I made my way up the stairs to the cafe. It was quiet at this time of night. Sarah was sitting in the corner, nursing a cup of tea. I made my way over to her and asked how Don was doing.

'They've moved him to a ward, so he's settled for the night.'

'What happened?'

'I don't really know. It seems his neighbour heard a lot noise, arguing, and knocked on his door. Whoever was in there ran straight out and fled. She called an ambulance and then me. That's all I've been able to find out. I can't speak to him until the morning.'

There was nothing more we could do for now. 'Where's Lauren?' I asked.

'I got a friend to look after her. She's happy to wait until I get home.'

'Good.'

I told her that Connor had taken the cigarettes.

'Does Niall know?'

'He can't know. It'd destroy him.'

'It's not healthy to keep secrets.'

'I haven't got a choice.'

She nodded her head in agreement, complicit in my decision. 'If you think it's for the best.'

I said it was.

Sarah took a notebook out of her coat pocket. 'I've been working, too.' She passed me her notes. 'Here's some more on the Palmer family. I decided to have a dig around.'

I skimmed through the notes. Sarah told me about Alan Palmer. 'He also worked with George Sutherland, back in the day.'

'Keeping it in the family.'

'When he wasn't in prison, obviously. Alan's got a history.'

'What about Carl?'

'He's not been to prison yet, but that's more through luck than judgement.'

Witnesses changing their minds about what they'd seen. It was a familiar story. I passed her the notebook back. 'He's dangerous, then.'

'In a nutshell.'

We sat in silence for a few moments before I told her there was nothing more we could do here for the time being. 'You should try and get some sleep. Keep things normal for Lauren.' Working for clients was one thing, but it's a different thing altogether when it happens on your own doorstep. At least Don wasn't in any immediate danger. I told her I'd walk her home. She was still shaken. 'I'll sleep on your settee tonight.

CHAPTER FOUR

I left Sarah's house early. My night's sleep on her settee had been uncomfortable and disjointed, not least because I was thinking about what had happened to Don. Sarah had woken me with a cup of coffee and toast. She didn't want Lauren to see me lying there. I understood what she was saying. Lauren was preparing to move up to senior school, so it was an important time for her. I'd quickly got myself dressed and on the move. As I walked back towards my flat to collect my car, I knew I had to help Don. I'd told Sarah that much. It was the least I could do. He'd gone the extra mile for me in the past. It was time for me to repay the favour.

I couldn't lose sight of my other problems, though. My call to Connor went straight to voicemail. I told him to call me back immediately. By the time I'd reached my flat, he'd returned my call. Connor hadn't wanted to give me Milo's work address, but he knew he had no choice in the matter. He sounded resigned to giving me the details. I could find it out. All he would be doing was saving me time. And, as I pointed out to him, time was what we didn't have a lot of.

Milo worked for his father's business, a public relations agency based on Priory Park. I negotiated my way through the maze of car dealerships which dominated the area and found the new-build offices at the back of the development. The reception area was light and airy, no doubt designed to put you at ease when you walked in. The walls were decorated with boards and posters promoting the developing green technology sector around the Humber. I could see similar boards promoting the new City Plan and City of Culture bid. Above the reception desk was the company logo and strapline. "Helping you to tell your story". It was bullshit. I didn't know what to make of it. The table in the middle of the room had trade magazines and brochures casually arranged on it. I leafed through them until a middle aged man appeared in front of me. He was casually dressed, yet smart enough to make it clear he was at work. Tricky to pull off the look, but he'd done it. It was something which eluded me.

'Can I help you?' he said.

I put the magazine down. 'I'm looking for Milo.'

'Milo?'

I nodded.

He smiled at me, understanding. 'You mean Miles? I can never get used to my son being called that.' His eyes narrowed. 'It's usually only his friends who call him Milo.'

'I'm more a friend of a friend.'

'I see.'

He was uncomfortable with the situation, but I was standing my ground. I was banking on the fact he didn't want a man dressed in jeans and an old jumper fouling up his reception area in front of clients. He eventually called out his son's name. Milo walked in, chewing gum, hands in his pockets. He was a clone of Connor with the same haircut, studded earring and tattoos creeping out from under his shirt sleeves. The smile on his face soon disappeared when he saw me. He was definitely scared of me. He told his dad he could handle it. We waited for him to leave.

'Take a walk with me,' I said.

'Can't we do it in here?'

I shook my head. 'No we can't, Miles.' It was a cheap shot, but I wanted to bring him down a peg or two by using his proper name. He reluctantly followed me outside. The Humber Bridge stood behind us, simultaneously beautiful and brutal looking. I walked until we were out of sight. He needed to know I wasn't messing about. I grabbed him by the shirt and pinned him against the nearest wall. I told him who I was.

'Connor's uncle?'

'That's right.'

'It was a laugh that got out of hand, that's all. We didn't mean any harm by it.'

'How can you not mean harm by it? You stole the cigarettes.'

The cockiness I'd seen when he'd sauntered into the reception area to meet me returned to his eyes now he knew I wasn't a direct threat to him.

He smiled at me. 'You can hardly claim the moral high ground, can you? Whose cigarettes are they, really?'

I released my grip and walked away. He was right. I wasn't really in a position to judge. I had to deal with the consequences of what had happened. It was as simple as that.

I switched the SIM cards and called Carl Palmer's number.

He answered immediately. 'I don't like being fucked about.'

'Calm down, Carl.' I was willing to bet only a handful of people used the number and all their numbers were likely to be stored in the mobile's memory. My number would have stood out like a sore thumb to him. Silence. I let him chew over the fact I knew his name.

He laughed. 'You're good. How did you get this number?'

I ignored the question.

'I want them back,' he said.

'They're yours?'

'I want them back.'

'I want to speak to their real owner.'

'Have you got them to return?'

'Not yet. That's what I want to speak to their owner about.'

Silence for a few moments. I waited for him to come back on the line. 'That can be arranged,' he said.

I wanted to do it in public. 'There's a Starbucks in St Stephens. I'll be there at mid-day.' I hung up.

I headed for Don's house. It wasn't much of a detour before heading to Starbucks. I had no master plan for the meeting with Palmer and his boss, so the sooner I got it over and done with, the better. I knocked on the door of Don's neighbour. A woman in her sixties answered.

'How is Don?' she asked. She didn't ask me in.

'He's on the mend.'

'Pleased to hear it.'

I told her that I used to work with Don.

Her eyes narrowed. 'In the police?'

'His more recent job.' It was clearly the wrong answer, as she took a step back into her house. I matched it and moved forward a little. 'Can you tell me what happened?'

'I've already spoken with the police.'

'I'm here to help Don.'

She looked me up and down, like she was weighing up whether I was to be trusted or not. 'There's not much I can tell you. The man ran out as I shouted Don's name.'

'Did you get a good look at him?'

'I'm afraid not. He was too fast for me. I'd say he was in his thirties. Big and muscular, but rough looking with it.'

'Anything else?'

'I heard him shout he'd be back. That's why the police said they would step up their patrols.' She pointed to the bag in her hallway. 'But you can't trust them, can you? That's why I'm going to stay with a relative until they catch this man.'

I told her I understood and thanked her for helping Don. She shouted after me as I walked away. 'The policeman left his card with me.'

I waited while she went and found it. She reappeared and held it out to me. I read the details. Acting Detective Inspector Coleman. He'd been promoted since our paths had last crossed.

Starbucks in the St Stephen's Shopping Centre was above the main row of shops, as if it was suspended in mid-air. I had a good view of people coming and going. More importantly to me, it was busy. I didn't know what I was getting into, so it had to be done in public. There were no seats free which had a decent view of the staircase, so I sat with my back to the entrance and waited. I watched as shoppers carried bags between stores. My concentration was broken by a hand gripping my shoulder. It squeezed hard but

I didn't flinch. George Sutherland slipped into the seat opposite me.

'This is a surprise, isn't it?' he said.

I couldn't help but smile. I'd been wrong about him. I'd considered him well under the radar, but there weren't many people in the city with the clout to smuggle in a quantity of cigarettes through the docks. Sutherland was obviously one of the small number who could. I remembered that his pub offered bed and breakfast. He could possibly justify importing the catering supplies which masked the cigarettes. I wasn't sure how it would work, but it made some sense to me.

'How's the wife?' I asked him. It was a cheap shot, but it was all I had.

He laughed. 'No idea, but I owe you my thanks for that. I couldn't give a fuck about her.' He pointed to the blonde a few tables away, flicking through a magazine. 'Worked out for the best, I reckon.'

I smiled. 'At least your wife will get some well-deserved money.'

'Fuck off, Geraghty. Have a look around. There's a recession on. I'm a humble businessman trying to scratch a living. I'm sixty years old soon. I've got fuck all to give her.'

'Right.' I didn't believe him.

'Ask my accountant. I believe you know Mr Millfield.'

'We're already acquainted.' I was surprised, but I didn't let it show.

'But we're not here to talk about that, are we? Seems like your brother has been a naughty boy.'

'Stupid, maybe.'

'Beside the point, really, given the circumstances.'

'Maybe you should have taken more care. If you trust someone like Gillespie to sort things out for you, maybe you should have kept the cigarettes somewhere else.'

Sutherland sat back in his chair. A waitress placed a large cappuccino in front of him.

He drank a mouthful of coffee. 'You might have a point there. I placed my trust in people and the cunts let me down.'

I thought about the beating my brother had been given. Sutherland must have known I was involved. He'd been playing with me, waiting for me to make a move. Maybe waiting to see if I could find the cigarettes for him.

'Gillespie is a piece of shit,' he said. 'I don't care for him. And I can't say I care much for your brother. If you want to play with the big boys, you're going to get hurt.'

I was getting angry with him. 'You leave my brother alone.'

Sutherland smiled again. 'I dare say you've spoken to Peter Hill, too. He's quite a useful man to know, so I'm sure I'll be dealing with that cunt soon enough. Plenty of people need to make things up to me.'

'What do you want?'

'I want them back, obviously.' He paused. 'Or I want paying.'

'Unlucky on both counts.'

He smiled again. 'That's not how it works.'

'I can't give you what I haven't got. They were stolen, but you already know that.' There was no way I was giving him Connor's name.

'Quite a fucking coincidence.'

'Indeed.'

'I'll make it clear, then. I can't get insurance for my line of business, so I have to enforce my own rules.' He shuffled forward and leaned in close to me. 'Believe me, I'll enforce them. I'm not prepared to be out of pocket or let people down.'

'How much are we talking about?'

'Fifteen grand for the cigs.' He shrugged. 'Make it twenty for the inconvenience and my time sorting it out.'

I laughed. 'I can't help you with that.'

'Don't be talking yourself down, Geraghty. You caught me out, didn't you?'

His was talking about his wife. 'You didn't make any attempt to cover your tracks.'

'And you think the people who've stolen the cigarettes are master criminals?'

'I want you to leave my brother out of this.'

Sutherland considered this. 'You want me to hold you responsible?'

I nodded. It was the only way. I didn't care much about Terry Gillespie or Peter Hill. I only cared about Niall and Connor.

He swallowed the last of his cappuccino. 'In that case, I'll be in touch.'

I need a distraction to occupy my mind. I was going to have think carefully about my next move with Sutherland. Kath Millfield's literacy charity operated from an office on Wright Street. I'd checked her website. They operated an open door policy. People were encouraged to simply drop in to see the work they did and maybe volunteer their time. Roger Millfield would be expecting me to make progress, so I decided I wanted to see his wife when she was in her comfort zone. I wanted to get a feel for the woman. I fed the parking meter and walked in.

Directly in front of me was a display board about their literacy work with children. It was impressive. At the bottom was a list of corporate sponsors. Her husband's firm was one of them. To the left, I could see the offices. They had glass fronts, so you could observe them at work. Kath Millfield was on the telephone. I looked again at the display boards. The charity certainly did important work around the city. The children on the photo were all smiles and laughter.

One of Kath Millfield's employees walked across to join me. 'The children get so much out of the process. A lot of them aren't interested in reading when they start with us, but we place the emphasis on fun.' She smiled. 'It's about learning without the pressures of targets and exams.'

'It's certainly impressive,' I said.

'We're always eager for men to get involved. We always need positive male role-models.'

Out of the corner of my eye I saw a man walk straight into Kath Millfield's office. She put the telephone down. The woman continued to talk to me. I nodded, as I kept an eye on the office.

She continued to press me. 'Are you thinking of volunteering with us?'

I said something non-committal. Kath Millfield was arguing with the man. The woman I was talking to was clearly embarrassed. We both watched as the man stormed out. Kath Millfield closed her office door after him. She didn't notice me. I picked up a brochure and said I'd think things over. There was no point in following the man. I recognised Neil Farr, the solicitor I'd seen in the photographs with Kath Millfield.

I found Don propped up in his bed in the far corner of the hospital ward. He'd been worked over, his face was a mess, but at least he was comfortable. I took a chair off the stack in the corner and placed it next to his bed.

'I can go home once they've finished running their tests,' he said.

'You should take your time.'

He stared out of the window at the panoramic view of the city. Under other circumstances, it would be breathtaking.

'Who did this to you, Don?'

'I don't know.'

'I spoke to your neighbour.'

'Keep out of my business, Joe.'

'I'm here to help you.'

'I don't need your help.'

I leaned forward. 'Sure?'

'Definitely.'

'Who did this to you?' I repeated. 'This isn't going to go away.' The man sounded like hired muscle to me. Which meant it was serious. There was a reason for what had happened.

He asked me to pour him a glass of water. I did as I was asked, even though I knew he was playing for time. This wasn't right. Don had set up as a Private Investigator as a means to keep himself occupied after taking early retirement. He had been happy to work the mundane cases. They'd kept him busy and in the loop with old colleagues. I knew he wasn't the sort to seek out trouble.

He took a mouthful of water before speaking. 'You don't owe me anything. We're not partners. Let it go.'

I changed the subject. 'Roger Millfield called me earlier.'

Don stared at me. 'Why would he do that?'

'He had a job for me.'

'I thought you were out of that game?'

'I've got to make a living.'

He shook his head. 'What are you doing with your life, Joe?'

It was a good question. I had no answer. 'At the moment I'm trying to help some old friends.'

'Don't keep me in suspense, then. What did he want?'

'He thinks his wife is having an affair.'

Don was shocked by my news. 'And he called you?'

'That's right.'

We sat in silence until the bell signalled the end of visiting time. Technically, he was a pensioner, but he was also ex-police. CID. He was nobody's fool. I leaned in close to him so no one else would hear. 'It's time to be honest with me.' I looked him in the eye. 'I can help you.' We'd had our problems and difficulties, but I knew what he'd given me. 'If you don't want my help for yourself, think of Sarah and Lauren. They're going to have to see you like this.'

Don said nothing. I straightened myself up and left him lying there.

CHAPTER FIVE

I forced my way through the crowd at the front of the hospital and headed for the car park. Acting Detective Inspector Richard Coleman was standing at the entrance. I suppose we had a grudging kind of respect for each other these days, but we certainly weren't friends. I nodded a greeting and tried to side-step him. He blocked my move, so I tried again. He mirrored my move.

'What brings you here, Joe?'

'Just visiting,' I said. 'I hear you've been promoted.'

'Not quite. Acting Detective Inspector.'

'Congratulations.'

'You still haven't said what brings you here.'

I told him again that I was a visitor.

'Don?'

He knew, so I nodded my agreement.

'Same here. I've come to take a statement.'

I tried to move away again. 'Best of luck with that.'

'Time for a coffee?'

I was curious as to why he'd want to speak to me. I agreed and let him lead the way back in to the hospital. We walked up the two flights of stairs to the canteen. I found a table and waited while he queued for coffee. The queue was long and the canteen understaffed. It gave me time to think. I was surprised to find a senior detective was personally taking a statement. It didn't make sense.

Coleman sat down and placed a mug of coffee in front of me. 'What happened to Don?' he asked me.

I shrugged and said I knew nothing. Don wasn't prepared to talk about it. I asked Coleman what brought him here.

'You know how it works. We take care of our own.' He sipped at his drink. 'We've all got pasts.'

He was playing it with a poker face, adding nothing further. I wasn't going to give him anything, either. He would have spoken with Don's neighbour, too. It was a stalemate.

'Are you going to tell me anything?' I asked Coleman.

'I haven't spoken to Don yet, so I haven't got anything to tell you.'

I finished my drink and stood up. 'See you later, then.'

He followed me out of the canteen. At the top of the stairs he grabbed my arm and pulled me back. 'Go careful, Joe.'

I put Coleman's warning to one side and called Terry Gillespie as I walked back to my car. He told me he couldn't talk. I told him he didn't have a choice. I suggested he made himself available. I was heading to his house and I expected him to be there. It took me fifteen minutes to make the journey.

'You can't do this,' he said, opening his front door to me. 'I've got a job to do.'

I brushed past him and went into his living room. We didn't sit down. 'Haven't we all?' I said. 'And don't give me any of that shit.'

'What do you want?'

'We're going to talk about George Sutherland. They were his cigarettes.'

Gillespie smiled. 'Hardly a surprise, is it?'

He'd known all along. He'd tried to play me for a fool to get himself off the hook, but it wasn't relevant now. 'I told Sutherland that he should consider it my debt.' I didn't mention the price tag. All twenty thousand pounds of it.

He laughed. 'Why the fuck would you do that?'

'For my brother.'

Gillespie shrugged. 'No skin off my nose.'

I leaned forward and grabbed him. 'Don't think you're walking away from this unless I say so.'

'Why would I care?'

I relented and released him. 'Niall said you used to work on the docks, back in the day.'

'Used to be a bobber, hauling the baskets of fish in off the boats. Loved that work, I did. It was honest work. Not like sitting on your arse all day, watching things come and go. But that's progress, I suppose.'

I walked over to the mantelpiece and picked up a leaflet for Sutherland's pub. It was advertising erotic dancers and gentleman's evenings. 'What's Sutherland up to?' I asked him.

'How would I know?'

'You were seen arguing in his pub.'

If he was surprised by what I knew, he hid it well. 'I argue in a lot places.'

'And you thought you'd drag my brother into your shit?'

'He's a big boy. He makes his own decision.'

I was starting to lose my patience with him. 'Don't fuck me about,' I warned him. 'I'm doing you a favour here.'

He didn't speak. I was wasting my time here. It was making more sense to me, though. Erotic dancers and gentleman's evenings. I finally got the subtext. No wonder Sarah had felt so uncomfortable in the place. Gillespie was most likely paying for sex in there. Or rather he wasn't paying. Sutherland had a grip on him. There was a debt to be paid. I was sure of it. He'd lied to me about his involvement, pretending he didn't recognise the photograph of Carl Palmer. He wasn't going to be any help to me. I balled up the leaflet and threw it at him.

Before driving away from Gillespie's house, I called Sarah and agreed to collect her from the hospital when she'd finished visiting Don. I had some time to kill. I wanted to get a feel for Kath Millfield's routines and habits. I headed for her office and parked up on the street. I had yesterday's newspaper on the floor of my car to help pass the time. I saw the assistant I'd spoken to leave the office for the day, so I figured Kath Millfield wouldn't be far behind. The city centre slowly emptied, the shops and offices depositing workers back onto the streets. I didn't have to wait long. Neil Farr stepped out of a car and walked across the road to knock on the front door of the office. A couple of minutes later, Kath Millfield appeared, kissed him on the cheek and locked up. I watched as they both got into Farr's car. I followed.

Farr turned on to Freetown Way and went straight across the lights to Spring Bank. The rush hour was coming to a close, so there was still traffic on the road. Two cars separated us and I stayed lucky with the lights. I followed his car on to Princes Avenue and watched as they took a left down the first side street. I did the same and saw Farr pull into a parking space. I drove straight past and parked a little further on. I watched them walk back to Princes Avenue in my rear-view mirror. I locked my car up and followed at a safe distance. I lost sight of them as they rounded the corner. By the time I arrived at the same spot, they were using the pedestrian crossing. I stayed where I was and watched, as they walked into an Italian restaurant.

Unsure of what to do, I stared in the nearest shop window for a moment. I'd come this far, so I decided to a chance. I crossed the road and headed straight in to the restaurant, making for the back. I sat down and had a clear view of the place. Millfield and Farr were sitting well away from me, close to the window. They were leaning in towards each other, so I was certain they had no interest in me. The waitress walked over to me and took my order. I asked for a bowl of pasta. I wasn't particularly hungry, but I could hardly just sit there. The food was pretty good, making it obvious why the place was popular. I didn't take my eyes off them as I ate. They ordered dessert, so I had to wait it out. There was no chance of me moving until they did.

Neil Farr eventually summoned the waitress across and settled the bill. I placed some money down on my table, ready to move. Farr and Millfield both laughed and joked with the waitress as they waited for the card machine to process the transaction. They waved as they left. I allowed them a minute and then followed. I noticed Kath Millfield had left her scarf on the chair she'd been sitting at. I picked it up and took it across to the waitress.

I held it out to her. 'The lady sitting there must have forgotten it.'

The waitress took it from me and nodded. 'That's very kind. They're regulars here. I'll make sure she gets it when they're next in.'

I smiled and said that was perfect. I walked back to my car, suspecting Roger Millfield was right about his wife having an affair.

I sat in the hospital car park and waited for Sarah. A stream of people filed past me, heads down, glad to be out of the place. It was the end of visiting time. I switched the radio off and waited. Sarah appeared and got into the car. I asked her how Don was.

'Probably no different to when you saw him. He's sore and uncomfortable, but it'll pass.'

'Did he say anything?'

She shook her head. 'He won't tell me. In fact, he said we should leave him alone.'

It was obvious the situation was upsetting her. I glanced up at the hospital tower block and wondered what was going on in Don's head. What was he so scared of? It wasn't the Don I knew.

'What have you been doing?' Sarah asked me.

I told her about what I'd seen at the restaurant. 'I'm going to have to speak to Neil Farr about it.' I shuffled in my seat. 'I've also found out who the cigarettes belong to.'

'Who?'

'George Sutherland. I met him earlier and told him I'd take the debt on.'

'That's a big commitment.'

She was genuinely surprised by my news. But what else could I do? It wasn't Niall's world. He had a family to think of. I didn't mention the amount of money involved.

I dropped Sarah off outside her house. Niall had left a message on my voicemail. He was asking me for an update, but I could tell he just wanted to talk. I called back and asked him where he was. He said he was at Victoria Pier. I knew it well. I headed straight there and found him stood by himself, staring out at the brown water of the River Humber. I locked up and made my way over to him. It was early evening and cold. I zipped my coat up and put my hands in my pockets.

I joined him in leaning over the barriers. To our left, the two North Sea Ferries were preparing for their outward voyages. 'Remember the ferries that went from here?' I said.

'I can remember going out on them.'

I did, too. Before the Humber Bridge was built, the ferry was the easiest way to reach the south bank. Our dad would take us over every other month or so when he went to see a former rugby team mate who lived in Grimsby.

'You always used to run up the stairs to the main deck while dad was parking his car up,' Niall said.

'You always thought you were too cool for that kind of thing.'

'I was.'

I laughed. I would have been about ten years old. I could still smell the boats. I'd never travelled well on them. Sometimes they had simply stopped halfway across the Humber, stuck on a sandbank. There was nothing you could do but wait it out.

'I'm in pieces, Joe. Ruth is so angry with me, especially because she knows I'm shutting her out of something. Connor's tiptoeing around, but at least he's old enough to sort himself out.'

'I'm doing my best,' I said. I risked a glance across to him and decided to tell him the truth. 'The cigarettes belonged to George Sutherland.' I outlined what I knew about the man. 'If I had the money, I'd give it to you.'

Niall shook his head. 'It's not your problem.'

'I've given the money I got from Debbie's life insurance policy to her sister. She needs it for a house move. I told her to pay me back when it all goes through.' I hadn't expected to need it back any time soon. It had sat in a bank account for several years now, untouched until recently.

'I wouldn't have taken your money, anyway. It wouldn't be right,' Niall said.

'It'd be a solution.'

We continued to stare at the water until he stretched and walked over to the far corner of the pier. I followed him.

'I always envied your freedom,' he said. 'Still do, I suppose.'

'I've not got anything you'd want.'

'You've always been your own man. I've always chased my tail, trying to make other people happy.'

'That's not true.'

'That's how it feels.'

'I've always envied you,' I said. 'You've got things worked out.'

He laughed. 'You reckon?'

'Apart from the cigarettes, obviously.'

We both turned our backs on the water. Niall spoke first. 'You definitely had it all worked out. Remember how proud Mum and Dad were at your wedding? Mum in that blue dress and Dad in his best suit?'

'His only suit.'

'He was just as proud at your wedding.'

I'd like to think so. It was a lifetime ago now. I could still remember the three of us throwing a rugby ball around on the field behind his pub. My mum would bring us drinks out and drag him back to work at the bar. A blast of wind snapped us back into our conversation.

'How's Sarah?' my brother asked me.

I thought about telling him what was happening, but decided to say nothing more than she was fine. As Niall had told me, he wasn't cut out for this kind of thing. He didn't need to know.

Niall told me he wanted to put in a couple more hours at the bar. It opened tomorrow night. We started to walk back down the pier toward our cars. Niall unlocked his and went to get in. He stopped halfway and thanked me. 'I needed to talk to someone.'

I nodded. 'It's what little brothers are for.' We embraced and I told him to look after himself.

'All I want is a quiet life, Joe.'

'Don't we all?'

He got in his car and opened the window. 'What are you going to do when this is over?'

It was a good question. I shrugged and walked away towards my car.

I watched my brother drive away before calling Connor. 'I need a word,' I said when he answered. 'Where are you?'

'Home?'

'Is your mum in?'

'No.'

'Put the kettle on, then.' I put my mobile back in my pocket and got in to my car. Connor had a coffee ready for me by the time I arrived. We went through to the kitchen.

'I've had a chat with your dad,' I told him. He wasn't getting off that easily. I said nothing, hoping Connor found the silence uncomfortable. A twinge of guilt hit me, but the time for being Uncle Joe had passed. This was man-to-man. Connor walked over to the patio doors. He was obviously struggling with whatever he had to say. I sipped my drink.

He spoke first. 'I had a word with Milo earlier.'

'Good.' I put the drink down and gave him my full attention.

'I told him how badly things had turned out.'

'What did he say?'

Connor shrugged. 'You know what he's like.'

I did. 'He's a dickhead.'

'Dad doesn't like him.'

'You can't really blame him for that.'

'I'm going to prove him wrong, though. We're going to get our club night off the ground. We're not messing about. We've got it all planned out. The theme's sorted and we know where we want to hold it. And if we can do that, we can go out around the country with it. The world, really. That's the brilliant thing with club nights. With the Internet you can reach out.'

I listened as Connor laid out his master plan to me. It was detailed and sounded convincing. I understood his passion and certainty. I was certain I'd play for Rovers and my country when I was his age. I'd win every honour there was to win and then I'd coach the club to even more success. You don't think about failing when you're young. I knew I had felt indestructible. It's only later you realise how fallible you are. Real life hadn't touched Connor yet. He didn't know illness, disappointment or loss. Bad things had threatened to make themselves known, but I could play my part in holding them at bay. And I would.

Connor spoke. 'I told Milo I had to know who he sold the cigarettes to.'

I was pleased he was making an effort. I listened as Connor told me the name of some brothers in Goole. The name meant nothing to me, but I would find out. They had a shop selling second hand furniture. It was worth a shot. They wouldn't be difficult to find. 'How much did you sell the cigarettes for?' I asked him.

He turned away from the patio doors. 'A thousand pounds.'

I asked him to repeat that. I couldn't believe it, even if it didn't really matter. 'What's happened to the money?'

'Milo's spent it on some promo stuff we needed doing.'

I shook my head. I hoped it was worth it.

'How's Dad doing?' he asked me.

'He'll be pleased when all this is over.'

'Can you sort it out?'

I drained my coffee and told him that was my plan. There was nothing more to be done today. I was heading home.

Hull, May 1980

Holborn shook his head and pulled out into the traffic. 'Can you believe some sad cunts went to watch City yesterday?'

Ridley wound down the car window and threw his cigarette butt out. 'Takes all sorts, I suppose.'

'It's a filthy fucking habit.'

'The smoking or the football?'

Holborn laughed and overtook a slow moving car. There was little traffic on the road. It was the day after the Challenge Cup Final. Hull KR v Hull FC at Wembley Stadium in front of 90,000 spectators. It was the biggest day in the rugby league calendar and Hull had been on show to the country. Hull KR in red and white at one end of the stadium, Hull FC in black and white at the other. Split down the middle, just like in the city.

'One of the lads at the station told me that someone left a banner on the side of the Humber Bridge. Last one to leave the city should turn the lights out. Can you believe that?' Holborn laughed. 'Cheeky cunts. Tell you something, though. Yesterday was the best day to get some fanny in this town. The field was clear.'

They continued past the city centre and headed east in the direction of Holderness Road.

'Where are we going?' Ridley asked.

'Just a couple of quick jobs before we go back. Won't take long. Need to have a word with some people.' Holborn glanced at Ridley. 'Alright?'

Ridley knew he wasn't being given a choice. They headed past Craven Park, home of Hull KR. 'Wouldn't piss on that place if it was on fire,' Holborn said. 'It's more than the cheating bastards deserve.'

Hull KR had taken the Cup, winning 10-5. One try apiece, but Hull KR kicked their penalties. Hull FC hadn't. Hubbard v Lloyd. Only one winner. Holborn pulled up in a pub car park.

The pub was nondescript, the area bland. A row of shops stood on the other side of the road. A butcher, a convenience store and a betting shop. It was the same as everywhere else. The pub was decorated in red and white. Holborn pushed people out of the way as he headed to the bar, daring them to challenge him. No one did.

Holborn spoke to Ridley, pointing to the man pulling a pint for a customer. 'I want you to meet Jimmy Geraghty, landlord of this shit-hole.'

Ridley nodded to the man in front of them. 'Alright.'

'Can I get you gentleman a drink?' Geraghty said.

'Bet you're fucking loving this, aren't you?' Holborn said, pointing to the Hull KR memorabilia.

'What can I do for you?'

'Let's do it in private shall we, Jimmy?'

Geraghty shook his head. 'I've got people to serve.'

Holborn smiled. 'I don't give a fuck, Jimmy. Your fan-club can do without you for ten minutes.' He turned to Ridley. 'Did you know Jimmy used to play for Rovers? Over 250 games for them, back when they were really shit. A fucking legend, weren't you, Jimmy?'

'If you like.'

'Upstairs.'

Geraghty led the way into the family living room and closed the door. Ridley looked around. The photographs covered the man's rugby career and his growing family with two young boys. Geraghty was about forty years of age, but any muscle he'd had was now fat.

'You know what we want, Jimmy,' Holborn said. 'Let's not piss about.'

'I haven't got the money.'

'I heard that, Jimmy, and that's what brings me here. It's the wrong answer. Try again.'

'I haven't got it.'

'Mr Salford's not going to be best pleased with your attitude.'

'I can't help that.'

Holborn laughed. 'That's not the attitude we're after, is it Don?'

Ridley said nothing, knowing this was heading in a direction which wasn't right. Holborn lunged forward and punched Geraghty in the stomach. Ridley watched Geraghty go down, winded.

Holborn shook his head. 'You try to help some people out but this how they treat you.' He bent down. 'Try again, Jimmy.'

Geraghty struggled to his feet. Holborn punched him back to the floor. 'Nobody said you could stand up.' He turned to Ridley and pointed at Geraghty. 'Be my guest. Take out some of the day's frustrations on the fat cunt.'

Ridley shook his head and walked over to the window. The street was quiet. If people weren't downstairs celebrating, they were no doubt still in bed nursing hangovers from yesterday's match.

'Fucking hit him,' Holborn repeated.

Ridley shook his head again.

'I've got the money,' Geraghty said.

'That's better Jimmy,' Holborn said. 'Much better. We're all friends here, aren't we?' He helped him stand back up.

Geraghty went over to a drawer and took out an envelope.

Ridley glanced at it and knew it was cash. Geraghty held it out towards Holborn.

'What the fuck are you thinking, Jimmy? You don't pass money to me. I'm a police officer.'

Geraghty lowered his arm, a beaten man.

'You pass it to Bancroft like normal. He'll be in soon enough to see you.' Holborn turned to Ridley and winked. 'You remember your mate Andrew Bancroft, don't you?'

Ridley didn't say a word, but thought back the altercation in the interview room. He knew him.

Holborn spoke to Geraghty. 'It wasn't that hard after all, was it Jimmy?' He nodded to Ridley. They were done here. Holborn headed for the door, but stopped before he left the room. 'I want you to be ready the next time we visit, Jimmy. Are we clear on that? I don't want to hear you've pissed Bancroft about again.'

Geraghty said he understood.

Holborn led Ridley back downstairs. The noise getting louder again. Victory songs from the Hull KR fans.

'Who do you support?' Holborn asked Ridley.

'I don't mind.'

Holborn laughed. 'Get a grip, Don. You can't live in this city and not have a team.'

'FC,' Ridley eventually said.

Holborn nodded his approval. 'Good choice, Don. These cunts can have their day in the sun, but we know the truth, don't we? They're small-time wankers. They'll do fuck all next year.'

Holborn pushed his way out the pub, back into the car park. Ridley stopped him from walking any further. 'Why did you have to do this to him today?'

Holborn smiled, took some money out and tucked it into Ridley's pocket. 'Times are changing, Don. You're not a bad detective and I know you're not a stupid bloke. You've already proved you know which the right team to support is. Make sure you don't choose the wrong one this time.'

CHAPTER SIX

I reminded myself Roger Millfield was paying me to do a job for him. Neil Farr had questions to answer. I needed to clarify a few things. I found a parking space on a meter before walking the short distance from Silver Street to Parliament Street.

His office was close to Roger Millfield's. All the solicitors and accountants grouped together in the area. Strength in numbers, I assumed. Farr's receptionist told me he was busy and wouldn't have the time to speak to me. I told her that if I didn't see Mr Farr as a matter of urgency, I'd be forced to take my business elsewhere. It was the best I could do. She probably didn't believe me, but eventually told me to take a seat while she double-checked his availability. Maybe it was a sign of the times. A few minutes later I was sitting in Neil Farr's office. It was indistinguishable from Millfield's, only the view changed.

'This is most irregular, Mr Geraghty,' he said, once he'd sat down.

'I'm an irregular type of guy.'

'And what line of business are you in again?'

'I'm in what you might call the people business.'

'I'm afraid I don't follow you.'

'I'm a Private Investigator.' I passed him one of my cards. I only had old ones marked up as 'Ridley & Son' in my pocket.

Farr laughed nervously. 'Come on, now. We're not in America.'

'I'm sure you use the services of one here.'

'Very rarely and only for routine matters.' Farr was flustered. He stood up. 'I think you should leave, Mr Geraghty.'

I shook my head and waited until he sat back down. 'We need to have a talk.'

'I can't imagine that we have anything to talk about.'

'Kath Millfield.'

'Kath?'

I nodded and repeated her name.

'What about her?'

'You're good friends?' I made sure I had his attention. 'I saw you with her last night.'

'Who do you work for?'

'I'm not prepared to discuss that.'

'Roger, I bet.'

I said nothing and waited for Farr to make a move. The silence was clearly making him uncomfortable. He eventually spoke. 'The man's a bully, always has been.'

'And she's just a friend?'

'I resent that comment, Mr Geraghty. I've known Kath for many years and she's a dear friend.' He leaned forward. 'And to be frank, you should look closer to home.'

'What does that mean?'

He held his hands up. 'I shouldn't have said that. Ignore me.'

It was too late for that. I was going nowhere until I heard whatever was on his mind. 'I should look closer to home?'

Farr swivelled back in his chair to face me. 'I'm not talking out of turn if I tell you Kath's marriage hasn't been the happiest or the smoothest. It's not a secret.'

'So why should I look closer to home?'

He pointed at me. 'Let's be clear Mr Geraghty, you're the one who came to me. You're the one who asked me the question.'

I told him we were clear on that.

He waved my card at me. 'She once had an affair with your Don Ridley.'

I wasn't expecting to hear that. I asked him when this affair had taken place.

'I'm going back a long way. I don't see how it's relevant. I shouldn't have said anything.'

'How long ago?'

'I don't know. More than a couple of decades ago. Ancient history.' He walked to the door, opened it and asked me to leave. 'I really shouldn't be having this conversation with you.'

I sat in my car and rubbed my face. I wasn't expecting to learn that Don had once had an affair. Nor did I know what to do with the information. I stared at Sarah's number in my mobile before I pressed call. I knew if I didn't call her, she'd call me.

'I've spoken with Neil Farr,' I said.

'Learn anything useful?'

'Not really.' I immediately felt bad for lying to her. Instinctively, I knew I couldn't tell her about Don's affair. It would break her heart. I told Sarah I'd keep trying and asked her if she'd found anything more out about George Sutherland.

'He's skint. His last accounts show that he owes money to a lot of different people. His business empire has crumbled due to the recession and no one wants to buy his house. Apart from the pub, that's pretty much all he's got. He's managed to lose everything else. It seems he's remortgaged what he could and there's nothing left.'

I thanked Sarah for the information. It explained why he was smuggling cigarettes into the country. He was desperate.

'What are you going to do, Joe?'

'I need to know more about Sutherland.' I knew that was the only way forward if I was going to sort this mess out. 'I need to find his weakness. I need an angle on him.'

'We'll find it.'

I could almost hear the smile in her voice. I ended the call, pleased I had someone to share the load with.

I headed for a cafe off George Street in the city centre. I borrowed their telephone directory and found the number for the police station in Queens Gardens. My call was eventually answered and I was put through to Acting Detective Inspector Coleman's office. I told him where I was, cut the connection and waited. His appearance at the hospital to speak to Don didn't make sense. There was something going on. Ten minutes later Coleman walked through the door. He spotted me, made his way over and sat down. He didn't bother ordering a drink.

'What's going on?' I said.

'You're the one who called.'

'What's going on?' I repeated.

He leaned forwards. 'You're the one who called me.'

I smiled and nodded. He wasn't going to give me anything easily. 'You implied that Don has enemies.'

'Only stating the obvious.' He relaxed into his chair, even though he didn't seem very comfortable with the situation. 'He was a policeman for long time. We make enemies. Nature of the beast.'

I'd given the possibility of someone holding a grudge against Don some thought and not made any progress. He'd been a well-respected detective for Humberside Police, but it had been a difficult job.. We'd also no doubt upset people when we'd operated as Private Investigators, but there was nothing obvious. Some of those cases had involved the police and the right people had gone to prison. The majority of work had been routine. There was no one we'd upset to the point they'd come looking for revenge. I needed a route into his police career. I asked him what Don had told him in the hospital.

'Nothing,' Coleman said.

'So what can you tell me?'

'I'm not at liberty to talk to you about ongoing police matters. You know that.'

'Off the record?'

'You know how it works, Joe.'

Stalemate again. But we both knew he held all the aces. He was part of a huge investigative machine. I was one man on his own.

'It could be something, it could be nothing,' Coleman said.

I finished my drink. 'You're bang on there.' I left him sitting there. I'd taken what I wanted from our chat. I'd chosen the place deliberately to see how long it would take him to arrive. His swift appearance and the mention of ongoing police matters told me everything I needed to know.

Something was happening that I wasn't aware of. I was right to be worried about Don.

I had things I needed to discuss with Roger Millfield, but his secretary made it easy for me. She told me Millfield was on a training course at the KC Stadium. He wanted to speak to me as soon as possible. I called Sarah to see if she was free. Don had been discharged, so I offered to take her to his house once we'd finished with Millfield.

We drove the short distance to Anlaby Road. We stood outside the main entrance to the stadium and looked upwards at the sloping West Stand roof. It had been built a decade ago with the proceeds from the council's sale of shares in local telecommunication company, Kingston Communications. The place still took my breath away a little.

The board in the reception area told me the accountancy course was in the Wilberforce Suite. Sarah shook her head when I told her I was going straight in. Millfield had called me, so I wasn't prepared to wait. There wasn't time for that. She sat down in one of the chairs placed around the glass table in the corner and waited. The lecturer stopped talking and the room fell silent as I entered. Millfield quickly excused himself and walked towards me. We stepped outside and walked around the stadium concourse. Sarah followed us.

He spoke to Sarah. 'I thought the old business had shut down.'

'Joe's asked me to help him out.'

Millfield stared at us both before taking an envelope out of his pocket. He held it out in front of me. 'I needed to give you this. There's no easy way of saying it, but I've changed my mind. It was a mistake. I don't need your services.'

I didn't understand. 'Why not?'

'I've changed my mind. Simple as that.' He glanced at Sarah. 'I had a word with Don after I'd spoken with you and he told me he'd sort it out.'

'I was sorting it out for you,' I said.

He opened the envelope and showed me the cheque inside it. It was made payable to me. 'I shouldn't have involved you with my problems. Split it how you see fit, but this the end of the matter. I need to spend my time at work, settling Rebecca into her new role.'

Sarah spoke. 'Why don't you tell us what's going on?'

'Nothing's going on.'

'Don's in hospital,' I said.

'What happened?'

'He was attacked.'

'How is he?'

'It's a good job he hasn't got any looks to lose.'

'But he'll be fine?'

I ignored the question. 'Don't take me for a fool,' I told him. 'You tell me you'd rather Don did the job and then he's attacked. I'm not a fan of coincidences'

He didn't break my stare. 'Don't go looking for something that's not there. I've changed my mind. That's all.'

I'd learned how to read people over the years. It was an essential skill to be able to look people in the eye and tell if they were lying or not. I knew Millfield wasn't being straight with me. I was about to say something about Neil Farr, but stopped myself. I wondered if Don's affair with Kath Millfield was relevant. Sarah didn't know and now wasn't the time.

'I don't want to talk to you about this again,' he said as he started to walk back toward the main entrance. 'Just do as you're told, please.'

It was only a short drive to Don's house. It passed in silence, both of us trying to make sense of what Roger Millfield had said. It would have to wait for now. It was clear Don wasn't as pleased to see me as he was Sarah. His appearance had improved a little. The bruising to his face was starting to come out a little more and his left eye had started to reopen. The mantelpiece had framed photographs of him on holiday with Sarah and Lauren. These were bookended with ones of Don with his wife. She'd died several years ago. I picked up the book he was reading. A Geoffrey Boycott biography. I smiled. Yorkshire to the core.

'How's the bowling going?' I asked him.

'It keeps me busy.'

'Good.' I'd been surprised to learn Don had taken up bowls in the local park, something to pass the time. Sarah had told me he was going to give it a go, but I hadn't expected him to stick with it. He wasn't the sort of person I imagined enjoying leisure activities.

Don spoke to Sarah. 'Put the kettle on, please.'

I sat down opposite him and waited for her to leave the room before speaking. 'We've spoken with Roger Millfield,' I said.

'Both of you?'

'Sarah's keen to help.'

He stared at me, like he wanted to say it wasn't a good idea, but eventually let it go. 'Did he have anything to say?'

'He told me he longer required my services.' Our eyes stayed on each other. He wasn't giving anything away. 'How come you're working for Roger Millfield?'

'He asked me to.'

'I thought you'd retired?'

He shrugged. 'We go way back.'

I wasn't buying it. 'You were attacked straight after getting involved.'

'Don't look for things that aren't there, Joe.'

'You must have enemies?'

'None worth talking about.'

'I'm not the only one concerned about you. I've been talking to Acting Detective Inspector Coleman.'

'He had a word with me.'

'Why would a man of that rank be interested? It doesn't make sense.'

Don simply shrugged. 'I'm one of them. It's the way it works.'

'He mentioned an ongoing investigation.'

'I wouldn't know. Only Coleman can tell you about that.'

Sarah walked into the room with our drinks. Don thanked her and said he had some washing he needed hanging out. I didn't dare look at Sarah. She knew he was excluding her from our conversation.

I waited until I heard the back door open before speaking. 'Why didn't you tell me about your affair with Kath Millfield?'

He wasn't surprised by the question. 'How do you know?'

'It's not important.' We sat in silence. I was waiting for him to speak.

He eventually sighed and spoke. 'There are things you don't need to know about me. Things Sarah certainly doesn't need to know about me.' He pointed at me. 'And you're going to keep them to yourself. Is that clear?' He couldn't look me in the eye. 'I'm not proud of myself. My marriage wasn't working back then. I was investigating some seriously sick people. I can't begin to explain what a strain it puts on you. I've seen the dead bodies of sexually abused children, children who were nothing more than punch-bags for their short lives, knowing how miserable their short time here was. I've seen bodies burnt beyond all recognition. I've had to intrude on families of decent people who were murdered because they were in the wrong place at the wrong time. It takes its toll on better people than me, I can tell you that much, and I've seen it all first-hand.'

'It doesn't excuse what you did.'

'I'm not saying it does.'

'How did you meet Kath Millfield?'

'Through her husband. He helped us out at with some investigation or other. I got to know her socially and one thing led to another.'

'One thing led to another?' I repeated. 'That's all you've got to say?'

'You leave the Millfields alone. I don't want you bothering them. Am I clear?' He sat back, his point made, and changed the subject. 'Sarah tells me your brother is in trouble.'

I told him about the smuggled cigarettes, the words sounding no less ridiculous than the first time I'd said them.

'Have you thought about going to the police?'

I smiled. Don knew I would have no intention of doing that. 'It's not on the agenda.'

'I didn't think it would be.'

'Niall's got a family to think about.'

He took the point. 'Start at the beginning.'

I told Don the whole story. I told him the missing cigarettes belonged to George Sutherland.

Don nodded. 'I know the name.' His eyes never left mine. 'What are you getting my daughter into?'

The honest answer was that I didn't know. But I also knew Sarah was tougher than he wanted to admit. If she wanted to be involved, neither of us would be able to stop her, not that I wanted to. I needed her help. Sarah walked back into the room. Don relaxed back into his chair, but he'd made his point.

I had a plan in mind. Talking to Don had jogged an old memory. I knew where to go, so I was pleased Sarah had agreed to help Niall at the bar ahead of the opening. I wanted some time on my own to see where it would lead.

Sarah broke the silence as we drove. 'What did my dad say, then?'

'Not much.'

'He wanted me out the room for some reason, did he?'

'He told me to leave Roger Millfield alone.' It was my turn to ask a question. 'Why is your dad doing this? I thought he'd decided to take it easy and enjoy his retirement?'

'So did I.'

We pulled up at a set of traffic lights. It didn't sit right with me, but the problem I had was that I didn't know how much I should tell her about her father. If it made me a coward, so be it. 'We'll sort it out,' I said.

'It's not like him,' she said. 'I'm worried. He's determined to shut me out.'

The lights changed. I put the car in gear and changed the subject. 'I told him about the cigarettes.'

'What did he say to that?'

'That I should go to the police.'

'Ironic of him, I suppose.'

CHAPTER SEVEN

I headed for Anlaby Road. If I wanted to know about Don's enemies, I knew a good place to start. I'd promised Sarah I'd get to the bottom of it, and if the person who'd attacked Don was hired muscle, as I suspected, chances were they were going to come back.

When I'd crossed Frank Salford in a previous case, myself and Don had spoken to an old police colleague of his. Gerard Branning had retired, but he retained an encyclopaedic knowledge of local criminality throughout the decades. He regularly drank in a one of the area's pubs. I remembered that he went in there most days after walking his dog. I parked up and made my way in.

I told the barman who I was looking for.

'He's not here.'

I asked for a Diet Coke and told him to keep the change.

'Last of the big spenders,' he said, passing me my drink.

'Have you seen Gerard recently?'

'Police?'

I shook my head. 'He's an old friend.'

The barman took a moment to make his decision before shouting across to a guy practising at the dartboard. 'What's the name of that place Gerard went into?'

The name of a care home was shouted back at me.

'He's been ill,' the barman told me.

The address I'd been given was in Hessle, a small settlement on the outskirts of Hull. I passed the Square and counted down the streets until I found the one I wanted. The place I wanted was at the bottom of a cul-de-sac. I'd been told Branning had undergone an operation. He had no family, so it was easier for him to recover away from his own home. I pressed the buzzer and waited. When it was answered, I said I was a friend of Branning's. Nothing happened. I assumed she had gone to check with him. Eventually I was allowed in and shown to a day room. The place was surprisingly noisy. Alarms and bells constantly sounded, the smell of overcooked vegetables lingered in the air and staff rushed from room to room. Gerard Branning sat in the far corner of the room, next to the window. The care assistant who had shown me through left us to it.

'Ridley's partner?' he said. 'I remember you.'

'That's right.' I sat down opposite him.

'At least you're a friendly face. I don't see too many of them stuck in here. I assume you went to the pub to find me?'

I told him that was exactly what I'd done.

'Hardly matters. Friend or enemy. It's the price you pay for working in the police. Besides, look at me, who's going to be interested in a man in my condition?'

I poured him a glass of water and told him the story I'd prepared as I'd driven to see him. 'I'm sorting out a party for Don and I need some help with the guest-list.'

'His 65th?'

I nodded. 'Who should I be inviting?'

Branning gave me a list of names. I made a note of them to keep up appearances. Some of the names I'd heard before, some were new to me. I let him reminisce for a while. It put a smile on his face, and truth be told, I enjoyed listening to his stories. I got us back on track. 'Is there anyone I shouldn't ask?'

Branning thought about the question. 'Don's a good man. He always did the job as it should be done. In fact, I don't think anyone worked harder than he did. And he worked some tough cases in his time. Do you remember Bruce Lee, the arsonist? He worked that one. It was tough. Three children dead.'

'I can imagine.'

'He worked the Christopher Laverack case, too.'

I knew that case had pushed Don to his limits. He would often speak about it. A nine year old boy sexually assaulted and battered to death. Sarah wouldn't have been much older than the boy at the time. I knew the case had resonated with him.

'As for enemies,' Branning said, 'there was Reg Holborn. He was a DI like Don, but they never saw eye to eye. I never pushed him on it. I never had any time for Holborn, either, but you learn to mind your own business.' He tapped his nose. 'You learn to keep that out.'

I wrote the name down and underlined it. I looked up at Branning. 'He wasn't on the level?'

'He made plenty of arrests'.

I waited for Branning to elaborate. He said nothing further, but I got the point. I tapped my pen on the pad resting on my knee and decided to take a chance. 'What can you tell me about George Sutherland?'

'He was very much Frank Salford's man. Obviously you'll know all about him. They both came up in the late sixties from the council estates and made names for themselves at the rugby and the football. Gang culture is nothing new, believe me. Sutherland was well in with Frank Salford, but so far as I know, he kept his head down. We could never prove anything against him, either. On paper, he was legitimate. We suspected he was money laundering for Salford in his pubs, but again, nothing stuck. Even the VAT man went in for a sniff around but didn't get anywhere. We couldn't prove it, but we knew Salford really owned the pubs. He must have been protected or Salford wasn't too bothered if he was skimming cash from him. All I know is they were tight.'

'Sounds like he hasn't changed all that much,' I said, thinking about his pub. 'Everything is cash-based.' I was ready to leave. I needed some fresh air and he'd given me something to work with. I thought about Sutherland's apparent change in character. He'd gone from an under the radar criminal to teeing up a significantly risky operation that would end with serious prison time if caught. With a sinking feeling in my stomach, I realised he was a man with nothing to lose. His wife of thirty years had left him and his business was failing. This was his chance to be a player. And I'd facilitated it. Dragging me into it all was going to give him a measure of revenge. I could see that now. I thanked

Branning and got as far as the door before he called out to me.

'It's Don's 64th this year.'

I stopped with my back to him and smiled. He'd known all along.

'You know where I am if you need me, Joe,' he said.

The History Centre housed the city's archives and local studies library. I wanted to review back issues of the Hull Daily Mail. It was quiet with only a handful of people at work, so I was able to persuade a member of staff to assist me. The archives had plenty references to Reg Holborn. I went straight to the article on his retirement. Holborn had retired as a Detective Chief Inspector and an event had been held in his honour at one of the city's boxing clubs. He had obviously been well thought of. I glanced through the details. Alongside Don, he'd worked on all the major murder investigations Hull had seen in recent times. The ones I'd spoken to Branning about, Bruce Lee and Christopher Laverack, were both included. As Holborn had moved up the ranks, he'd taken the lead on the doorstep stabbing of driving instructor Keith Slater in 1988, and then in 1994, the doorstep shooting of Shane George. That had been the first time I could remember such an incident in the city. It had felt like a definite shift, a move to more violent and final solutions. I knew from the stories Don had told me how difficult the job had been, especially if you were leading the investigations. Holborn had done a tough job for several decades. My helper brought me more items to review. I looked at photographs of Holborn taken at various civic events. He'd done a lot of work for his favourite charities, particularly those which benefited young people. He had been a patron of a well-known local boxing club, which made sense, given the venue for his retirement celebration. I read the accompanying article. Holborn had been taken to the place as a youngster and he'd felt it had given him some purpose in life and he wanted to pass it on. Boxing had been his passion and escape from the rigours of the job. I'd thought Don's escape had been his family life, but that assumption had been turned on its head by what Neil Farr had told me. I turned to the photographs of Holborn standing alongside various Lord Mayors and local members of Parliament. They were always Labour. It was that kind of city. Holborn had moved in impressive circles, seemingly a popular man. I stared out of the window at Freetown Way. Cars hurried past, skirting around the edge of city centre. I went back to the screen and checked the most recent mention of Holborn. I read the story again. He'd died in a house fire a couple of weeks ago.

I left the History Centre with several photocopies. I'd read the articles in depth later. Gerard Branning had played me like a professional. He'd wanted me to find out about Reg Holborn's death. He was still sharp. The Hull Daily Mail's coverage of Holborn's death stated he lived on Winchester Close, a small estate of bungalows in East Hull. My dad had told me Rovers had once owned the land, before deciding to build the original Craven Park a couple of miles closer to the city centre on Holderness Road. I knew the area well. My dad had been landlord at the Barham Pub, which stood at the top of estate. Before heading there, I tried calling Neil Farr. I wanted to speak to him again, but I was told he was in a meeting. I knew I was being lied to, but there was no point pushing my luck.

I hadn't been back to the area I'd spent most of my childhood in for years. The small row of shops had changed. What had once been a large playing field behind the pub was now sheltered housing for the elderly. The estate was enclosed and easy to navigate. Holborn's house was easy to spot. I could see the damage the fire had done. I pulled out my mobile and started to call the number on the estate agent's board. I stopped and put my mobile away before the call was answered. I had a better idea. I parked up and approached the house. No curtains were up, so I peered in. There wasn't much to see, but it got me the attention I wanted.

'Can I help you?'

Holborn's neighbour was a woman in her sixties. She was holding a trowel in her hand and had appeared from the back of her bungalow. Her front garden was immaculate. I pointed to the estate agent's board. 'I was thinking about having a look around for my dad. It's the kind of place he'd be interested in.' I gave her my best smile and told her I'd just been looking through the window. 'There was a fire?'

She nodded. 'A terrible business.'

'What happened?'

'It seems Reg dropped a cigarette on the chair he was sat in. By the time the fire brigade arrived, it was too late.' She shrugged. 'Most of us around here are elderly, you see. We're not built for dragging people out of houses. Reg was more or less infirm, so the poor man never stood a chance.'

I sympathised with her before turning away and taking a deep breath. I'd thought I'd come to terms with Debbie's death, but stories like this brought it back all too vividly, leaving me wondering if I could ever put it fully behind me.

I snapped back into our conversation when she spoke. 'He kept himself to himself, but I knew he had other health problems. It can't have helped.'

'I suppose not.' Reading the newspaper reports in The History Centre had fixed Holborn into a particular time frame for me. I couldn't picture him as an old man with failing health.

'His children don't live in Hull,' she said. 'One's down in London and the other one works abroad. It's the way of the world, I suppose. My two aren't much different. They both moved away for work, too. Lucky if they call me more than once a month. Do you have children?'

I shook my head. 'No children.'

She looked at me again, taking my face in. 'I knew you were familiar to me. You're Jimmy's lad, aren't you?'

There was no point lying. I said I was. She was confused, so I told her what I was really doing here. I gave her one of my cards. She might have blown my cover, but I was pleased my dad was still remembered around here.

She walked across the driveway to me. 'The really strange thing about all of this is that I never saw him smoke a cigarette in his life.'

CHAPTER EIGHT

Neil Farr still hadn't returned my call. I knew there was a library close by. My parents had taken me there as a child. Pulling up outside of it, it was clear not much had changed here, either. I went inside and got the information I needed from the telephone directory. Neil Farr lived in the exclusive village of Swanland. It was situated outside of Hull on the edge of the Yorkshire Wolds. I headed straight there. It was a twenty minute journey, but Hull felt a million miles away. I drove slowly past the village pond, looking for the address I needed. There was a large 4x4 BMW parked outside of it. The private registration plate made it clear that it belonged to Farr. It was the same car I'd seen outside Kath Millfield's office. I parked at the end of the cul-de-sac, well away from his house and headed back towards it. I walked slowly down his drive, giving him every opportunity to spot me. He didn't, so I hammered loudly on the front door. I told the woman who answered that I needed to speak to her husband. It was a quiet village, not the kind of place where dishevelled people like me turned up to ask questions. She shut the door on me. Eventually Neil Farr reopened it and stood in front of me.

'What do you want?' he said. 'This is my home. You can't do this.'

'You didn't return my call.'

'I don't return many calls.'

'I need to talk to you.'

He took a step back. 'How did you find me?'

I told him professional people were invariably listed in the telephone directory. I didn't know why, but it was a lesson I'd learnt over the years.

He shouted to his wife that he was popping out before turning back to me. 'The pub's only a short walk away.'

I followed a step behind him. We didn't speak until we reached the bar of The Swan and Cygnet, the local village pub. He told me I was buying. I passed him half a pint of bitter and we found a quiet corner.

He took a sip and placed his drink down. 'You've got my attention, Mr Geraghty. What do you want?'

I leaned across to the table to make sure I had his full attention. I'd tried to get the logic straight in my mind as I drove to his house. I knew there was a link between Don and Kath Millfield because they'd had an affair, but Roger Millfield was adamant he didn't want me involved in investigating his wife's alleged infidelity any further. And Don was equally adamant that I should leave it alone, saying he was now taking care of it, despite being hospitalised. It didn't make much sense, but Coleman had suggested that Don had enemies from his days with the police. I had to do something, as I'd made a promise to Sarah. Maybe there wasn't a direct line between them, but I had to follow things, wherever they took me. I had too many questions and not enough answers. Farr had made it clear he was fond of Kath Millfield. Maybe he'd throw me something. 'You met Roger when you were training?' I said.

'When I was networking, really. It was encouraged. You need a book of contacts in every line of business. You know that as well as I do. I'm a solicitor, he's an accountant. It made sense.'

'Do you get on with him?'

'I suppose I must have to start with.'

'What changed?'

'Kath.' He looked resigned to telling me the truth now he knew I wasn't going to let it drop. 'You'll only hear it somewhere else if I don't tell you, but Kath and I had a relationship many, many years ago.'

'Before she met Roger?'

'She left me for him.'

I tapped my fingers on the top of the table. I didn't want to antagonise him. I wanted him to continue talking. 'Roger made a move on her?'

'He was always the sort to take what he wanted.'

'You don't like Roger very much, do you?'

'I'd have thought that was pretty obvious. It wasn't just the situation with Kath, though. You learn to move on and start again. It enabled us to be the best of friends.'

I thought about asking what his wife made of it all, but he continued to talk.

'It was all about him. He became arrogant very quickly. Once he finished his training, he changed, almost overnight. He quickly climbed the ladder, but for me, there are ways of doing things and there's no difference between your private life and your personal life. Not in my book. You treat people properly. I've always considered myself to be an honest man and I've always tried to do my best for my clients.'

I glanced at the menu above the bar to give him a moment to gather his thoughts. I realised I was hungry. I hadn't eaten all day. I turned my attention back to him. 'Roger has never shared my ethics,' Farr said. 'His bottom-line is profit, pure and simple. He's not particularly concerned about who he acts for, if you follow me.'

'Like George Sutherland?'

He didn't seem surprised by my mention of the name. In fact, he smiled. 'Roger has acted for him for a number of years, even though Kath begged him not to. Roger wouldn't listen to her, though.'

'Why would Kath be so bothered about what her husband did at work?'

'George Sutherland has a grip on Roger. He always has done.'

'Why?'

'He goes back even further than I do with Kath. I think they were brought up on the same street. Kath knows exactly what the man is.'

I went back to my flat and showered. I turned the water to cold, as I often found the shock of the ice-cold blast cleared my mind. It allowed me to start again. Only this time when I'd finished, the problems were still there. A non-smoker dying in a house fire from a dropped cigarette didn't sit right with me, especially when he was ex-police like Don. I heated up the last tin of tomato soup in my cupboard and stared out of the window as I ate. I didn't believe in coincidences. I was also puzzled by Roger Millfield's willingness to act for George Sutherland, given what I now knew.

Once I was finished eating, I headed out to Niall's bar launch. It was busier than I expected it to be. I recognised some of the faces. Niall had obviously been on the phone to his old mates and they'd come out in force for him. The night was drawing in, so I got to see the bar lighting at full effect. Niall knew people in the trades. A lot of them weren't busy, so he'd persuaded them to do the work for a decent price. The spirit bottles behind the bar twinkled under the spotlights. It was great. I was proud of the way he'd met the challenge of getting the place on its feet. I squeezed my way through the crowd, stopping to shake hands with Niall's rugby mates, who'd also come out in force for him. It was great to see people smiling and enjoying themselves. I saw Sarah. I nodded to her and smiled. We'd talk later on. I was tempted to take a drink for myself, but I still had things to do. Connor was helping out behind the bar. That was pleasing. I spotted Niall fiddling with his mobile by the toilets. I guided him towards the kitchen door, closing it behind us. It was eerily quiet in contrast to the buzz around the bar. I pulled up two chairs and told him to sit down.

'Ruth doesn't believe my story about being mugged,' he said.

I tried not to laugh. 'It wasn't the best story in the world.' His face was better already, the bruising fading.

'She's making me sleep in the spare room until I tell her the truth.'

I felt bad for nearly laughing. 'I'm doing my best.'

He looked like he was going to say something before he simply nodded.

'It's nice to see Connor here,' I said.

'I think his mother has had a word with him.'

'He's a kid trying to find his way. It was hard enough for us to do, wasn't it?'

'It wasn't that hard, I'm sure.'

'Different world now.'

Niall rubbed his face. 'I suppose it is.'

'He's told me about his plan to be a nightclub promoter.'

'I'll believe it when I see it.'

I don't think my brother had ever sounded more like our dad than he had at that moment. 'You've got to let him try. If he fails, so what? What's he lost?'

'Time.'

'Time?'

'Time that could be spent on a proper career, building something worthwhile.'

'Like working on the caravans?' I regretted saying it as soon as it left my mouth. Niall stood up and paced the room. I said I hadn't meant it like that.

'You think I've wasted my life?'

I shook my head. 'I mean you can't put all your eggs in one basket these days, can you? No one's going to work their entire life in one job.'

'It's you who needs a job, not me.'

'I haven't got a clue about pulling pints. You saw how shit I was at it in Dad's pub.'

Niall couldn't keep a smile off his face. 'That's true.' He walked back to his chair and sat down.

'I've got a problem,' I said.

'What kind of problem?'

I took a breath and told him. 'What would you do if you knew something a friend didn't? Something important.'

He shrugged. 'Depends on what you knew and who the friend was.'

'It's a close friend.'

'Sarah?'

I nodded. There was no point in pretending. It felt like I'd re-established myself with her again of late. I'd missed her company. I had no idea where what had happened to Don was going to take us, but holding secrets back did no one any good.

'Going to tell me, then?' Niall said.

I checked we were alone before speaking. 'I know Don had an affair when Sarah's mother was still alive.'

'And Sarah's got no idea?'

'None at all.'

'How did you find out?'

'It doesn't really matter.'

He blew out his cheeks and shrugged. 'I really don't know what to say. But I'll tell you this. If you don't make the decision and do something about it, someone else will find out and tell her. If you know, it'll come out. It always happens and that will make the situation twice as bad for you.'

Niall went back to work. I spotted Sarah and made my way over to her. I knew what he'd said was right, even if I didn't want to acknowledge it.

'Where have you been?' she said.

I nodded to the front door. We went outside, leaving the noise behind us. Chanterlands Avenue ran parallel to Princes Avenue. The latter was the livelier and more developed. It had reinvented itself with countless bars and restaurants. The street we were on was playing catch-up. None of it was my scene, but I knew you got peaks and troughs in this type of industry. Places and areas came and went in popularity. If Niall offered quality, people would stay loyal. It was the same as in any business. Maybe I'd learned a thing or two from the partnership with Don. There was a bus shelter a little further along. I told her we should sit in there. It'd shut out the noise of the traffic.

'It's like being teenagers,' I said as we huddled up close together against the cold night.

Sarah smiled. 'I think we're well past that, Joe.'

Maybe it was late at night and seeing my brother's bar doing so well, but I told her I hadn't felt so low since the end of my rugby days. I was sure it wasn't jealousy, or anything negative. It was more something that was missing within me.

'You've never really told me what happened to you,' she said.

Sarah was right. I'd never really spoken about it. I didn't know where to start, but it felt like the right time. 'It felt like my life was over just as it was getting started.' It was difficult finding the right words. 'I'd worked so hard to get my contract at Rovers, and to have it ripped away from me after only a handful of games, it left me in pieces.' I smiled. 'Literally'. Gallows humour.

'What happened?'

'My knee. The guy at St Helens tackled me and made sure his weight came down it. It just collapsed underneath me.'

'Deliberate?'

I nodded. 'He was after me right from the kick-off.' I'd stayed in a Merseyside hospital for a couple of days until I had been able to travel back home. 'I kicked against it when I was told I'd never play again. I wouldn't listen to the doctors or their advice. Not even Debbie could sort me out.'

'But she was there for you?'

'She sorted me out eventually. I did the odd shift in my dad's pub, but I couldn't take it seriously. I couldn't knuckle down to things like Niall had. My dad had been right. He'd told me not to put all my eggs into one basket with the rugby, but I hadn't listened to him. He wanted me to get a proper job.'

Sarah smiled. 'It wasn't for you?'

'I went abroad for a bit, labouring and working on building sites, mainly. It did me good. I got to see a bit of the world and Debbie understood why I needed to do it. I was only away for a few weeks at a time, but I came back with bit more of a clue and eventually sorted myself out.'

'It's normal to want the best for your kids.' She laughed. 'If Lauren doesn't become a solicitor or an accountant, I'll be very disappointed.'

I laughed, too. I knew she didn't want that, but I got the point.

'All I want is for her to be happy. And I bet that's all your dad ever wanted for you.'

'He hid it well, then. Niall tried to help us keep things civil, but it was a struggle. I was blaming anyone and everyone for what had happened with the rugby. Niall was there for me when I needed him. He got me through it, really. That's why I've got to help him now.'

We watched people go by in silence. Sarah eventually spoke. 'I like your dad's rugby shirts.'

'They make a nice feature.'

'I wasn't there when he died.' It just came out. 'I was working in Germany. Niall called me to say he'd been taken into hospital, but I couldn't get back in time. He suffered a brain haemorrhage. The doctors said it was one of those things which could have happened at any time.'

'Do you think it was to do with rugby?'

I didn't have an answer. 'It could have been.' I knew she meant well, but it was stirring up too many bad memories. I didn't want to talk about it.

Sarah stood up. 'You'll understand, then. I need to know what happened to my dad.' She paused for a moment. 'And if it's going to get any worse.'

The bar grew increasingly busy as the night went on. My mood changed when I saw George Sutherland making his way through the crowd towards me. I hadn't spent much time trying to sort the cigarette problem out.

He pointed at me as he approached. 'I want a word with you.'

I didn't respond. The people standing close to me started to drift away.

'I thought it was time we had a catch-up about our mutual business interests,' he said.

I shook my head. 'It's not convenient.'

'I think it is.' He beckoned me closer. 'We can do this the easy way or the hard way.'

He glanced over to the door where Carl Palmer was standing and smiled. 'Come for a drive with us or I'll need to have a word with that brother of yours.'

I got into Sutherland's car. We headed down Spring Bank and crossed the city centre, picking up speed as we hit

Hedon Road. There was little traffic on the road heading east. I asked where we were going, but received no answer.

Sutherland waved the question away. 'Any news for me?'

I told him I had nothing new.

'Not much of a detective, are you?'

'Probably not.'

'I want my money, Geraghty.'

I didn't reply. We passed the docks and Sutherland spoke again. 'What do you think to all this green technology shit they keep banging on about, then? Might even make a more suitable career for you if you're lucky.'

Palmer laughed at his boss's joke.

'Who knows?' I said.

We lapsed back into silence and slowed down as we pulled off Hedon Road. We headed past the flattened site of Fenners and took a right turn at the Preston Road traffic lights.

Sutherland spoke. 'We need a word with someone. Seems like he hasn't learned his lesson, either.'

'Who?'

He smiled. 'Another debtor.'

Palmer pulled off the main road and drove slowly down a dense road of terraced houses. Every speed bump he hit acted as a punch to my stomach. I realised that I'd been here recently. Palmer pulled up and Sutherland told me to get out of the car. I thought briefly about refusing, but it would be pointless. Whatever was about to happen, I was going to have to be a part of it.

Sutherland knocked on the door, took a step backwards and waited. I was looking at the neighbour's house. They were either in bed or out. They certainly weren't going to challenge three men banging on a door at this hour. Sutherland knocked again, louder this time. When the door was opened, Sutherland stepped to one side and let Palmer take his place. Palmer didn't wait to be invited in, instead forcing his way through into the house.

'After you,' Sutherland said to me.

I did as I was told and followed them into the living room. Terry Gillespie was already on the floor, Palmer standing over him. Sutherland nodded and Palmer dragged Gillespie up before throwing another punch, this one breaking Gillespie's nose. The smell in the room was disgusting. It had been takeaway pizza and cheap lager for tea. Sutherland picked up a chair from the dining table and placed it in the middle of the room. I kept myself out of Gillespie's eye-line. I didn't know how he'd react to seeing me. Palmer threw another punch and Gillespie's head lolled to one side. He took a length of rope out of his pocket and tied Gillespie to the chair. I looked away as Palmer continued to beat him.

It stopped when Sutherland spoke. 'You let me down, Terry.'

Gillespie could barely focus. He didn't answer.

'If you can't pay me back, you need to make it up to me.'

Gillespie smiled. 'Fuck you.'

Sutherland sighed and stepped aside. Palmer threw another punch. Gillespie's head snapped back.

'Try again,' Sutherland said to Gillespie.

I needed to get out of the room. The kitchen was as bad as the living room, but it gave me some breathing space. I knew full well why I'd been brought here. Sutherland wanted me to understand the full consequences of letting him down. I took a deep breath and walked back into the living room. Sutherland was breathing heavily and flexing his right hand. He'd joined in the fun. Gillespie's right eye had closed up.

Sutherland turned to me. 'Hit the cunt, then.'

I shook my head. 'No.'

'Hit him. You're here with us, so fucking hit him.'

I was rooted to the spot. I wanted to get out of the house and away from them all. Sutherland repeated the order. Palmer moved closer to me. Gillespie slowly started to focus on me. I could tell he recognised me. He looked at Sutherland and started to say something, but it made no sense. I had no idea what he was going to say about me. I stepped forward, closed my eyes and hit him.

Sutherland nodded to me. 'See. We're not that different after all.'

It was made clear to me I wasn't getting a lift back. Sutherland had also made it clear that nothing had changed. I still had the debt to settle and he expected progress. I stuck to the main road and jumped on the first bus heading to the city centre. I stared at my reflection in the window as the city flashed past. What had I become? However bad things were, I certainly shouldn't be getting involved in George Sutherland's activities. I turned away, not wanting to look at myself. I'd crossed a line, regardless of what I thought about Terry Gillespie. I should have stopped what was going on, not contributed to it. I was lying to myself. There was no way I could have stopped the beating. I wasn't even sure I'd wanted to. Gillespie had dragged my brother into this mess and was now paying the penalty. I realised I didn't give a shit about Gillespie, even when he was being beaten by Palmer. What did that say about me? Maybe Sutherland was right. Maybe I wasn't so different to him after all.

CHAPTER NINE

I'd slept on the settee again and was woken by the sun pouring into the living room. I made a coffee and stared out of the window and thought about the previous evening. I told myself I needed to get a grip. I was under no illusions as to the danger Sutherland posed to me. He would continue to push me, but I had to protect Niall from him. I searched through my mobile and found the number I had for Coleman. I wasn't sure what I could do about Sutherland. I needed to think about it, but I also needed to focus on Don's problem. Coleman was working an active case and he had an interest in Don. It was time to take a chance, see if I could make something happen. I sent a text message containing the name Reg Holborn to Coleman and sat down and waited.

The reply came quickly. Fifteen minutes later, he was in my flat. I brewed a fresh pot of coffee as Coleman paced around my living room, flicking through the CDs and books. I'd suggested meeting him close to the station, but he was adamant he would come to me. We were both playing our cards close to our chests. I was sure he had something to tell me. Otherwise, he wouldn't be here.

'Like The Clash?' he said, pointing to *London Calling*.

I nodded. 'What's not to like?'

'One of my favourites, too.'

I was surprised, but didn't show it. 'Must be a bit different to your house, I'd imagine.'

'Maybe.' He walked across to the window. 'Nice view.'

'It does for me.'

'It might do for me, too.'

I was puzzled. 'What does that mean?'

'My wife's kicked me out.'

I said nothing. I wasn't sure why he was telling me this, but I listened. I saw him glance at my photo of Debbie. 'I've moved into a flat on Park Avenue. We're practically neighbours now.'

'Right.' That was why he'd arrived so quickly.

He put his coffee down. 'Doesn't seem to be an improvement, though.'

I knew he had a young daughter. It clearly wasn't an easy situation for him.

'The old cliché,' he said. 'Too many hours at work and not enough of them at home. It takes its toll.'

His card stated 'Acting Detective Inspector'. Everything comes at a price. We weren't exactly friends and never would be, but we'd reached an understanding when dealing with each other. I felt sad that he was telling me about his domestic troubles. I suspected he had no one else to talk to.

Coleman got to the point. 'You wanted to speak to me.'

'Shall we talk about Reg Holborn?'

'He was a well-respected detective.'

'In the past tense.'

'He retired years ago. Well before my time.'

'I meant past tense as in dead. House fire.'

'These things happen.'

'Not if you don't smoke.' Coleman didn't hold my stare. He didn't need to say anything more. 'It wasn't an accident, was it?'

'I'm going by what I've been told.'

'And what's that?'

'It was an accident.'

'And this is the ongoing investigation you mentioned?'

'I'm not prepared to talk about it.'

'Holborn didn't get on with Don,' I told him.

'Well before my time, Joe. There's no one around who remembers that far back.'

'Depends where you're looking. I talked to people who suggested Holborn wasn't all he seemed.'

'I can't really comment.'

I leaned forward. 'But people must talk. Old war stories, past glories, that kind of thing.'

'Not what I've heard.'

'Do you want your wife back?' I asked.

He was surprised by what I'd asked him. 'What kind of question is that?'

I shrugged and settled back in my chair. Let him work it out for himself.

'Of course I do,' he eventually said to me.

'You'll understand, then. There are things we've got to do, whatever the cost. This is the least I can do for Don,' I told him. 'Wherever it leads.'

Coleman thought about it and came to a decision. 'Of course people talk. Don was a good policeman. You won't find anyone who says otherwise. I'm here unofficially. Off the record, right?'

'Of course.'

'You might want to look at a man called Andrew Bancroft.'

Coleman left without saying anything further. I wrote down the name he'd given me. Once I was ready, I left my flat and headed to the nearest library. It was busy with a group of toddlers sitting together singing nursery rhymes in one corner. In another, an old guy was reading a newspaper. The librarian set me up on a computer and left me to it.

I entered the name Andrew Bancroft into Google and got too many hits. I tried to narrow it down by putting Hull in alongside the name. I scrolled down the first two pages and found nothing of interest. The woman on the computer next to me complained as I drummed my fingers on the table. I smiled an apology, but she'd already gone back to whatever she was doing. It had been a long shot. Whatever Bancroft had done would be buried in the past and possibly off the record. But it linked to Don and Holborn. It had to be something tangible if Coleman was interested. I would have to do my research using the old school method. I would have to knock on doors and ask questions. It felt like I was slowing making progress.

I headed for Niall's bar with something like a plan in mind. The door to the bar was locked. I peered in to see him sweeping the floor. One of his mates was restocking the bar. Niall spotted me and let me in.

'I need a word,' I said. 'In private.'

He led me through to the office and sat down. 'What happened to you last night?'

I took the chair opposite him. 'George Sutherland wanted a word. I was given a warning that I should sort the problem out quickly.' I paused. 'I didn't feel like coming back to the party.'

'What a mess.'

'I had to watch as Terry Gillespie was given a beating.' I didn't go into details.

'It's not going away, is it?' Niall said.

'No.'

Niall stared at me. 'I can't let this go on, leaving it all to you. I've got to make a stand. I've got to take some responsibility.'

I cut him off. 'You need to concentrate on this place and leave it to me.'

Niall shook his head. 'What about if I ask my mates to back me up? We'll go and see Sutherland and tell him the deal's off. We can outnumber him. He'll have to listen.'

I told him this wasn't a playground argument. 'Sutherland and his crew are criminals. They won't go away because you've got some mates.' I felt bad for saying it, like he was a child, but I needed to spell it out to him. 'Sutherland will take whatever you throw at him and then come back twice as hard. He won't give a second thought to having you seriously hurt, or attacking this place.'

We sat in silence, Niall staring at the wall. I told him I appreciated the thought. It was true, I did appreciate it, but he had to know the truth of the situation. I had one last throw of the dice. 'I've got a lead on where the cigarettes went to,' I said.

'How did you find out?'

'It doesn't matter.' I could hardly tell him Connor had told me. I told him I needed to borrow some of last night's takings.

I headed east on the M62 in the direction of Goole, ready to speak to the Horton brothers about the cigarettes Milo had sold them. I wanted them back. I saw the two water towers as I approached the centre of town. The salt and pepper pots as I'd heard people refer to them. Goole was a town sat between Hull and Leeds. It was far enough away to feel like alien territory. I parked in the train station car park and decided the best bet was the nearest pub. I headed into the first one I came to. I was the only customer. The landlord was bent over, stocking up a cabinet with soft drinks.

I pointed to one of the bottles of juice. 'I'll take one of them, please.'

He held his hand out for payment.

I passed him a five pound note. 'Expecting a busy day?'

'Doubt it.'

It was going to be like that. 'I need some furniture,' I said. 'I've been told I should see the Horton brothers.' I took the piece of paper I'd written their address down on and asked him for directions.

He took it from me, looked at it and told me where I needed to go. I thanked him and held my hand out for my change.

I found the shop easily. A man was unloading cardboard boxes from an old red van, the name of the brothers on the side of it. I locked my car up and walked inside the shop. The quality of the furniture they were selling was variable, mainly house clearance stuff, but it was certainly cheap. Eventually I was joined by another man. He was tall, fat and in his mid-twenties. He was chewing gum and smiling at me with an easy confidence. It was kind of smile that was meant to tell me that this was his territory. I was beginning to sense I was about to make a mistake, but there was no going back now.

'Help you, pal?' he said.

'I'm new to the area,' I told him. 'Just getting a feel for it, really.'

He nodded. 'It's all good quality stuff and cheap. Moving here for work?'

'Thinking about.'

'Brave man.' He folded his arms and continued to stare at me. 'What line of business are you in?'

'This and that.' I held my hand out. 'Joe Geraghty.'

He shook it. 'Steve Horton.'

'So you're the men to see, I take it?'

'Definitely.' He passed me a cheap card.

I took it from him. It stated his name and mobile number. I put it in my pocket and walked closer to the where the till was. I could see the other man unloading the van and stacking boxes in the storeroom. 'Keeping busy, then?' I said.

'We're always busy.'

He stared at me, trying to work out my angle. I didn't flinch, feeling more confident about the situation. They were small town crooks. Given their size, they'd no doubt bully the locals, but they were getting mixed up with more dangerous people. They would end up as collateral damage if they weren't careful. I glanced again at the stack of cardboard boxes. 'I'm looking for some cigarettes' I said.

Horton smiled and stepped towards me. I tensed, ready for his attack. I watched as he went for his pocket. He pulled out a packet of cigarettes and lit one for me. 'Have one of these, and if you're not buying, I suggest you be on your way.'

I threw it on the floor and stubbed it out. 'I want my cigarettes back.'

Horton shouted for his brother to join us. It was the man I'd seen unloading boxes. He appeared from the back room. It was two against one.

'This cunt thinks we've got something of his,' Horton said to his brother.

'I know you have,' I said.

'Don't know what you're talking about, pal.'

It was a stand-off. I repeated that I wanted the cigarettes back.

Horton laughed. 'Even if we had them, why the fuck would we want to give them to you?'

'I'll buy them back,' I said.

Steve Horton stepped closer to me. 'Have you got the cash to do that?'

His brother followed him. I stared at them, my heart pumping a little faster. I eventually nodded. 'I've got it.'

'On you?' Steve Horton said.

'I can cover what you paid for them and give you some profit. I know the lads you bought them from and it's causing some bother for them.'

'So what?'

'They weren't their cigarettes to sell.'

'Sounds like their problem, not ours.'

'It's going to become your problem if you don't give them back.'

Steve Horton laughed. 'You didn't answer my question. Have you got the money on you?'

His brother walked around me and guarded the door. I was boxed in and outnumbered. I'd made a mistake. Steve Horton stepped forward and threw a punch which landed square on my jaw. I fell backwards and before I had time to defend myself, his brother followed through with a kick to my stomach. I collapsed to the floor. The next thing I knew, I was being hauled up and thrown out of the front door. I no longer had the money.

I drove back to Hull. I ached a little, but it was mainly my pride which was suffering. I'd been stupid to think I could reason with the Horton brothers. I was done with diplomacy. I had to change my angle of attack. I knew very little about Sutherland as a man. I had to know more if I was going to find a weakness I could exploit and get him off my family's back. My advantage was that I'd once worked for his ex-wife, Brenda. If anyone could help me, it was her. I didn't know where the paperwork for the case was, but it had amounted to little more than a selection of long lens photographs of her husband and his mistress. It had been very straightforward. Fortunately, I still had her contact details in my mobile. She was surprised to hear from me, but was willing to meet, even after I told her what I wanted. She lived in a flat on Peel Street, off Spring Bank.

The area had changed a lot in recent years. War and social unrest in Europe had brought people from around the world to the area. I knew Lauren's class at school contained children from Eastern Europe, Iraq and Africa. She'd told me about them with a look of excitement on her face. When I'd been at school, new class members from the other side of the River Hull had been greeted as if they were aliens.

I arrived at Brenda Sutherland's flat. She let me straight in and offered me a drink. I told her I was fine and sat down. The furniture was sparse and basic. A small portable television perched on a unit in the far corner of the room. She had a bookcase full of paperbacks.

'Bit of a change since we last spoke,' she said. 'I'm still waiting on him to sell the house.' She shrugged. 'I didn't know he'd re-mortgaged it. It's not too bad around here, though. Everyone's friendly enough and I'm making new friends. It's fine for now.'

I was pleased to hear it. In fact, I admired the way she was making a go of things. It would have been easier for her to turn a blind eye and carry on living in more comfortable surroundings than this. 'I know we never talked much about your husband when I worked for you, but I need to know more about him for something I'm working on.'

She shrugged, not interested in the details. 'If it helps, it'll be my pleasure. Believe me.'

'How much do you know about how he makes a living?' I asked.

'I know exactly what he is, if that's what you mean. I won't lie to you, Joe. When I first met him, it was that edge he had which attracted me. Every girl loves a bad boy, don't they? He was a little bit dangerous and that scared people. It meant we got special treatment when we went out, and I liked it at first. We were treated like royalty, but it wasn't real.'

'How much did you know about his business?'

'Not a lot.'

'You knew he worked for Frank Salford?'

She nodded. 'He was the boss. If Frank called, George went running. That's the way it was.'

'What did he do for Salford?'

'He always told me he looked after Frank's businesses for him. Management.' She shook her head. 'I don't really know. I knew what Frank was, so I didn't ask for the details.' She shuffled forwards. 'I always thought George reckoned he was entitled to more from Frank, that he didn't get the respect he deserved.'

'What happened?'

'George took what he thought he was entitled to.'

'He was skimming the cash?'

'All but admitted it to me.'

'What happened after that?'

'They didn't work together again.'

'Never?'

'Not so far as I know.'

I nodded. It was a reasonable assumption that they both knew where the bodies were buried. It would have been a case of mutual destruction if one or the other had gone to the police. I asked her how dangerous her ex-husband was.

She thought about the question. I waited as she lit a cigarette and took a long drag. 'He likes to be the big man when he's got a crowd, but he's really nothing more than a bully and a coward. Nothing physical, just the type of comments that are designed to chip away at you and make you feel worthless. He's a manipulator, always looking for an angle.'

Her hand was shaking slightly. I angled myself away from her so she couldn't blow smoke in my face. She took another deep drag and put the cigarette down in an ashtray. 'Tread carefully, Joe. But whatever he's done, make sure he pays for it.'

I left Brenda Sutherland's flat with plenty to think about. I wanted to give Roger Millfield another shake. I still hadn't banked the cheque he'd given me at the KC Stadium. It was the excuse I needed.

His receptionist tried to stop me making my way in to his office, but I wasn't going to be fobbed off. He was on the telephone as I entered. My entrance left him speechless. It took him a couple of seconds to pull himself together and tell whoever was at the other end of the line that he'd call them back.

He looked at me. 'I thought I'd made myself clear. Our business together is finished.'

I shook my head and passed him the cheque back. 'I'm not done yet.' I could have used the cheque to repay some of Niall's takings I'd lost in Goole, but I needed him to talk.

He waved the cheque away and tried to busy himself with the paperwork on his desk. 'If I don't require your help, I'd say we're finished. Take the money and leave it there, please.'

'That's what Don said I should do.'

He stopped what he was doing. 'Maybe you should take his advice, then.'

'You didn't tell me your wife knew George Sutherland.'

'I don't see how that's relevant. Many of my clients are known to me personally. It's perfectly normal.'

We sat in silence. I hoped he would crack first, but he didn't. He busied himself on his laptop.

'She knows him from when they were kids,' I said, wanting his attention back.

Millfield laughed. 'You've been talking to Neil Farr.'

'It doesn't matter who I've been talking to.'

'Just so long as you realise who the man is. That's all.'

I took the bait. 'Who is he?'

'The man who settled for second best. He always wanted Kath, but she never wanted him.'

I didn't want to talk about Farr. 'Your wife was brought up in the same street as Sutherland?'

He shrugged. 'It's a small city. You know that.'

'Why do you still act for him, then?'

He was puzzled by my question. 'He's a client.'

'But your wife doesn't want you doing it.'

He wasn't surprised that I knew. 'Kath doesn't like the man. Can't say I blame her really, but it's business. Simple as that.'

'Even though he worked with Frank Salford?'

He tried to pretend he didn't know the name. He was a bad liar. He was sweating and refusing to meet my eye. I wondered why a professional man like Roger Millfield was happy to associate himself with a known criminal.

I let it hang there for a moment before continuing. 'I've got a problem with Sutherland,' I leaned toward him. 'A serious problem.' I wanted to pressurise him a bit. Let him know the lie of the land. I was certain he'd crack. I made sure I had eye contact before speaking. 'I need to take him down.'

Millfield cut me off and held the cheque back out to me. His hand was shaking a little. 'Take it and leave me alone.'

I knew I was going to need to find another route in George Sutherland. I also needed to give some attention to Don's problem. My best bet was to go back to Gerard Branning. He'd made it clear he'd help if asked. The door at the care home was answered by the same woman. 'I'm back to see Gerard,' I told her.

She shook her head and blocked my entrance. 'I'm afraid not.'

'He said I could visit him any time.'

'He's not receiving visitors at the moment.'

I took a step back. I didn't understand what had changed.

She leaned in to me. 'He changed his mind after he had a visitor earlier.'

She was enjoying herself, so I played along. 'Not family, then?'

'They showed me their ID cards.'

I nodded. Police. I asked her to describe the visitor to me. She might as well have handed me a photograph of

Coleman. I thanked her and headed back to my car. I was
being used. Branning had led me to news of Reg Holborn's
death. And now he wouldn't speak to me. And Coleman, the
man who had pointed me in the direction of Andrew
Bancroft, was closing my avenues off. It didn't make sense.

CHAPTER TEN

I knocked on Don's front door and stepped back. If he saw me, he was likely to pretend he wasn't in. I was banking on him being curious enough to open up if he couldn't see me standing there. It was the nature of the man. He'd always told me that once you were police, you were always police. It reminded me of Coleman saying they took care of their own. Don didn't let me down. As soon as the door was open slightly, I had my foot wedged in the door so he couldn't close it.

Once he saw it was me, he stepped back and opened the door fully. 'No need for that, Joe. I would have let you in.'

I smiled and followed him through to the living room.

'Put the kettle on,' he said, as he sat down.

I did as I was told. I looked at the photographs on his wall as I waited for the kettle to boil. There were more photographs of Sarah as a child and then as a woman. There were photographs of Lauren and some of his wife. There were also photographs of them together as a family. It was all built on lies. I walked back to Don, passed him his coffee and sat down opposite him.

'What can I do for you, Joe?'

'Told Sarah yet?'

He leaned forwards. 'I thought we understood each other on that.'

'She'll hear it from someone else,' I told him. I knew that if Sarah found out I had knowledge of her dad's affair with Kath Millfield and I hadn't said anything, she wouldn't talk to me again.

'No one knows about it and that's the way it's going to stay.' Don turned away from me. Topic closed.

I asked him if he'd spoken with Roger Millfield.

He stared at me, but didn't answer.

'He's still desperate for me to stop working for him,' I said.

'You should listen to him, then.'

'That's not how I work.'

Don shook his head. 'Got your cigarettes back yet?

'Not yet.'

'Any leads?'

'One or two.' We sat in silence with our drinks until I spoke. 'Who attacked you Don?' I wasn't letting it go. Sarah was depending on me. We both knew that it wasn't going to be the end of things. It never was. They'd be back. 'I can help you.' He was running scared, like Millfield was.

'I don't need any help,' Don said.

'Sure?'

'Quite sure.'

'I could certainly use some help,' I said.

Don stared at me. 'I'm not in that game now.'

'Tell me about Reg Holborn.' I watched for any reaction to the name.

'What's he got to do with anything?'

Don had played it straight. No reaction. 'He was your ex-colleague,' I said.

'I know who you mean.' He continued to stare at me. 'Who have you been talking to?'

'I caught up with Gerard Branning.' I didn't mention that he now wasn't speaking to me.

Don smiled. 'I trained you well.'

'It's my job.' I knew I was making progress. Before getting involved, Don was leading the life of a retired man, which made his involvement with Millfield's problems all the more puzzling, especially as he didn't want knowledge of his affair with Kath Millfield to surface.

Don continued speaking. 'You'll know I didn't see eye to eye with Holborn, then?'

'I've heard that.'

'There's no doubting the man was a good detective, even if some of his methods were a bit out of order in my opinion. He was ruthless and wasn't bothered who he trod on, whether it was a colleague or a criminal. He got results and that made him popular with the bosses. Once you're on a roll, you're on a roll. Promotion soon follows.'

'Did he ever cause you any problems?'

'I stayed away from him.'

'He died in a fire recently.'

'So I heard.'

Of course he had. It was the nature of the job.

'I didn't go to the funeral,' he said. 'It would have been hypocritical of me.'

'Dropped a cigarette the newspaper said. The fire got a grip too quickly for help to reach him.'

'It happens. What more can I say?'

I left it there about Holborn. He wasn't going to say anything further. I changed the subject again. 'Tell me about Andrew Bancroft.'

Don put his mug down and stood up. 'It's time for you to go, Joe.'

I walked into Niall's bar. I had to tell him I fucked up with the Horton brothers in Goole. He spotted me and led me across to an empty table. I was still thinking over Don's reaction to the mention of Bancroft's name, but I wasn't surprised. Little was surprising me at the moment. I turned to my brother. 'I've lost the money,' I said, once we were sat down. I explained what I'd done. 'It was a stupid idea.'

Niall sighed and leaned towards me. 'What do we do now?'

He wasn't too disappointed. It was a minor blow in comparison to what else had happened. I told him about my visit to Sutherland's ex-wife. 'I'll find a way to get Sutherland off our back. It just takes a bit of time.'

My brother wasn't convinced. One of his mates came over and said he needed his help in the kitchen. I told Niall not to worry as he left. He was as uncertain as I felt, but I had nothing more comforting to say to him.

I stared into space, unsure of what I should do next. Sarah finished serving a customer and came over to me.

'Any news for me?' she said.

I shook my head and asked if Don had said anything more about Roger Millfield.

'Nothing.'

I brought her up to date. 'I can't believe I was stupid enough to think I could sort things out so easily.' I paused, deciding I had to take another chance. 'I've had a name given to me. Andrew Bancroft.'

'Who's he?'

'That's the question. I asked your dad, but he wasn't talking.'

'I'll ask around if it helps?'

I nodded. I knew she'd ask Don who Bancroft was. I was stirring something up. I hoped I was doing the right thing.

Sarah stood up, ready to go back to work. 'Don't shut me out, Joe.'

My mobile vibrated in my pocket. I read the text message from Connor. He was outside my flat and wanted to speak to me urgently. I left the bar and headed straight there.

I found him sitting on the doorstep, clearly upset. We went up to my flat. The best I could offer him was a glass of water. I told him to sit down and calm himself. 'What's happened?'

He ignored me and paced the room, running his hand through his hair. 'This bloke stopped me and asked what the time was. I got my mobile out to check and he boxed me in against the wall, told me he knew all about me, that it was time to pay up.'

I was listening more seriously now. 'He threatened you?'

'He was right in my face.'

I told him again to sit down. We needed to go through it from the beginning. 'So he asked you the time first, right? That was the first time you noticed him?'

Connor nodded. 'And then he jostled me down an alleyway.'

'Where?'

'On High Street. I was cutting through to meet a mate from college.'

I knew the area had lots of narrow cobbled alleyways. They were quiet enough to drag someone down without it being noticed. A lot of the old warehouses were now student flats. The chances of any potential witnesses were slim. 'What happened when he had you out of sight? Did he take your wallet and mobile?'

'He didn't take anything.'

'Nothing?'

'No.'

'You said he knew all about you?'

'He said he knew what I'd done and I was to pass on a message to my dad. He said they wanted the money for the cigarettes.'

It was George Sutherland's work. 'You didn't ring the police, did you?'

'No.'

'Good.'

'I should tell dad the truth. It's gone too far.'

'Leave it for now.' In this case, the truth didn't seem such a good idea.

'What are you going to do?'

I told him I was going to take him home before I did anything else. Then I had a visit to make. George Sutherland had made it clear Niall had no protection, but this was overstepping the mark. I wasn't standing for it.

'Order a drink first,' the barmaid said to me.

'I don't want one.' I eyeballed her and repeated that I wanted to speak to George Sutherland.

She laughed and picked up an empty glass from the bar. 'Fuck off before I throw you out.'

I stood my ground. The drinkers weren't making eye contact with me. I repeated myself.

'Don't be thinking I need any help in throwing you out,' she said.

I smiled. 'I believe you.'

She eventually relented and shouted out for Sutherland. I thanked her and waited.

He eventually walked into the bar. 'What the fuck do you want?' he said before pointing at his barmaid. 'I hope you haven't given this cunt a free drink?

She laughed and shook her head. 'Told him to fuck off, didn't I?'

'Good.' He told me to follow him through to his office. The only thing of interest to me was the bank of CCTV screens in the corner. One camera was focused on the till at the bar, another was watching an empty bedroom. There was a rack of DVDs on his desk. Niall's colleague, Terry Gillespie, had a leaflet advertising gentleman's evenings and had paid for sex here. It looked to me like Sutherland was filming the extra-curricular activities as a side-line. The man repulsed me. I pointed to the screen. 'Peeping Tom?'

He told me to sit down. 'What the fuck do you want, Geraghty? I haven't got time for this.' He lit a cigarette. The smoking ban obviously didn't apply to himself in his own kingdom.

'I've just seen Connor,' I said.

'Who's he?'

'Don't take the piss. He's my brother's lad.'

'Never had the pleasure.'

'I got the message last night.'

Sutherland leaned forwards. 'I should hope so, too.'

'Leave my family out of it.'

'Your brother is fair game if you don't pull your finger out.'

I walked to the door. I'd said what I needed to. I turned back to Sutherland. 'You don't touch him or his family. You come to me if you've got a problem.'

'Sit the fuck down Geraghty and be civil. Otherwise I'll be offended.' He smiled at me and leaned back in his chair. 'I keep asking myself, are you trying hard enough? And I don't think you are.'

'That's your opinion.'

'Thing is, I'm still not sure if you're on my side or not.'

'I want this sorted out.'

'Pleased to hear it.' His attention was diverted by a man moving into shot on the bedroom CCTV. A woman followed. I wondered if he knew he was being filmed. Sutherland turned back to me, not interested in the scene.

'So the thing is, I need to be sure. You're coming with me on another job tonight.'

'No chance.'

'I'm not giving you a choice.' He picked the telephone on his desk up. I watched the barmaid pick up the call at the other end on the CCTV screen. She passed the telephone to Carl Palmer. Sutherland told him to come to the office. 'He'll escort you off the premises,' he said to me.

I returned to my flat, filled the kettle and put a pot of coffee on. Caffeine would help me think about how I was going to handle whatever George Sutherland was about to throw at me. I called Sarah's mobile and asked her if she'd had any luck in relation to Andrew Bancroft.

'Absolutely nothing,' she said. 'No one is speaking about him. It's a closed shop.'

'Anyone else you can ask?'

'I've tried everyone I can think of.'

'Not even a hint?'

'Stonewalled.'

It wasn't a surprise. 'Has your dad said anything about Roger Millfield?'

'Not a thing.'

I wasn't surprised to hear that, either. I thanked her and said I'd see her soon. I sat back on my settee and closed my eyes. For some reason, Coleman had given me Bancroft's name, but nobody would talk about him. It wasn't right. I was sure Coleman wanted me to do his dirty work for him. I woke fifteen minutes later and took a shower, hoping it would perk me up. It did the job and I walked back into the living room feeling much more alert and ready for whatever the evening would throw at me.

I noticed the red light on my answerphone was flashing. I pressed play and listened to the message from Reg Holborn's son, David. He wanted to speak to me as a matter of urgency and left a number. He'd be available until midnight. I replayed the message and made a note of the number. The dialling code was for London. I found a notepad and pen before returning his call. He answered on the second ring.

'Joe Geraghty,' I said. 'You called.'

He told me he was putting me on hold until he was back in his office. The line went dead and I waited. I was surprised he was working so late. A moment later, he picked back up.

'Late night?' I said.

'It's always a late night at the moment. It's an important case. I'm a barrister.'

'Right.' That was all I needed.

'I got your number from the card you left with the lady next door to my father's house.'

That made sense. 'What can I do for you, Mr Holborn?'

'Your card says you're a Private Investigator. I want to know why you were there asking questions.'

I wasn't sure how to play it. I was dealing with a man who was both more intelligent and more aware of the law than me. I decided it would have to be the truth. 'His name came up in relation to something I'm looking into.'

'And what would that be, Mr Geraghty?'

'I'm not at liberty to give you the details. Client confidentiality. I'm sure you appreciate that.'

'I do indeed, but I'm not asking you in a professional capacity.'

'I'm still unable to help you.'

'I'm sorry that's the line you're taking.'

'It's the necessary line, I'm afraid.'

'Maybe I'll have to take it further, then.'

'Acting Detective Inspector Richard Coleman is the man you need. Queens Gardens Police Station.' I smiled to myself. He wasn't expecting me to give him a name like that. I decided to push him a bit. 'I understand your father wasn't a smoker.'

'Listen to me, Mr Geraghty. I don't know what your game is, or why you're interested in my father, but I'll tell you this. My father was an excellent detective with an impeccable record. He not only took countless serious criminals off the streets of Hull, but he was also a well-respected man. Ask anyone that. Maybe ask your Acting Detective Inspector. If you take the time to do your homework, you'll see my father was a passionate man who supported many good causes around the city and made it a better place to live. Can you say you do the same? What I won't tolerate, and what I'll take the strongest possible action over, is any suggestion from yourself that my father was anything but what I've outlined to you.' He took a breath. 'Do I make myself clear?'

'Perfectly' I said, before ending the call.

Queens was busy. I had an hour before Sutherland would come looking for me. The landlady asked me if I wanted my usual. I hadn't been in for a while, so it was nice to be remembered, though I didn't want to think about what else it said about me. I ordered two pints, found an empty table and sent Coleman a text message. I told him I'd drawn a blank on Andrew Bancroft. The time had come for him to give me something. Coleman walked in ten minutes later. He sat down opposite me and thanked me for the drink.

'Not a problem,' I said.

'It's good to get out, to be honest.'

I asked him if he was still in the flat.

'Decorating next time I get a couple of days off.'

'No going back then?'

'She's got someone else.'

'Must be tough.'

Coleman picked his pint up. 'What can you do?'

'Fair point.'

He laughed. 'I could look him up on the computer at work and then kick the shit out of him, but it doesn't work like that does it?' He shook his head. 'I'm not the first it's happened to and I won't be the last.'

I thought about Don. He'd tried to justify his affair by blaming the pressures of work. Maybe I didn't understand as well as I thought I did. I told Coleman it was a mature attitude to take.

'Still fancy kicking the shit out of her new bloke, though.'

I smiled and finished my pint. It was his round. He forced his way to the bar. There was football on the big screen. I had no idea who was playing. News was starting to pass me by. It was always the way once an investigation started.

Coleman returned and placed the drinks in front of us and asked again about Sarah. 'I always thought you two would make a good couple. I'm sure Don would approve.'

'Doubt it. Not these days.'

'What happened with you and Don? You had a good little business going there.'

'We didn't see eye to eye. Let's leave it there.' I was sure Don thought I'd let him down. I'd always had a tendency to stick my nose in where it wasn't wanted and had proved I couldn't let things go. Don's approach to our work had been more pragmatic. It was a job and we owed a duty of care to our clients. No more than that. He couldn't work with me and certainly didn't need me bringing trouble to his door. All that was true, but I still owed the man a debt of gratitude.

I swallowed a mouthful of my drink and got to the point. 'Who's Andrew Bancroft?'

Coleman took a piece of paper out his pocket and asked if I had a pen. I passed one over and watched as he wrote down a name.

'Andrew Bancroft's brother,' he said. 'You should talk to him.'

I left Coleman sitting in Queens. He was going to drink away his troubles, and I couldn't really blame him. Normally, I would have given serious consideration to doing the same, but my problems were about to knock on the front door of my flat. I walked back there and saw Sutherland's car parked directly outside. The back door opened as I approached. I got in and said I'd nipped out to do some last-minute shopping. There was no point fighting it.

The doors locked behind me. Carl Palmer was in the driving seat. Sutherland sat next to him. He turned to speak to me. 'Don't get smart with me, cunt.'

I knew the trip to Gillespie's house the previous evening had been the warning. Wherever we were going now was going to be worse for me. I tried to control my fear and remain alert. We headed down Spring Bank and across the city centre, towards the east side of the city, back in Sutherland's territory.

I leaned forwards. 'How's your dad?' I said to Palmer.

He laughed. 'Ask him yourself if you give a shit. He spends his days sat with the other tramps near the City Hall, drinking and getting pissed.'

I was hoping to push his buttons a little and stir things up. If I could unsettle him, it would cause Sutherland a problem. But it wasn't working. He didn't give a shit about his dad, or the fact I knew about him. The rest of the journey passed in silence. The car pulled up outside of Sutherland's pub.

Sutherland spoke. 'You can either walk in there or I'll get you carried in. Your choice.'

I glanced at Palmer. He was itching for me to step out of line. 'I'll walk.'

'Good choice,' Sutherland said.

I was on my guard as we walked in. The pub was quiet with a handful of drinkers standing at the bar. The football I'd been watching in Queens was still under way.

'Up there,' Sutherland said, pointing to the stairs.

I braced myself as I walked up them first. The expected attack didn't come. I stared at the three doors in front of me, unsure of where I was supposed to be going.

Sutherland joined me and pointed to the door on the right. 'In there.'

I could hear grunting noises coming from the room next to it. The female noises sounded fake.

Sutherland repeated himself. 'In there.'

I did as I was told and walked into a bathroom. There was a toilet in one corner, a sink with a mirror above it in the other. The floor was bare except for a dirty bath mat on the floor. There was no carpet. I barely had time to register the fact that the bath was full of water before Connor was pushed into the room by Palmer. He'd taken a beating.

Behind him, a man I didn't recognise was holding a baseball bat.

'Think I don't talk to people, Geraghty?' Sutherland said to me. 'Do you think I'm some kind of fucking amateur?'

I didn't have chance to reply or process what he was saying to me. Palmer dragged Connor across to the bath and forced his head down into the water. I shouted out, but the man with baseball bat stepped forward and hit me in the stomach. I buckled in agony and went down. Connor's head was dragged out of the water. He was thrown down next to me.

Sutherland stepped forwards and bent down to my level. 'I know all about the Horton brothers and your trip to see them.' He laughed. 'I heard all about you giving them your money.' He stood back up. 'Let's see if I've got your attention now, shall we?' He pointed to Connor. 'He was given his warning.'

Palmer gripped the back of Connor's head again. He was pushed back under the water and held there. It can't have lasted for more than several seconds, but it felt like a lifetime before he was released. He spat the water out and took in a deep mouthful of air.

'I want my money,' Sutherland said to me.

'I need more time,' I said.

Sutherland nodded to Palmer. Connor's head was back under water, this time for longer. Sutherland looked at me. 'Change the record, Geraghty.'

Palmer eventually pulled Connor back up for air. I watched as my nephew coughed and vomited. I tried to think of something I could give Sutherland, something that would bring an end to the situation.

He dropped to his knees again and leaned in close to me. 'You're going to try harder?'

I nodded. He was now attacking my family. I had little left to give.

He stood back up. 'I'm glad that we understand each other at last.'

Hull, March 1984

Ridley pushed his way into the interview room. Gary Bancroft was waiting for him. Bancroft was in his late twenties and already had a long list of convictions to his name. The room was grey, drab and far too hot for the time of year.

Ridley closed the door and sat down. 'What can I do for you, Gary?'

'Nice to see you, too, Mr Ridley.'

Ridley took out his cigarettes and offered Bancroft one. 'I haven't got time for this.' What he wasn't going to tell Bancroft was that they'd just found a nine year old boy in Beverley Beck. Some poor bastard was going to have to tell his family the news.

'I'm in deep shit this time, Don.'

Ridley glanced down at the paperwork he had. 'I agree. It's looking like prison time to me.'

Bancroft shuffled forward. 'Can you make it disappear?'

Ridley placed the charge sheet between them and leaned back. 'It's not that simple.'

'Sure?'

'How's your brother? Behaving himself better than you?'

'I thought we could speak about Andrew.'

Ridley leaned forward. 'Go on.'

'Can you help get me out of here?'

Ridley looked again at the piece of paper, this time more seriously. 'It needs to be good.'

'I've no time for our kid. Fuck him. You know he works for Frank Salford, right?'

Ridley said he did.

'What do you want to know about their relationship?'

Ridley found Reg Holborn sat in the canteen. He was with two other detectives from CID. 'Guess who I've got in custody,' Ridley said.

Holborn answered. 'Surprise me, Don.'

'Gary Bancroft.'

Holborn took a moment before smiling. 'So what, Don?'
He nodded to the detectives and told them to disappear.

Once they were alone, Ridley sat down. 'Seems there's been a falling out in the family.'

'What's that got to do with me?'

'It's got everything to do with you.'

Holborn told the others to leave them to it before leaning in closer and lowering his voice. 'You've made your choice, Don, and I respect that, but keep your nose out of my business or we're going to fall out.' He stirred another sugar into his tea. 'And we don't want that, do we?'

Ridley shrugged. 'He's told me all about his brother working for Frank Salford.'

'Frank's a legitimate businessman. You know that as well as I do. He creates employment in this city of ours, and in case you hadn't noticed, there aren't many jobs about at the moment. This city needs entrepreneurs like him.'

'You can do better than that.'

'You know that's the word from upon high. Mr Salford is a very generous donor to our benevolent fund, so I wouldn't want you to go forgetting that in a hurry.'

'Bullshit.'

'Whatever, Don, but I'm advising you to think very carefully here. The boss isn't going to be impressed with this carry on. You think you can come in here, in front of people, and start acting the cunt? You want to get your own house in order first before you come to me, issuing threats.'

'Who's issuing threats?'

Holborn smiled. 'Sounds like you are, Don. But like I said, sort yourself out first. You're not whiter than white. Everyone knows you can't keep your cock in your pants. You're becoming an embarrassment.' He relaxed in his chair and waved the other detectives back. 'You go and tell Gary Bancroft you can't help him, that things have gone too far for that. And then you can leave it with me. Can't say fairer than that, can I?' He stood up. 'Now if you'll excuse me, I've got a murder inquiry to be working on.'

CHAPTER ELEVEN

I woke late, made myself coffee and buttered a slice of toast. I managed one mouthful before deciding I didn't want it. I picked up my mug. The coffee tasted bitter. I threw the food into the kitchen bin and walked back to the living room and checked my mobile for messages. There was nothing from Niall. There was nothing from Connor, either. I'd let my nephew down. I hadn't protected him as I should have done. I felt like shit.

I picked my mobile up and scrolled through for Sarah's number, and after debating with myself for a moment, I called her. Something Coleman had said in the pub had touched a nerve with me.

'How's it going?' I said when she answered.

'Don't ask.'

I could hear empty bottles being thrown out in the background. 'You're at work?'

'Just started.'

'What's going on?'

'Niall's in a mood with himself. He won't talk about it.'

I walked over to the window. 'Spoken to your dad?'

'Last night.'

'How is he?'

She sighed. 'Still unwilling to talk to me, even though I'm his daughter.'

I was sure Don wouldn't tell us anything, but something would bring the situation to a head, and whatever it was, he seemed determined to face it alone. I had to follow the trail to Gary Bancroft. I heard my brother swear in the background. I was glad of the distraction. It saved me having to answer difficult questions about Don and what I knew.

'What's going on with Niall?' she asked me.

I told her what had happened to Connor.

'Is he alright?'

'He'll get over it.' I hoped I was right. Regardless of the rights and wrongs of the situation, he didn't deserve what had happened. 'He'll heal over.' It was the mental scars I was more worried about.

'What are you going to do?'

Sutherland was increasing the stakes. I told Sarah I still needed to find a way to get him off my back.

The library was much quieter than during my last visit. The piece of paper in front of me had the name Gary Bancroft on it. Coleman said I should talk to him. I repeated the search I'd done on his brother. This time I got a result. Gary Bancroft was a low-level career criminal. I found plenty of links to court cases in the Hull Daily Mail. The most recent report from less than a year ago told me the street he lived on. A few more searches and I had the house number. I wrote it down. There was no time like the present.

The address I had was off Boulevard, which in turn cut across Hessle Road. In a former life, the area had been the heart of the fishing industry. Now, as I drove down it, it was clear those days were long gone. It never failed to shock me, even though I knew the area well. Boulevard was once the jewel in the area's crown, but now it was downtrodden and decaying. So far as I could see, the regeneration of the area had ground to a halt. I'd once worked a case with a businessman who had big plans for the area. They'd come to nothing, but I wondered if he'd really been the man the area had needed to bring about change.

The old rugby league stadium, which the black and white half of the city had once thronged to had been bulldozed, a new academy school in the process of being constructed in its place. Back in the day, it had been one of the places the trawlermen, the three day millionaires, headed for during their shore leave, eager to release some pent-up frustration. I'd never played there, and judging by stories I'd heard, it had been no place for the opposition.

I found the house I wanted, and as usual, drove past, turned around and parked a hundred yards away from it. It was a precaution in case I didn't want my car recognised. I wasn't anticipating trouble, but the past few days had demonstrated that trouble had a way of finding me.

The house was shabby from the outside. I was standing in a small front yard. Litter from the street had blown in and weeds were creeping through the concrete. The downstairs window frames were wooden and in desperate need of updating. I knocked and waited. An old woman opened the door. She stared at me, almost like I was expected. It unnerved me.

'Is Gary in?' I said.

She stepped back into her house. 'You best come through.'

I followed her into the living room. It was dark and fusty. She sat down in her chair and lit a cigarette, her eyes never leaving me. It was sparse. I glanced at the handful of framed photographs on the mantelpiece.

'There's nothing left for you to take,' she said.

She wasn't wrong. There was nothing of value. She took a drag on her cigarette. I guessed she was well into her seventies, but she wasn't worried about having me in the house.

'Don't think I haven't already dealt with your sort a hundred times before,' she said.

'My sort?'

'Parasites. You don't scare me.'

I tried to find a place to sit on the settee. I hadn't noticed the dog, sleeping in the corner. 'I don't want anything from you.'

'Who are you, then?'

'I need a word with Gary.' I passed her a card.

'Why?'

'His name came up in something I'm looking into.' I didn't have a better story than that. She was suspicious. I placed a twenty pound note on the coffee table which sat between us. She gave me a small nod. 'He doesn't live here.'

'Where will I find him?'

She ignored my question. 'Always in trouble with the police, that one.'

'So I understand.'

'And at his age, too.'

From the newspaper reports, I'd worked out that he was around fifty years old. I asked again where I would find him.

'No idea.'

'Take a guess?'

'I'm not his keeper. Drops in to see me when he feels like it.'

'You must have some idea where he goes?'

'Probably the bookies or the pub.'

We were starting to get somewhere. 'Not working, then?'

'He's never had a steady job.'

'Not many of them about.'

She snorted. 'Not for the likes of Gary.'

'I suppose not.'

She sat forward. 'You're a Private Investigator?'

'That's right.'

'You can find people?'

'Sometimes.'

She pointed to a photograph on the mantelpiece. 'Have a look.'

I walked across and picked it up. I was looking at a young man in his early twenties. He was smiling for the camera. In one hand he was holding an ice-cream. I recognised the setting. The photograph had been taken in Scarborough. I could see the castle in the background. I placed it back where I'd got it from.

'My other son,' she said. 'Andrew. He's been missing for nearly thirty years now.'

I sat in my car, but didn't switch the engine on. I stared at the house and thought over what I'd heard. Andrew Bancroft had been missing for almost three decades. Experience told me people can disappear without leaving a trace, even if it was unusual. Thirty years ago, you wouldn't leave an electronic trail. It was possible to do. But Coleman had linked this to Don for me. I was sure Coleman could tell me more, but it wouldn't work like that. I would have to dig a bit deeper before I went back to him again. I needed something to bargain with. I'd left my card with Gary Bancroft's mother and she'd seen I had cash. He would get the message. I was sure he'd call me. Otherwise, I would have to come back and find him. I took one last look at the house and drove away.

Niall was working alone in the kitchen. I closed the door behind me. I wanted to make sure he was ok after what Sarah had said. He put his knife down and turned to stare at me before launching himself across the room. He pinned me to the food preparation table. I tried to shake him off, but he was too strong. I was going nowhere.

'What the fuck are you doing?' I said.

'Why didn't you tell me?'

I continued to struggle. 'Tell you what?'

He shouted. 'The truth. The fucking truth, Joe. I know Connor took the cigarettes.'

I closed my eyes. Niall released his grip on me. He picked up an empty pan and threw it at the wall. 'Fuck's sake, Joe. I've seen him. I've seen the state of his face.'

I stood back up and rearranged my clothes.

'Say something, then,' he said.

There was nothing to say. I couldn't believe Connor hadn't told me he was going to tell his dad. This was why it wasn't a good idea.

Niall walked towards me. 'Aren't you going to try and justify it to me? Tell me why you thought I shouldn't know that my son stole from me, what he was getting involved in?'

'It was for the best.'

He shoved me in the chest. 'It was for the best? Are you out of your mind? Even Connor had the balls to front up to me and tell me truth. What have you got, Joe? You watched as your nephew took a kicking in front of you.'

He continued to push me. 'I'm not going to fight you,' I said. I wanted to tell him not to take the moral high ground. We were talking about smuggled cigarettes. We were all in this shit together.

Niall squared up to me again. 'You always know best, don't you, Joe? Always have done, but I'll tell you this for nothing, I'm fucking sick of hearing it from you.'

I shoved him away from me. 'You didn't need to know. I'm sorting it.'

Niall sneered at me. 'Sorting it? You've only made things worse.'

I took a breath. Making it worse? 'I'm doing my best,' I said.

My brother stared at me before deflating in front of me, like he'd got the worst out of his system. 'He told me everything, Joe.'

'Right.'

'You should have told me.'

'I made a decision.'

'I've kicked him out.'

'Why?'

'You wouldn't understand.'

It was my turn to shout. 'Understand what?'

'What it's like to have a son.'

He looked ashamed as soon as the words left his mouth. I was too angry to care. I ignored him and headed for the door.

'I didn't mean that, Joe,' he shouted after me.

I carried on walking. 'Fuck off, Niall. Maybe you should stick to building wardrobes in your lock-up.'

I had to decide what to do. I felt bad for what I'd said to Niall and thought about calling him to apologise. But we both needed some time to calm down. I called Connor instead. 'Where are you?' I asked him.

'At Milo's dad's place.'

I cut the connection and put my mobile back in my pocket before taking one last look around the office.

Milo's dad stared at me as I walked into his office. 'Problem?' He shook his head. I immediately felt bad. He was probably as worried for his son as Niall was for Connor, even if my brother couldn't admit it. Connor stared at me.

The state of his face following the attack at Sutherland's pub made my heart sink. I nodded to the door. He followed me out to the car park. I watched the trail of traffic leaving the city on the A63. I wondered if I should be using it, too. Was I doing any good being here? For a moment I thought about travelling the world. I hadn't seen much of it. I smiled at the thought, like I was still a daft teenager with everything in front of me. I knew where I belonged, and that was here, sorting out my family's problems whether they wanted my help or not. Connor leaned against my car.

'I'm sorry,' I said to him.

'It's not your fault. I deserved it.'

It wasn't the point, but there was nothing more to be said. 'Why did you tell your dad?'

Connor shrugged. 'It seemed like a good idea at the time.'

'That's it?'

'I thought it was the right thing to do. It's my problem to sort, not yours.'

'I was sorting it.'

'We were lying to my dad. You shouldn't have to do that.'

'It was for the best.' It sounded weak, I knew that, but it was the truth.

Connor put his hands in his pockets and shrugged. 'It was still a lie.'

He was right, but no good had come from Niall knowing the truth. It didn't make any difference whether it was Connor or someone else who'd taken the cigarettes. They were gone. I walked around the car and leaned on the bonnet next to him. 'Feel any better for doing it?'

He took his time before answering the question. 'Not really.'

'What happened when you told him?'

'He went mental.'

'Can't really blame him for that.'

'It's my mum I feel bad for. He was shouting at me, calling me all sorts of names, but she was just crying. I thought he was going to hit me at one point. It's what I deserve.'

'He wouldn't hit you.'

'Felt like he might do.'

'He wouldn't,' I repeated. I was pretty certain he was going to hit me, though, back at the bar. 'He's proud of you.'

Connor shook his head. 'Doubt that.'

'I was there when he brought you home from the hospital as a baby and I saw his face at your christening. He was the proudest man I've ever seen.'

Connor smiled weakly. 'Even so.'

'We're all at fault here.'

It was what was actually happening that was important. The idea of fault or blame wasn't of interest to me. I'd always been someone who simply tried to sort things. 'Where did you stay last night?'

'At Milo's.'

'With his parents?'

Connor shook his head. 'He's got a flat.'

'Right.' I didn't like the fact he wasn't supervised. 'I've got the space for you to stay at my flat.'

'I don't want to cause you any trouble.'

I would have laughed if the situation wasn't so serious. For a moment, I caught a glimpse of my nephew as a boy again. He was scared, so I made light of the situation. 'I can keep an eye on you, for a start.'

Connor nodded. 'Thanks.'

'Not a problem. You can have the settee.' I glanced back at the office. Milo's dad was staring at us from the window. Once he realised I was staring back at him, he turned away. At least he'd given Connor a chance. I owed the man an apology. 'You can pay me some board,' I said to Connor, as I passed him the key to my flat. 'And don't bother going out.'

Once I was back in my car I checked my mobile. There was a text message from Gary Bancroft. He was in the Whalebone pub on Wincolmlee if I wanted to buy him a pint. I wasn't surprised to hear from him, but I was surprised he'd strayed so far away from his Hessle Road patch.

The pub was close to the River Hull on the edge of the city centre. It was one of the few pubs still standing in the area. The housing had long gone and the industry was slowly dying away, taking the passing trade with it. The Whalebone was small with black and white photographs lining the walls. The majority were of long gone pubs in the city and football memorabilia. It was a proper old-fashioned pub, the kind my dad would have loved. Under other circumstances, I would have enjoyed a visit.

Even though I had no idea what Bancroft looked like, the only customers were three men sat together around a small table. I walked up to them. They were all about the right age. They all stared at me with dead eyes. I got the message. They'd all eaten people like me for breakfast. Even though they were older than me, I didn't want to take my chances. I didn't know the lie of the land in here.

One of them spoke. 'Geraghty?'

I nodded and assumed he was Gary Bancroft. He was rolling tobacco on the table. His slow and deliberate movements were those of a man whose body had been ravaged over the years by alcohol.

'Buy us all a drink,' he said.

I went to the bar and waited for the landlord to appear. When did he, I ordered three pints of lager.

'For yourself?' he said, placing the glasses in front of me.

'Nothing.'

'Treat yourself.'

I told him to take the money for a diet coke and walked back to the three men. I told the two who weren't Bancroft to leave us alone. They eventually walked away with their drinks.

'Old habits die hard?' I said.

Bancroft picked up his drink. 'What do you mean?'

'The welcoming committee.'

He set his glass back down and shrugged. 'My mam said you wanted a word.'

'Good of her.'

'What do want?'

'Your brother's name has come up in an investigation of mine.'

'I doubt that.'

'Because he's been gone for thirty years?'

'Something like that.'

I assumed he would be upset at the mention of his brother's name, but I'd seen things and learned something about human nature. I took a couple of twenty pound notes out of my wallet and put them in front of him. I didn't need to be subtle with him. 'Tell me about your brother.'

'There's not much to tell.'

I let him take his time. If he wanted to show he was in charge, that was fine. Bancroft pocketed the money. 'Our kid always was a selfish wanker.'

'I'll take your word for that, but no birthday cards? No Christmas cards?'

'Nothing.'

'You weren't close?'

'Not really.'

'Your mum seemed pretty upset by it.'

'That's up to her.'

'You didn't get on with him?'

'Take him or leave him, to be honest.'

'Even though he was your brother?'

He leaned in closer to me. 'Don't think you can be coming in here telling me what to think.'

I conceded the point. 'Did you look for him when he disappeared?'

'What could I do? He was a grown man. He could do as he pleased.'

'But you must have been able to have a guess where he went. Places you knew he had friends? Places where you've got family?'

He relaxed. 'Not really.'

'Did you speak to his mates?'

'Can't say I did.' He finished his pint and slid the empty glass across the table to me. I took it back to the bar, returning with a fresh pint for him. He took a mouthful before speaking. 'I was working away. What could I do?'

I was genuinely taken back by his attitude. It was his brother. Even after our bust up, I would still do anything for Niall. 'What about the police?' I asked him.

Bancroft smiled. 'The police?'

'They'd have helped.'

'Don't take the piss out of me, Geraghty. You know as well as I do that they don't give a shit.'

'Because you've got a record?'

'And the fact he was a grown man who could make his own decisions. My mam contacted them, but that was her lookout.'

'Nothing happened?'

'Didn't give a fuck, did they? We're scum to them.' He paused. 'How's Don doing these days?'

I leaned forward this time. 'What's Don got to do with anything?'

Bancroft smiled again. 'The card you left had his name on it.'

The old cards. Don Ridley & Son. 'Why do you want to know about Don?'

He was obviously pleased he knew something I didn't. 'Because when our kid went missing he was the only policeman who took it seriously and wouldn't let it go. Like a dog with a bone, you might say.'

'Don Ridley?'

'The very fucking one.'

CHAPTER TWELVE

My talk with Gary Bancroft had left me with more questions. I made slow progress down Anlaby Road towards Don's house, the city traffic as bad as ever. There was a car parked outside his house. I recognised it straight away as Sutherland's. As I got closer, I could see Carl Palmer in the driver's seat. There was no sign of George Sutherland, so I assumed he was inside talking to Don. I drove to the end of the street and parked up. My heart was racing at what it meant. I waited it out. Sutherland left Don's house about twenty minutes later, getting straight into the passenger seat alongside Palmer. I stayed where I was for five minutes in case they came back. Once I was satisfied they were gone, I got out of my car and walked to Don's house. I wondered what I was going to find. I knocked loudly on his front door. No answer. I took a step back and bent down to look in the window. The feeling of dread was growing. I wasn't sure what to do. The decision was made for me when he opened the door. He was genuinely surprised to see me.

'I was washing the pots,' he said, composing himself quickly. He turned away, but left the door open.

I followed him through to the kitchen. The house had been tidied. 'Had guests have you?'

'I had Sarah here earlier on.'

It was a half-truth at best, but I went with it. 'She won't let it go, you know? She's worried about you.'

'I've told her she's got nothing to worry about. I can take care of myself.'

I smiled. 'She's her father's daughter. It's not in her make-up to let things go. Or mine. How's Roger Millfield? Still working for him?'

He didn't answer me, but I wasn't too bothered. It wasn't why I was here. I waited as he finished washing the two mugs in the sink. He put the dishcloth to one side. The bruising on his face was starting to fade, but he still wore the scars of the attack he'd suffered. He wasn't going to mention George Sutherland to me, though. I nodded in the direction of his dining table. 'Shall we sit down?' I waited for him to join me. 'Andrew Bancroft' I said.

'We've already been through this. You've already tried to get Sarah to do your dirty work for you. The name doesn't mean anything to me.'

I stared out at Don's back garden. He'd had the turf relaid so Lauren had somewhere to play. 'Don't lie to me.'

'I've no reason to lie to you. I don't recall the name.'

'He went missing thirty years ago.'

'Hardly breaking news.'

'I spoke to his mother. It still means something to her.'

'Only natural.'

'I spoke to her other son, Gary. He's a character.'

'Plenty of them about, too.'

'And his name doesn't mean anything to you?'

Don shook his head. 'Can't say it does.'

'Coleman gave me Andrew Bancroft's name.'

'Why would he do that?'

That was a very good question. Why had Coleman given me the name of a man who disappeared decades ago? I'd let him use me so far, but that was going to have to change. I needed something, too. 'I know you looked into Andrew Bancroft's disappearance.'

'I looked into countless disappearances,' he said. 'Grown man decides to leave and start again? Doesn't sound like a stand-out case to me.'

'Really?'

'I've seen things you can't even begin to imagine.'

'Gary Bancroft said you took it very personally.'

'I took every case personally.'

I knew Don was right. He'd worked in CID for decades. Of course he'd seen things I couldn't imagine. But that didn't excuse the fact he was lying to me. He was still sharp and I had to respect that. I only had one shot at asking him why he was speaking to Sutherland and that needed to be done on my terms. Connor's beating had increased the stakes. I could feel my two problems starting to converge. Whatever was going on between Don and George

Sutherland was probably going to give me my chance to resolve all my problems. I told him this was his last chance to tell me the truth.

'There's nothing to tell,' he eventually said.

I drove into the city centre, left my car on a meter and walked to Queens Gardens Police Station. I told the officer on the front desk I wanted to speak to Acting DI Coleman.

'Geraghty, isn't it?'

I nodded. I now knew more about Andrew Bancroft, but it was time for Coleman to tell me what he knew. The man didn't make any move to pick up the telephone and call Coleman's extension. I looked around as I waited. The same old tired posters on the walls, the same old tired faces waiting to be attended to. I was losing patience. The man was going through the motions of filing paperwork. 'Are you going to ring him, then?'

He reluctantly picked up the telephone. When his call was answered, he asked to speak to Coleman. He listened to the response and put it back down. 'He's about to go into a meeting.'

'It's important.'

He smiled. 'Lovers tiff, is it?'

'What's that supposed to mean?'

'Bit matey with the Acting Detective Inspector, aren't you?'

His distaste was obvious, but I wasn't letting it go. 'Call him back and tell him I've spoken to Gary Bancroft.'

'He's busy.'

'Try again.'

He did so. 'Still about to go into a meeting.' He put the telephone back down. 'Anything else I can help you with today?'

Sutherland's pub was almost empty. There was no sign of the barmaid I'd spoken with previously. Maybe Sutherland was right and he was skint. He might benefit from the regeneration around the docks in due course, but I doubted the city's politicians had this place in mind when talking about a new Hull. The closer I looked at it, the more I realised what a shit-hole it was. The décor was tatty, the furniture didn't match and the carpet was stained.

I stood and waited. If I rattled Sutherland's cage, word would get back to Don, I was sure. That might force him to talk to me.

Carl Palmer appeared. 'What do you want?'

'A word with your boss.'

'Our boss?'

I smiled. 'Never going to happen.'

'Order a drink first.'

We were playing that game again. 'Just get him for me.'

Palmer laughed and walked away from me. I waited it out.

Sutherland eventually appeared. 'Got my money, Geraghty?'

'No.'

He moved closer to me so the handful of drinkers couldn't hear us. 'So what the fuck are you doing here?'

'I didn't get chance to speak to you at Don's earlier.'

Sutherland stared hard at me before smiling. 'You best come through.'

I followed Sutherland through to his office and sat down opposite him. The CCTV images were filtering through to the television screens as before.

Sutherland spoke. 'If you haven't got my money, why the fuck aren't you doing something about it?'

'What were you talking to Don about?'

He relaxed in his chair. 'What's it got to do with you?'

I said nothing and waited for him to speak. He eventually repeated that it was none of my business.

'How was he?' I asked.

'Don't waste my time, Geraghty. I'm not in the mood.'

'Odd that Don didn't mention it to me.'

'You're his minder now, are you?'

'I've got his best interests at heart.'

Sutherland smiled. I wanted to lean across the table and wipe it off his face. 'I didn't have him down as a mate of yours,' I said.

He thumped his fist on the table. 'You watch your fucking mouth. I can have you and your family hurt whenever I want to. Just you remember that.'

We stared at each other and he calmed down. 'We go back. Nature of the place, isn't it?' he said. 'Can't fart in Hull without someone else knowing about it. I always bump into people I know when I'm out and about.'

The telephone on his desk sounded. He answered without taking his eyes off me. He swore before saying he'd be down immediately. He stood up and left the room.

Once I was sure he wasn't coming back, I took my opportunity. I moved across to Sutherland's desk and flicked through the rack of DVDs. They all had names on the front cover. I glanced at the CCTV camera covering the bedroom. They were alphabetical. I flicked through. The names meant nothing to me until I reached Roger Millfield. I could hear Sutherland shouting as he walked back towards the office. I quickly stuffed the DVD into my coat pocket. Sutherland stared at me as he walked in. 'You still fucking here, Geraghty?'

I held my hands up. 'On my way.' I headed for the door before stopping. I needed him to know. 'My nephew is off limits, do we understand each other? I don't care who you are, or how many people you've got on your side. You can do what you like to me, but if you pull another stunt like that, I will come for you without giving a fuck about the consequences.'

Sutherland laughed. 'Get my money sorted, Geraghty, before I lose my patience with you.' He stood up and faced me. 'And keep your nose out of my business.'

I put the DVD on top of my television. I stayed standing and looked out to Westbourne Avenue. It was a normal day for the people walking past. I went into the kitchen and made myself a coffee. My mobile was silent. No word from Niall,

Sarah or Connor. Nobody was talking to me. I put the drink down and picked up the DVD to stare at it again. The cover was plain. All that was written on it was the name, Roger Millfield. I took the disc out. His name had been scribbled on it, but this time there was also a date. It had been filmed six months ago. I put the disc into my DVD player. The picture sprung into life. The bedroom which appeared on my screen was the one I'd been staring at on the camera in Sutherland's office. A young girl walked into shot. She was in her late teens or early twenties. She busied herself, plumping up the pillows before touching up her hair and make-up. I wondered if she was aware she was being filmed. I fast-forwarded the footage. I pressed play when a man walked into shot. It was definitely Roger Millfield. I pressed fast-forward again and watched as the girl undressed. I let it play again and listened as he referred to her as Tiffany. I'd seen enough. I switched it off, sat back and closed my eyes. I needed to get out of my flat.

I knocked on the door and took a step back. The living room curtain twitched. I turned to face it so Bancroft's mother could get a proper look at me. She eventually opened the door and let me in. I followed her through into the house. I had to continue giving things a shake.

'I was hoping you'd come back,' she said.

I told her I'd spoken with Gary earlier in the day. 'I owe you an apology. When I spoke to you earlier, I didn't know about Andrew.' Her hand was shaking slightly. I felt terrible for stirring up bad memories, but I had to know about her relationship with Don.

She nodded. 'It wasn't what Andrew was like. People like Andrew don't just disappear.'

I'd been thinking about it. Sometimes people did disappear into thin air. In Hull, it wasn't unheard of for people to simply fall into the water. Sometimes their bodies were found, sometimes only the nagging doubt that maybe something else had happened remained.

'I know my lads aren't perfect,' she said. 'I certainly know that, but my Andrew was the better of the two. He was a good lad, really.' She took a tissue out from the sleeve of her cardigan and blew her nose. 'I could never control them, though,' she said. 'How was a woman like me supposed to control two boys? Men, really? They wouldn't listen to me.'

'How about their dad?' I asked.

'Waste of time from start to finish.'

'Working on the trawlers?'

She laughed. Given that we were sitting close to Hessle Road, it had felt like a reasonable guess.

'Howard wasn't exactly what you'd call a hard worker. He was more a hard drinker. The trawlers were certainly too much for him. He went out once, but that was it for him. He reckoned he suffered from severe seasickness and couldn't do the job. He called himself a painter and decorator, but he always more interested in painting the town red.'

I smiled. It was obviously a rehearsed line she gave everyone.

She glanced at a photograph of Andrew. It had been taken on holiday, outside a caravan. 'He wasn't a bad lad. It was his brother leading him astray. Andrew loved his rugby. He was always playing or watching at The Boulevard. I thought that was going to be enough to keep him out of trouble. Sport's usually good for young men.'

Thinking about myself, I wasn't so sure I agreed with her. I asked her to tell me more about Andrew.

'What do you want to know?'

'Whatever you can tell me about him.' She didn't seem to know where to start. 'When did he leave school?' I asked, hoping to get her started.

I watched as she did the arithmetic in her head. '1976, a couple of years after his brother. He went to Trinity House. He passed all the entrance exams, so he was definitely brainy.'

I knew of the school. It was a boys-only nautical school in the city centre. The pupils wore navy-themed uniforms and caps. 'He didn't fancy going to sea when he left?'

'It wasn't for Andrew, either, but he never found a proper job. He did a bit of labouring here and there, but there wasn't much going on in Hull back then. A bit like now, I suppose. I couldn't stop him, but his brother got him involved with a bad group of people. As hard as I tried to stop it, they became his friends. He wouldn't listen to me telling him that they were no good.'

It reminded me of Connor's story. It was certainly enough to make me feel uncomfortable, though hopefully I was doing something to sort him out. 'What happened to Andrew?'

'The police got involved. Just a warning at first, but his dad wouldn't do anything. I said he should give him a clip around the ear, but he wasn't interested.' She shrugged. 'And things went from bad to worse.'

'And then he disappeared?'

She nodded. 'I went to the police.'

'Don Ridley?'

'He was very good to me. I liked Don. You could tell he was a good man.'

I was beginning to wonder how true that was, but she had my attention. 'Can you tell me what happened?'

She sat back in her chair and stared, weighing me up. She'd probably been ignored and written off countless times. I held her stare, so she knew I was really listening.

'1986,' she eventually said. 'That was when Andrew went missing. I remember sitting in the reception at Queens Gardens. Horrible place it was. It was Don who spoke to me.'

'What did he say?'

'Like you'd expect, he promised to look into it for me.'

'What did he find out?'

'Nothing.'

'Nothing at all?'

'He did his best. I know that. He spoke to people and stayed in touch with me, but I suppose he had other cases to deal with. He went the extra mile for me, so I can't complain.' She paused. 'Is he dead?'

I told her Don was absolutely fine.

'Why don't you talk to him, then? He'll be able to tell you more.'

'I will do, don't worry about that.'

'Doubt he'll even remember Andrew these days,' she said.

'Is there anyone I can talk to? Anyone who might be able to tell me more about what happened?'

She thought about my question. 'I know Don spoke to one of Andrew's friends on a few occasions.'

'Have you got his name?'

She shook her head. 'It doesn't matter.'

'It might help.'

'He died in a car crash years ago.'

I finished my coffee. It was another dead end, another thread I couldn't unpick.

'He came to the house, you know,' she said.

'Who did?'

'His workmate, if that's what you'd call him. He came round with some money.' She paused. 'What was he called?' she said to herself. She tapped the arm of her chair with satisfaction. 'It was a man called Alan. Alan Palmer.'

I kept my face neutral, but I felt something click into place. Alan Palmer meant Frank Salford and George Sutherland. The link Coleman had given me pointed to Sutherland. I couldn't overlook the fact he was working a live case. Everything seemed to be narrowing. 'Did you tell Don about this?'

'He said he'd speak with Alan Palmer about it.'

'What happened?'

'I don't think anything happened. He certainly never told me about any developments.' She picked up the card I'd left during my last visit and looked at it. 'Can you help find out what happened to my son?'

Without thinking, I found myself nodding. 'I'll try my best.'

CHAPTER THIRTEEN

I left Bancroft's mother and returned to my car. I couldn't believe I'd made such a rash promise to her. I pushed the thought to one side for now. I needed to speak to Sarah and keep her up to speed. The night was drawing in and I'd spent the day running around without giving her a second thought.

I headed straight to her house. She was surprised to see me, but invited me in. 'Where's Lauren?' I said.

'Upstairs asleep. Be quiet.'

I walked through to the kitchen and sat down at the table. Sarah put the kettle on and made the drinks. 'How's Niall?' I asked.

She sat down opposite me. 'Still pissed off. You should have told him, Joe.'

I still couldn't believe that would have been the best course of action. 'He's a kid,' I said. 'He took the beating, but the message was for me.' We lapsed into silence. I broke it by telling her Connor was staying at my flat for a bit. 'That way I can keep an eye on him. He needs my help.'

She nodded. 'You have to look after your own first.'

I winced at the barb, but was surprised by her attitude. I was expecting a bit more understanding, but I knew she had her own problems to think about. It wasn't a massive leap to see the situation through her eyes. I looked at her and thought about Don's affair with Kath Millfield. I could see how worried she was about him. Worse than that, I could see that I hadn't given her the help she'd expected. I knew she wasn't being heartless. It was me. I changed the subject. 'I found Andrew Bancroft's brother,' I said.

'You didn't say you knew he had one.'

'Coleman told me.'

'Why didn't you let me know?'

I was about to explain, but she waved my explanation away.

'What did you find out?' she said.

'Andrew Bancroft's been missing for almost thirty years.'

'What does missing mean?'

'He worked for Frank Salford.' I didn't need to say any more. What I didn't know was how Don fitted in, but there was something there to be found. 'It's all speculation and guesswork,' I said. 'Especially if your dad won't talk about it.'

'But he's involved somewhere.'

It was a statement rather than a question. 'It seems likely.'

She softened. 'I'm worried about him, Joe.'

I didn't know what to say to that. There was nothing I could say that would make it sound any better.

'Tell me what's going on, Joe.'

'I just did.'

Sarah walked across the room. 'The truth,' she said. 'What's going on with my dad? I know he's in trouble and I know the two of you aren't telling me everything.'

Over the years we'd become close friends, even if nothing else was going to happen between us. She knew me better than I knew myself. Yet I was still prepared to lie to her. Or at least shield her from the truth as best I could. 'I'm still trying to put it together.' It only felt like a small lie.

'You can do better than that, Joe.'

She was right. It was no answer. I was making excuses for Don, but it wasn't my place to tell her what I knew. I stood, ready to go. 'You need to speak to your dad.'

It felt like I had a jigsaw puzzle in front of me, but none of the pieces would fit into the right place. I watched from the pavement as Sarah closed her curtains. It felt like I'd let her down. It broke my heart to admit it, but I had to put it to one side, even if it had cost me the one person willing to help. I took my mobile out and called Coleman again. He answered quickly. 'We need to talk,' I said. 'The old office in about twenty minutes?' It was the first place I'd thought of.

I parked my car next to Holy Trinity and walked the short distance to the office. Coleman was waiting outside for me. He put his mobile back in his pocket as he saw me approach. 'Just about to ring you.'

I walked straight past him and unlocked. He followed me in. I flicked the light switch on.

'Someone's been busy,' Coleman said, as he looked around the empty room.

There were no chairs left. It was empty. I settled for leaning against the window with my hands in my pocket, ignoring his remark.

'What's the plan, then, Joe? Set up and go it alone? Isn't that how you Private Investigators should operate? Lone wolves?'

'We'll see.' I told him about Niall's bar and that I couldn't see myself doing the same. Sinking my money into a new business like that wasn't me. Maybe Coleman was on the right track. This was what I did. This kind of thing was me. 'They were taking the piss at Queens Gardens when I asked to speak to you.'

Coleman continued to pace the room. 'On the desk?'

'Asked if we'd had a lovers tiff.'

Coleman smiled. 'Fuck them.'

'Pretty much what I thought.' I told him I'd spoken with Gary Bancroft.

'Good.'

'I tracked him down to a pub on Wincolmlee. He seems to be one of life's drinkers.' Coleman was giving nothing away, so I continued. 'I know his brother hasn't been seen for pretty much thirty years.' He was still giving me nothing. 'I spoke to his mum about it. Poor woman's still in pieces.'

Coleman stopped pacing the room. 'What else?'

It was as if I had to give him the golden piece of information, the one thing which would trigger him into giving me something back. I took a deep breath and controlled myself. Losing patience wouldn't do me any good. 'I know Don was involved in the investigation to find Andrew Bancroft, and by all accounts he took it a lot more seriously than his colleagues.'

'But he didn't get very far?'

'Don certainly won't speak about it, but I know Andrew Bancroft was working for Frank Salford.'

'Correct.'

I pushed myself upright and walked across to Coleman. 'Cards on the table?'

Coleman agreed. 'Cards on the table.'

'I've got a problem with George Sutherland.'

'Doesn't surprise me, Joe.'

He could see I was surprised by that. He held his hands up. 'A lot of people have a problem with Sutherland. Want to tell me about it?'

I shook my head. 'Not really.'

'I'll buy you a drink,' he said. 'But let's do it somewhere more comfortable.'

We walked across Lowgate to Silver Street and headed in the direction of Ye Olde White Harte. Coleman bought the drinks and we found a quiet corner. The pub was famous for being the place in 1642 where it was resolved that the King wouldn't be allowed access to the city, triggering the English Civil War. Tonight wasn't going to be quite so momentous, but it felt like an appropriate place to be sitting. I didn't touch my drink. I wanted to hear what he had to say.

Coleman picked his drink up and drank a mouthful. He didn't take his eyes off me. I waited it out. He put his drink down. 'Can I trust you, Joe?'

I had no idea what the right answer to the question was. We did different jobs and often we were on different sides of the line. I wasn't going to forget that. 'You're going to have to spit out whatever's on your mind.'

'I've been speaking to Dave Johnson,' he said.

It felt like the room had started to spin. My stomach lurched. It was a name I never wanted to hear again.

'He wants out of prison,' Coleman said. 'He's realised that as things stand, he's going to die behind bars.'

'Good.' Dave Johnson had been Frank Salford's right-hand man. Salford had died, but Johnson hadn't been so lucky. Although Dave Johnson wasn't the man who'd set fire to the house my wife had died in, it had been done on his orders, and that made him responsible in my eyes. I took a moment to compose myself.

Coleman took another mouthful of his drink. 'I know it's hard for you.'

I leaned forwards. 'You know it's hard for me? Are you taking the piss?'

Coleman shook his head. 'I'm not taking the piss.'

I looked down at my drink. He'd bought me a coke. 'I need a proper drink.' The car could stay where it was. I needed to buy myself some time to think. I returned from the bar and sat back down. 'Why are you doing this?'

'Johnson contacted me. He thinks he's got information I might be interested in.'

'Only thinks?'

'More a hint of information to come.'

'And you've brought me out here to tell me that?'

'It's a difficult situation to handle.'

I'd heard enough. I stood up, ready to leave. 'You can fuck off.'

'Sit down, Joe.'

I headed for the exit. Coleman followed me. I headed through the alleyway and back to Silver Street. I walked towards Whitefriargate, heading in the direction of the Market Square and Holy Trinity. I was on autopilot. Coleman matched my stride. He grabbed my arm and told me calm down. I spun round and forced him against the doors of the indoor market. 'Don't tell me what to do.' The heavy doors rattled as he struggled until I released my grip. We were toe to toe, staring at each other.

It was Coleman who spoke first. He was perfectly calm. 'Johnson won't talk until there's a deal on the table.'

I shook my head and continued to walk. Coleman wouldn't leave it and was again by my side. I stopped and turned to face him. 'What is on the table, out of interest?'

'That depends if the information he's giving me is any good.'

'Why does that concern me?'

'It's not official yet.'

'Fuck's sake.' I walked over to the benches in front of the church and sat down. Coleman followed and did the same. I couldn't believe what I was hearing. Neither of us spoke for a moment.

'I need someone to check his story out,' Coleman eventually said.

'No chance.'

'Hear me out, Joe.'

I assumed my world was about to get an awful lot worse.

'Andrew Bancroft,' Coleman said. 'Johnson gave me his name.'

'What about him?'

'Johnson won't say specifically. He mentioned George Sutherland. He was involved, too.'

'For definite?'

'Stands to reason given the Salford link. I know it's not easy for you, Joe, but have a think about it.' Coleman stood up and looked down at me. 'I'll be talking to Johnson tomorrow. If you want, you can come along and see what he has to say.'

I watched Coleman walk away from me. It was a big ask. I paced around, angry with Coleman for bringing it all back. I knew the feeling of loss had never left me and never would, but knowing Johnson was behind bars and Salford was dead gave me some measure of satisfaction. I found myself walking up to the doors of the church. I had no idea why. I certainly wasn't a religious man. The church was lit up by a series of lights around the courtyard. I could only stare in awe at the building, like with the Humber Bridge, even though they couldn't be more different structures. The spell was broken by the sound of a drunk being sick on the street corner. His mates cheered him on. I walked back to the benches, sat down and tried to make a decision.

The deal on the table from Coleman was clear. He was offering me a line into George Sutherland. I watched as the man who'd been sick was carried away by his mates. He'd have a hangover in the morning, but nothing more serious.

My problems weren't so easily resolved. I had no better plan for removing Sutherland.

The bench was cold and uncomfortable, but I wasn't ready to move. I was pretty sure I had a handle on Coleman's motives. He was yet to be confirmed as a DI, so he was no doubt looking for a final push over the line, the one case that could confirm his promotion. It appeared he was talking to Johnson off the record, and it made sense that Johnson had some serious stories to tell. But even a careerist like Coleman wouldn't risk turning a man like Johnson free unless there was something there. Maybe I was being used. Maybe this was Coleman's way of proving he had some worth after his wife had left him and it would be a pointless exercise. The ultimate irony of the situation was that to help my brother and Don, I had to help the man who was responsible for my wife's death.

Connor was waiting for me in my flat, drinking a bottle of beer and looking sorry for himself. At least he'd done as he was told and stayed in.

He looked up at me. 'How's it going?'

I took my coat off and threw it in the corner. 'Get me a beer, please.'

Connor went to the fridge and passed me one over. I opened it and drank from the bottle. I walked over to the front window and stared out on to the street. My reflection in the glass stared back at me. I turned away and sat down.

'Are you hungry?' Connor asked me. 'I was about to order a takeaway.'

I shook my head. 'Not especially.'

He ordered food and we both sat down in silence. I watched him fidget with his mobile. 'What's on your mind?'

'I was curious, really,' he said.

'What about?'

'Did you get on with your dad?'

There was a question. I thought about it before answering. 'Maybe not as well as I should have.'

'Didn't the rugby make it easier?'

'Rugby was the problem.'

'You wanted to be like him?'

I shook my head. 'Not really. All I wanted was to play, but he knew what a toll it took on your body and how hard it was to combine it with a proper job. He didn't want me following him down the same road. He wanted better for me, but I couldn't see it at the time.'

Connor smiled and took a drag on his bottle of beer. 'Sounds familiar. Did you fall out with him?'

'A little bit, I suppose.'

'After the injury?'

What he was really asking me was what happened after I'd failed, after my dad had been proved right. I wasn't going to lie. 'We argued,' I said. 'I worked in his pub for a bit, but it wasn't for me. I couldn't handle people coming in on their way to the match, reminiscing about the good old days with him. All that stuff. It brought back bad memories, and to be totally honest, it was starting to make me bitter.'

'How did you patch it up, then?'

I turned to face Connor. I wanted to make sure he got the message loud and clear. 'We never really patched it up all that well. That's my biggest regret.'

Connor nodded, like he understood. 'So how do you go about patching things up?'

I offered my bottle up for a toast. 'That's the question you've got to figure out an answer to. The only way you can convince your dad about the night club stuff is to go out and make it work. Make it a success. Prove to him that it can be done.'

The buzzer to my flat interrupted us.

'The food.' Connor said.

'I'll get it.' I walked down the stairs and opened the front door to the delivery driver. George Sutherland threw a bag of hot food at me.

'Bumped into the guy at your door. Thought I'd save him the trouble.' He pointed to his car. 'Get in.'

Carl Palmer stood behind him, smiling at me. I weighed up the situation. The odds were stacked against me and

Connor was upstairs. I didn't want him involved. I followed Sutherland and Palmer out of the building. Palmer drove with Sutherland next to me in the back.

'I was up your end of town,' Sutherland said. 'I thought we'd go for a drive.'

The journey passed in silence until Palmer pulled up down North Road and stopped outside what had once been the South Stand entrance to Boothferry Park, former home of Hull City AFC. It was now a building site.

Sutherland stared out of the window at the construction work. 'It's a fucking disgrace. I had some of the best days of my life here. Now it's going to be fucking houses.'

I didn't say anything. Like with the rugby, time moves on. He continued talking, like I was his mate. I didn't like it.

'I remember when Chelsea played here in the Cup, back when it meant something. Me and Frank on the rampage down in London for the first time, even though we were only teenagers. Great day. Two goals for Waggy, as per fucking usual. Showed them cunts how it's done. Shame we didn't finish the job when we got back here, though.'

'Not really my game,' I told him.

'I forgot you were an egg-chaser.'

'My dad went to both games.'

Sutherland shuffled around in his seat to stare at me. 'I thought he was a rugby man, too?'

'It was a big match.'

Sutherland opened the door and got out. 'Take a walk with me. My mate's the site foreman. I've borrowed the key off him.'

Palmer was smiling at me though the rear view mirror. I got out and followed Sutherland. He was already opening up the gate to the site. An icy wind blew around the open spaces of the building site, cutting straight through me. Sutherland beckoned me forward. Palmer had locked the car and was standing behind me. No one else was around. I did as I was told and walked into the building site. My shoes sunk down in the mud. Sutherland shouted at me to keep up. Palmer had closed the gate behind us. It was dark, but my eyes slowly adjusted and I followed Sutherland out into the site, leaving the completed houses behind. He came to a stop in the middle of some new plots.

'Just digging the foundations,' he said. 'Funny how weird places like this are when the machines are switched off and no one's around.' He pointed to the plot we were standing next to. 'Amazing how deep they are these days.'

He was fucking with me and I wasn't in the mood. 'What's your point?'

He took an envelope out of his pocket. 'Have a look.'

I took it from him. Inside was a printout with details of the overnight Hull to Zeebrugge ferry.

'Cat got your tongue, Geraghty? You've had your chance to put the situation right and you haven't done it, so here's what's going to happen. You and that brother of yours are going across to pick up some more cigarettes for me. You're going to drive a van over, load it up and drive it back again.'

I said nothing. If it went wrong, it meant serious prison time. Sutherland was an idiot, but I didn't have a better plan.

'What precautions have you taken?'

He laughed. 'I've got you driving the van.'

'You got the last lot through. You don't need me.'

Sutherland ignored my protests. 'You're doing it. I'll be having a word with Peter Hill. That cunt owes me, too.'

Sutherland was desperate if he was prepared to go over with effectively no insurance policy. We were going to be winging it. He plan was madness. 'I'm not doing it.'

Palmer and Sutherland both took a step towards me. 'Give me my money, then,' Sutherland said.

He knew I didn't have it. I held his stare before eventually conceding with a nod.

Sutherland smiled. 'We'll be in touch, then.'

I was left to walk back to my flat. Connor was sitting in the living room.

'Where did you go?' he said.

'George Sutherland wanted a word.'

He stood up and walked around the room, clearly scared by what had happened. I took the bottle of beer he was drinking from and swallowed a mouthful. 'Don't worry about it. It's going to get sorted.'

He sat back down, but didn't speak. I told him he should go to his girlfriend's house if he wanted. He was glad to get away. I stared at the printout Sutherland had given me before putting it to one side. I hadn't been on a ferry for years. I had no idea how stringent the security was. I had no idea what would be waiting in Belgium. I switched the lights off and sat in the darkened room and came to a decision. I took my mobile out of my pocket and sent a text message to Coleman. I had no intention of getting on a ferry to collect cigarettes on Sutherland's behalf. Whatever Coleman's plan involved, I was in.

Hull, June 1986

Don Ridley walked into Queens Gardens Police Station. The mother of the Bancroft brothers was waiting for him. He asked what he could do for her.

    She stood up. 'I need to report my son missing.'

    'Which one?'

    'Andrew.'

    Ridley nodded and led her out towards Queens Gardens, found an empty bench and sat down. 'Shall we start at the beginning before we go back in there and make it official? How long's he been missing for?'

    'Two days now.'

    'Have you spoken to his friends?'

    'All of them. No one's heard from him.'

    'What about your Gary? What does he have to say?'

    'I don't see much of him. He took a job somewhere in the Midlands. Just went off one day. One of his friends fixed it up for him. He sends cards.' She lit a cigarette. 'It's not asking a lot to expect a call every now and again, is it?'

    'I suppose not. Do you think Andrew's taken himself off for a break?'

    'He told me he was skint. Spent it all on that girlfriend of his.' She looked at Ridley and blew smoke in his direction. 'He left his toothbrush. If you're going away, you don't leave your toothbrush behind, do you?'

    Ridley agreed that it wasn't rational behaviour. 'I thought he was working for Frank Salford?' She took a drag on her cigarette but didn't answer. 'It was an observation,' Ridley said. 'That's all.'

    She ground her cigarette out on the bench arm. 'He told me it was quiet, but he had something on the go.'

    'What did he have on the go?'

    'He didn't say.'

    'Didn't you ask?'

    'It's his business, not mine.'

    It was fair enough. They both knew what her son was. He didn't need her to say any more.

Ridley walked upstairs to the CID office, nodding greetings to the people he knew. The board at the front of the room contained details of a murder enquiry. On it were photographs of the victim. The one to the left had been taken with his family during a caravan holiday. The one to the right had been taken of him following his death. The man had suffered a violent assault before his death. Notes were stuck to the board, mainly details of known movements and associates.

Holborn's space was marked out with partition walls. He walked over to where Ridley was standing. He pointed to the photographs with his mug of tea. 'It happens to scum. You should know that. A lucky find really. A dog walker in the area had spotted the body. Whoever slung him out with the rubbish hadn't even been bothered enough to do it properly.'

'Where?'

'Don't be concerning yourself with big boys' work, Don.'

Ridley walked towards Holborn's office. 'I want a word.'

Holborn followed him in. 'Watch the game last night?'

'Can't say I did.'

'Load of shit, really. I don't know if I hate that cunt Maradona more for cheating or that cunt Shilton for not stopping it.'

Ridley ignored the football talk and got down to the reason he was there. 'Andrew Bancroft is missing.'

Holborn sat down and smiled. 'And why should I give a shit about that?'

'Given that he works for your mate, Salford, I thought you might be concerned?'

'Close the door.'

Ridley did as he was told and sat down. He looked at the photograph of Holborn with his wife and son on his desk. It had been taken in London, next to Big Ben.

'Spit it out, Don.'

Ridley leaned in closer. 'What do you know about Bancroft's disappearance?'

'Why would I know anything about it?'

'Because he was working for Frank Salford.'

Holborn picked up his mug of tea. 'I repeat, Don. So what?'

'You're in Salford's pocket.'

Holborn stared hard at him. 'Say that again?'

'You heard me the first time.'

'I suggest you think very carefully about that type of accusation, Don. Saying things like that could get you into a lot of trouble with the wrong type of people.'

'Like who?'

Holborn shrugged. 'I'm not best pleased with it for a start.'

'No?'

'Not in the slightest.'

'Bancroft's mother isn't going to let this go.'

'A grown man goes missing? Why would we give a shit? Happens every day.' Holborn smiled. 'It's been nice catching up, Don, but here's a word to the wise. Keep the fuck out of my way, alright?'

Ridley readied himself to leave. 'I'll be looking for Andrew Bancroft.'

'And I wish you the best of luck with that, Don, I really do, but I don't think you're in any position to take the moral high-ground with me. I know you, Don, and I know what you are.' Holborn walked to the door and opened it. 'Andrew Bancroft was scum. He won't be missed. Do yourself a favour and take the hint. Fuck off out of here and let it go.'

CHAPTER FOURTEEN

I woke up on my settee. I was firmly back in the habit of sleeping in the living room, worrying about my problems. And seeing as I was sleeping on what was effectively Connor's bed, it was clear he'd spent the night at his girlfriend's. I eased myself up and stretched. I could already feel the effect of the night on my back. I slowly moved into the kitchen and poured myself a glass of water. Things were going from bad to worse with George Sutherland. And today was going to rake up things which I didn't really want to think about. I had no choice, though. Coleman had sent me a text message. He'd arranged for us to speak with Dave Johnson at eleven o'clock. HMP Hull Prison. I felt sick at the thought.

I had time to make one last attempt to sort things out before the meeting with Johnson. I walked into the city centre, hoping the fresh air would help me think and prepare for what was to come. It didn't. My car was where I'd left it. I drove to the park. If you didn't look down at the dog shit and broken glass on the path, it was a pleasant enough place. A row of unused football pitches stood next to what was once an outdoor five-a-side court. Now it was covered in graffiti. The cafe was closed, seemingly abandoned.

I walked around the immaculately tended square of grass where Don was bowling with three of his friends. They were all dressed in regulation white. He was crouched down, feeling the weight of the bowl in his hand, working out the force he needed to put behind the delivery. He released it and followed its flight down the green. I stood close to the jack and waited for Don to straighten up. When he did, it was obvious I wasn't a welcome guest.

'I need a word,' I said.

He knew I wasn't going away. He nodded to the benches which lined the duck pond. 'Give me a couple of minutes.'

I walked over and made myself comfortable. A small girl was with her grandmother, feeding the ducks. She screeched with delight as the birds circled, waiting for her to throw the bread to them. For a moment, I forgot about my problems.

Don sat down next to me and crashed me back into the present.

'Sarah's not happy,' I said. 'She wants to know what's going on. You should tell her.'

'I've already told you. I'm not going to do that and nor am I going to help you with your wild goose chase about Andrew Bancroft.'

'Things have changed.'

'I doubt it, Joe.'

'Bancroft's mother said you spoke to Alan Palmer.'

'It was a long time ago. I've really got no idea.'

'Sure about that?'

'Perfectly sure.'

I sighed. It was like talking to myself. 'This really is your last chance to tell me.'

'Tell you what?'

'Whatever you know about Andrew Bancroft.'

'We've been through this.'

'Are you being blackmailed?'

Don laughed and shook his head. 'Is that the best you can do?'

I told him about the DVD I'd found in Sutherland's office. 'Will I find any more surprises in that pile?'

'Chance would be a fine thing these days. Get a grip of yourself.'

I continued anyway. 'Is that why Millfield wanted your help?'

'Maybe he's just stupid and doesn't know when he has a good thing? Have you considered that?'

I had no answer to his suggestion.

'Whatever it is, you leave him be,' Don said.

We sat in silence and watched as the young girl was led away from the duck pond. 'I'm desperate,' I said.

'Aren't we all?'

'Sutherland has come up with a plan for me to repay Niall's debt.' I didn't tell him what it entailed. All I told him was that I didn't want to go through with the plan. 'I'm scared.' It was a truth I wouldn't have said to many people. But Don had been my mentor, the one person who'd taken a chance on me when I'd needed it. I hoped he'd understand.

'I don't want to hear it, Joe.'

'What are you scared of?'

'I'm an old man I'm not scared of anything.'

I had nothing more to say to him. His police background made him more than a match for me. I told him I was going to speak to Dave Johnson.

He was unable to keep the look of surprise off his face. 'Johnson?'

I nodded. 'Coleman's taking me to see him.'

'After what he did?'

I didn't need Don to say it. I knew no good would come out of the situation for me. I was focusing on the fact it might help Niall. 'He knows something about Andrew Bancroft's disappearance. He's already mentioned George Sutherland.'

'You can't trust scum like Johnson to tell you the truth.'

'I know.' I'd thought it over the previous night. I would have to control my emotions when I spoke to Johnson. I couldn't let my hatred of the man overpower me, or only hear what I wanted to.

'And you can't trust Coleman, either. He's only in it for himself.'

That much was true, too. I couldn't disagree with him on that point, but I had to throw my lot in with someone.

Don slowly straightened himself up. 'Rather than you coming here to tell me it's my last chance, you should think of this as being your last chance to drop it all.' I remained sitting. He looked down on me. 'Go to the police and tell them what your brother's done. You're not stupid. You can work a deal out with them and drop all this nonsense.'

I stood up and faced him. 'Don't you think I would if I could? Do you think I'm enjoying doing this?'

Don looked at me, like he was weighing my last question up.

I had one last roll of the dice. 'I saw Sutherland at your house.' I took a breath and told him about Connor's role with the cigarettes. And how Sutherland had beaten him for it.

Don's poker face held. He eventually shook his head and started walking back to his bowls match.

I reached for my mobile and called Gary Bancroft. It was tight, but I had time before speaking to Dave Johnson. I'd stored his number when he'd made contact with me. I glanced across to Don before leaving. He'd edged away from his friends and was staring back at me. I held his stare and I waited for Bancroft to answer. When he did, I turned away from Don. 'I need another word,' I said.

'I'm on my way to the office.' I was confused. Bancroft laughed when I didn't say anything. 'I'm signing on.'

'Where?'

'I'm in town. Meet me at Admiral of the Humber. You know it?'

I said I did. It was a Wetherspoon's pub on the corner of Carr Lane, next to the bingo hall.

'I want an all-day breakfast, too.'

I found Bancroft sitting in a booth by himself. He didn't have a drink. As I approached, he told me he wanted a pint of lager. He shouted a reminder about the food as I headed for the bar. I didn't want either. I hadn't eaten today, but there was no chance of doing so before I'd spoken with Dave Johnson.

I sat back down at the table and passed him the laminated card with an order number on it. 'It won't be long.'

He put the card down and shrugged before picking up the pint of lager I'd bought him.

'I had another chat with your mum,' I said.

He eyed me suspiciously and put his pint down. 'You don't want to pay too much attention to what she says.'

'She said Alan Palmer gave her some money when your brother disappeared.'

That got his attention. He played for time and took another mouthful of lager. I didn't take my eyes off him.

'I don't remember,' he eventually said. 'I wasn't around much then.'

'Your mum was pretty sure Alan Palmer worked for Frank Salford.'

Bancroft shrugged. 'Maybe.'

'That's definitely what happened.'

'So what?'

I was pleased to be getting under his skin with my questions. The waitress brought his all-day breakfast over. He took his time applying ketchup. He was stalling me again. I could read him like a book. I waited until he picked up a slice of toast. 'Why did he give her the money?'

Bancroft put his toast down. 'Maybe he wanted to help out?'

'Seems unlikely to me.'

He shrugged and took another mouthful of his pint. 'She never looked a gift-horse in the mouth.'

'What did your brother do for Salford?'

He picked his toast back up. 'Never really spoke about it. Bit of this, bit of that. Probably did what he was told to do.'

'Just following orders?'

He took a bite and nodded. 'I reckon so.'

I leaned in across the table. 'Try a bit harder.' I took the toast out of his hand. 'We're talking about your brother.'

Bancroft snatched the toast back. I'd rattled him. He was a man with a short fuse. He took a breath and composed himself before emptying his pint glass. He smiled. 'I'll take another one of them.'

I went to the bar and watched as he continued to eat his food. He was doing his best to keep a lid on his temper, but I was needling him. I returned to the table and changed my line of attack. 'If your brother went away, why didn't he take his toothbrush?'

He sneered at me. 'You shouldn't listen to everything my mam says. It's easy enough to buy another.'

'Did Palmer say that your brother had gone away?' I sat back. 'I bet he did and you took the money without asking any questions.'

Bancroft jabbed his fork at me. 'You know nothing, so I suggest you watch your mouth.'

I checked the time. 'I'm talking to Dave Johnson soon. You'll remember him? He was Frank Salford's number two. He's going to have stories to tell.'

Bancroft picked up his pint and drank it off in one. He didn't take his eyes off me. He stood up.

'Aren't you going to finish your food?' I said.

He shook his head and pushed his chair back in. 'My brother disappeared and he isn't coming back. That's all you need to know.'

I sent Coleman a text message to say I'd be at my brother's bar when he was ready for me. Niall was working on his laptop when I walked in. He didn't acknowledge me. I coughed to get his attention. He relented and looked up. 'You can be angry if you want, but we need to talk,' I said.

Niall stopped what he was doing. 'I've got nothing to say.'

He'd said some unpleasant things to me, too, but I'd put them to one side and carried on anyway. I told him I had news on the cigarettes. I took the printout from my pocket and held it out to him.

He took it from me and read through the information before holding it back out to me. 'I don't understand.'

'We sail on tomorrow night's Zeebrugge ferry. George Sutherland wants to go over with a van to make a collection.' Niall stared at me. I could tell he was scared. 'I don't want to go, either,' I said. 'It's a bad idea.' I was about to say something more when Coleman appeared.

He said the place was looking good before walking over to study the display of my dad's rugby memorabilia.

Niall spoke. 'How's Connor?'

'He's fine,' I said.

'His mum was asking.'

'Right.'

Coleman walked back over to us. 'I didn't realise,' he said. 'Quite a player.'

'Can't argue with that,' I said.

'Fancy a drink before we go?'

I shook my head. 'I'm ready.'

Niall asked where we were going.

'You don't want to know.'

Coleman pulled up in the prison car park. I took a deep breath and stepped out. I looked up at the imposing Victorian building. It was grim and unwelcoming. No doubt that was the point.

'Ever been inside?' Coleman asked me.

I said I hadn't.

He nodded to the Visitors' Entrance. It was a discreet door next to where the prison vans drove in an out. 'Ready?'

'As I'll ever be.'

We passed slowly through the security checks with Coleman nodding greetings as we moved forward. We were led through a series of corridors, well away from the actual prisoners. The more we walked, the more I was aware of the feeling of being caged in. The prison was playing tricks with my mind. We came to a stop outside a featureless room. The prison officer opened the door and said Johnson would be along shortly. Inside there was a table and three chairs. Nothing else. Not even a window. Coleman rearranged the chairs. Johnson would be sitting on one side of the table, Coleman and myself on the other.

I stayed standing, leaning against the wall. The room was stuffy and uncomfortable. All I could think about was Debbie and how she'd died in the house fire, how she must have suffered. And how it was all Johnson's fault.

I put the thought to one side when I heard a knock on the door. Coleman looked at me. I nodded. I was ready. Coleman walked across the room and opened the door. Johnson's escort brought him into the room before leaving and closing the door behind him. Johnson smiled, never taking his eyes off me. He was pushing sixty years of age, but he was in good shape. He read my mind.

'Been working out,' he said. 'Got to keep yourself active, haven't you?' He sat down and waited for me and Coleman to follow suit. His eyes never left mine. 'Got a new bird yet, Geraghty?'

I flew across the table at him and landed a glancing blow to his face before Coleman was able to restrain me. Johnson laughed. I struggled free, kicked my chair back and paced the room, trying to compose myself.

'Sit down, Joe,' Coleman said to me.

Johnson laughed and pointed at me. 'You can have that one for free, now do as your boyfriend says and sit the fuck down.'

Coleman spoke. 'Watch your mouth, Johnson.'

Johnson held his hands up and offered an insincere apology to me. 'I shouldn't be so rude to my ticket out of this place.'

I sat back down and told him I was nothing of the sort.

'Not how I see it.'

Coleman stepped in. 'Joe's agreed to look into your claims.'

Johnson stared at me but continued to speak to Coleman. 'Why would he do that?'

'Because it suits me to,' I said.

He answered me. 'What's in it for you?'

I stared at him and decided it had to be the truth. 'I've got a problem with George Sutherland,' I said. I was appealing to his ego, knowing he didn't like Sutherland, either. There was history between them. Johnson had taken over as Salford's right-hand man after the falling out with Sutherland. I'd been told he hadn't enjoyed the same rewards, though.

'Bitten off more than you can chew, have you?' Johnson said. 'Wouldn't surprise me. It seems to be a speciality of yours.'

'How is prison?' I asked him. 'Shit, I hope.'

'I've got a bed and a television.' He shrugged. 'I don't get any trouble. What's not to like?'

It was my turn to smile. Nobody wanted to be in here, whatever the perks.

'Andrew Bancroft,' Coleman said, bringing things round to business.

'What's on the table?' Johnson asked.

I was pleased he was so desperate to know. It meant he was sick of being in this place, regardless of what he'd just told me.

'There's nothing on the table yet,' Coleman said.

Johnson weighed things up. I knew he was sharp. He might have been Frank Salford's muscle, but you still needed a bit of nous to survive in the criminal world. I noticed Coleman wasn't recording our conversation or taking notes. Johnson would also have noticed that this wasn't official yet.

'Like I said, Joe's going to look into what you tell us,' Coleman said.

Johnson nodded. 'Fair enough.'

'What happened to Andrew Bancroft?' I asked him.

Johnson shrugged. 'Any number of things could have happened to him, I suppose. He could have been given some money and told to leave town? Sounds plausible to me.'

'Or he could have been killed?'

'He could have been.' He stared at me. 'Can't trust the police and their investigations, can you? Plenty of corruption about, isn't there? Always has been.'

He was pressing my buttons. It was obvious I was meant to infer something from his comment.

Coleman ignored it and leaned in to show him who was in charge. 'Let's work on the assumption Bancroft was killed, then. What did he do to deserve it?'

Johnson shrugged, but didn't answer the question.

Coleman sighed. 'I assume other people are involved in this, some of them still alive?'

Johnson nodded. 'Sounds likely.'

'Who?'

A smile broke across his face. 'I'm not giving you names.' He stared at me. 'Not yet, but I reckon I can help with your problem.'

'Sutherland was definitely involved?' I said.

Johnson confirmed that he was.

'In what way?'

Johnson smiled, but said nothing.

'You've got to see it from our point of view,' Coleman said. 'If you can't give us anything, how can you expect us to help?'

This time Johnson smiled again. 'I've definitely got something for you.'

'What?'

'I know where Andrew Bancroft's wallet is.'

Johnson was taken back to his cell and we left the prison. I was glad to breathe in the fresh air, even if it was polluted by the fumes of the lorries thundering past. Meeting Johnson hadn't been as bad as I feared. It was the fact my assistance might get him out of prison early that weighed heavily on me. The past or the future? Debbie or Niall and Connor? It was my decision to make. Either way, I knew Johnson couldn't hurt me now, and that was something to take away.

Coleman took a packet of cigarettes out of his pocket and lit one up.

I stared at him. 'Since when did you smoke?'

He took a long drag on it and shrugged.

'Fancy a drink?' I said. We had things to discuss.

'Around here?'

'I know a place.'

Like on my previous visits, Sutherland's pub wasn't busy. No wonder he was exploring other avenues to make some money. I could only see one drinker in the place. He was sitting at the bar, nursing a pint of lager. My favourite barmaid was back on duty.

I smiled as I got her attention. 'Two orange juices, please.'

Her eyes narrowed as she looked at Coleman. She had him marked down immediately for what he was. Coleman sat down as I waited for the drinks. She poured them and took my money. As I walked away, she picked up the telephone. I knew who she was calling.

I took the drinks across to the table. I made sure we could both keep an eye on the bar, just in case of any surprises. Coleman hadn't put up any argument when I said we should come here. He knew it was all about notching up the pressure on people like Sutherland, letting them know you were watching. That was when they eventually cracked and did something stupid.

I took a mouthful of my drink and spoke. 'Do you believe what Johnson's saying?'

He rubbed his face. 'I don't know, but it still needs checking.'

'We know he was never happy being Salford's right-hand man.'

'You think he's bullshitting?'

I shrugged and asked the question which had been nagging away at me. 'Why is he speaking to you now? What's changed?'

Coleman repeated what he'd told me before. 'He doesn't want to die behind bars. He's not stupid. He'll know what's going on out here. If he thinks he can use it to his advantage, he will.'

I agreed, unable to think of a more compelling reason. 'What do you think about the corruption he hinted at?'

Coleman shrugged. 'Not an easy one to prove.'

I had to agree. 'Where are you at with Holborn's death?'

'It was an accident.'

'That's the official line?'

'For now.'

His neighbour had told me Holborn was infirm. It wasn't hard to image someone else starting the fire and leaving. It was certainly a possibility. 'I spoke to his son last night. He was at pains to tell me what a great man his father had been.

I'm sure he'll be speaking to you shortly.' I smiled. 'He didn't like the tone of my voice.'

'I look forward to it.'

'He's a barrister in London.'

Coleman laughed. 'Perfect.'

Carl Palmer appeared and stared at us from behind the bar. I was pleased our presence bothered him so much. I thought about Johnson's suggestion he knew where Andrew Bancroft's wallet was. The implication was if Bancroft had simply left Hull, be it of his own free will or otherwise, he would have taken his wallet with him.

I asked Coleman about it. 'What did you make of what Johnson said? Could be a lie. It could be an old wallet.'

'Easily checked, though.'

'But it implicates Johnson in a potential murder?'

Coleman shook his head. 'Any number of ways out of it.' He turned to look at me. 'Especially if he's assisting with inquiries.'

And that was the truth of the matter. Politics always won the day.

Coleman continued. 'He's got nothing to lose, has he? If he does nothing, he's staying where he is with no chance of getting out.'

He wasn't wrong. The wallet was Johnson's insurance policy. He'd been holding on to it until the time was right. It was obviously meant to implicate Frank Salford, but he was dead. It had to implicate others, and that meant George Sutherland. Coleman didn't need to say this was all being done off the record. Johnson had told us where the wallet was being kept. It was down to me to retrieve it.

CHAPTER FIFTEEN

Carl Palmer blew me a kiss as we left the pub. Coleman offered to drop me off back at Niall's bar so I could collect my car. We spoke more about Johnson on the way, but it was academic. Nothing could happen until I'd collected the wallet. That would dictate the next move. I didn't go into the bar. I collected my car and headed for the city centre. I had something I needed to do. I needed some time to think about the deal with Johnson before making any decisions. A meter was free next to the BBC building on the edge of Queens Gardens. I walked to Queen Victoria Square. In front of me, the City Hall stood proudly. Behind me was the Maritime Museum. Benches ran around its perimeter. Rather than being taken by shoppers, they were home to a collection of tramps. Some were drinking discreetly, all of them peacefully watching the world go by.

I headed across to the nearest bench and spoke to the two men sitting there. I told them I was looking for Alan Palmer. One of them pointed to a man sitting by himself on the next bench. I thanked them and made my way over and sat down. Alan Palmer didn't acknowledge me. We watched in silence as shoppers hurried by. Like Johnson, Palmer was around sixty years of age, but he definitely hadn't been keeping himself in such good shape.

I told him who I was and handed over a card. 'I was hoping for a word,' I said.

He didn't look at me, but eventually nodded. 'How did you find me?'

'Your lad told me about you.'

'Haven't seen him in months.'

'Ironic that he works for George Sutherland, though.'

'We all make choices. I decided to kick the booze at long last.'

I nodded. 'Fair play to you.'

'Problem is, it makes you remember the things you've done.' He shuffled on the bench, but still didn't look at me. 'I don't know who you are, but I know why you're here.'

I asked him how he knew what I wanted.

'There's always a price to pay. I spend every day sat here. I'm not hard to find if you're looking for me. That's how Gary Bancroft found me.'

It confirmed a few things for me. Plenty of people were now running scared. It seemed to me that Palmer had spent long enough running away from things. 'What did Bancroft want?' I asked.

'My silence.'

'Why would he want that?'

'Because I was ordered to pay his family off all those years ago.'

His brother's disappearance. 'On Frank Salford's orders?'

'You're well informed.'

'What happened to Andrew Bancroft?'

'I don't want to tell you that at the moment.'

There was nothing I could say to that. I was relying on his goodwill, even if it was pretty obvious to me what had happened. I shuffled forwards again. 'What did Andrew Bancroft do for Salford?'

'He was a dogsbody. Run of the mill muscle. Someone like George Sutherland would go out on his rounds to collect protection money, so Bancroft would often be sent as back-up. Nothing major. Just shops and pubs. The low level stuff, nothing which required a brain.'

I decided to take a chance. 'Do you remember a policeman called Reg Holborn?'

Palmer was still refusing to look at me. He nodded, though. 'He was always around. He was friendly with Frank.' He paused. 'Boxing clubs,' he eventually said. 'The ones kids go to.'

'Was he corrupt?' I asked.

I was sure I saw a smile start to form on the side of Palmer's mouth. 'He had a strange taste in friends for someone in his job.'

I knew I had to weigh that up against the fact times were different. Things were done differently. I let it go, knowing if I pressed Palmer, he might walk away and disappear.

He finally looked at me. 'I'm not proud of the life I've led, but it was a living. If there has to be a reckoning, then so be it.'

'Where will you be if I need to speak to you again?'

'I'm always here. The council are about to kick me out of my flat, so I've got nowhere else to go. If I have a good day and make some money, I'll have an orange juice in the Old Town pubs later on. I'm not going anywhere else. You seem like a clever bloke to me. You'll be able to find me if we need to talk more.'

The address I'd been given to collect the wallet from was in Withernsea, a small seaside town east of the city. I'd returned to my car and stared at the address. I drove past the prison and the docks before BP Saltend signalled the end of the city and the start of the quieter country roads of Holderness. I drove through the isolated villages of Thorngumbald, Keyingham and Patrington. I was on auto-pilot, as I knew the route well. If Scarborough was the jewel in the crown of East Yorkshire's coastline, time had forgotten Withernsea. Even as a child, I could tell it was a dying resort. The train link to Hull had long gone, cutting the place off. I drove past the new Tesco store, the only sign of progress I could see, and on to the seafront. The beach was quiet, only a handful of dog owners exercising their animals. The town centre loop took me down Queen Street. It was mainly takeaways, charity shops and empty units. I checked for the address I needed. Johnson was a man who had enemies, and given what I knew about Salford not being a good payer, this town was perfect. It was relatively isolated and comparatively cheap.

I counted the houses off until I found Johnson's. I stared at it for a moment before getting out of my car. It was like any other on the street. Rather than having front gardens, the properties came with small walled off concrete yards which led directly to the pavement. There wasn't much room for anything other than the householder's dustbins. I knocked on the door and waited. A woman who I assumed was

Johnson's wife answered. I didn't know her name. She was smoking a cigarette and wore a care home uniform.

She took a drag on her cigarette before speaking. 'If you're a Jehovah's Witness, you can fuck off.'

I shook my head and started to speak.

She interrupted me. 'Geraghty, is it?'

'That's right.'

She closed the door on me, leaving me standing outside. I took a step back. She saved me from knocking again when she opened the door and passed me a jiffy bag. 'That's what you came for.'

I sat in my car and stared at the jiffy bag I'd been given. I decided I wasn't going to open it. I had no idea if the wallet had any forensic value, but I certainly didn't want my own fingerprints on it. I tried calling Coleman, but he didn't answer. I didn't leave a message. I took one last look at the package and placed it on the floor before deciding to visit Gerard Branning again. I now had something to talk to him about. I was sure he'd know about Andrew Bancroft.

The care worker shook her head and put her arm across the door. 'I'm afraid Gerard still isn't receiving visitors.'

I'd anticipated hearing I wasn't welcome. 'If you could tell him I've come with news of our mutual friend, Andrew Bancroft.' I put on my best smile. 'He'll really want to hear the news.' She seemed uncertain. I told her I'd wait while she went to check with him. I sat down on the only chair in the reception area. She eventually relented and said she wouldn't be long.

I only had a short wait before I was ushered through to the day room. Gerard Branning sat in the far corner, away from the other residents.

'I'll leave you to it,' the care worker said, before turning to Branning. 'Shout if you need anything, Gerard.'

She stared at me as she left. I took a chair from the table and carried it over so I could sit next to Branning. A solitary old lady was sitting nearby, talking to herself.

'Ignore her,' he said. 'She's harmless.'

I sat down. He was looking a little better, like the recuperation time was doing him good.

'I knew you'd be back,' he said.

'Why wouldn't you talk to me before?'

'Coleman asked me not to.'

I smiled. 'Always loyal?'

'Always.'

I could understand his attitude. He owed me nothing. I leaned in closer to him. 'Who's Andrew Bancroft?'

'I thought you'd have figured that one out for yourself by now.'

'Not quite,' I confessed. 'I'm here for your help.' I explained that George Sutherland was the key. I knew Branning had tried and failed to bring down Frank Salford over the years. I hoped he'd see this as his chance to do that, even if it was by proxy. I was appealing to his vanity. I told him I needed to know about Reg Holborn. 'I don't believe in coincidences any more than you do. I can't buy the fact all this is happening and Holborn, a non-smoker, dies in a house fire started by a dropped cigarette.'

Branning nodded and stared out of the window. He eventually nodded, the decision made. 'I suppose what you've got to appreciate is that those times were different. It wasn't unusual for the occasional beating to be handed out back then if you needed to exert some authority. That's the way it was, and let's say Reg Holborn wasn't afraid to do that, even if he did go too far sometimes.'

'In what way?'

'He had a gang and they would go well over the top. He walked a fine line at the best of times.'

'He was pals with Frank Salford through the boxing? I've seen the photographs.'

Branning nodded, impressed with my work. 'Holborn was into his boxing. Probably not surprising, given the nature of the man. He was a patron for some of the young lads' clubs, always going around the station with raffle tickets and a begging bowl.'

'Bit naïve to be hanging about with Salford, though, even if they supported the same causes?'

'It wasn't exactly encouraged, but if he could keep tabs on what Salford was doing, then it was considered useful.'

'Keep him in check?'

'In theory.'

'In theory?'

'I don't need to spell it out, surely? You're better than that.'

'I'd rather you did spell it out for me.'

'I can't offer you any proof, which makes it worthless.'

Branning didn't say anything further, so I attempted to press him. 'But you think he was corrupt?'

'There were half-hearted attempts to investigate him, but it was all off the record. Nothing came of it.'

'What about George Sutherland?'

Branning made sure he had my attention before speaking. 'He was there every step of the way. Whatever Salford was doing, Sutherland was involved. I suppose they both knew too much about each other, even when Dave Johnson came up through the ranks.'

I found myself nodding my agreement. It made sense. Whatever Johnson was offering had to put Sutherland in the frame. And keep himself out of it.

'What can you tell me about Andrew Bancroft?' I asked him.

He repeated what Alan Palmer had told me. Bancroft had been one of Salford's musclemen, employed to enforce, collect money, and hand out beatings. Dispensable muscle. 'What went wrong?'

'Bancroft started dipping on the cash take, so the story went. He got too big for his own boots and I assume the temptation was too much. There was always plenty of cash sloshing about.'

I was running the scenario through my mind. 'I assume Salford wasn't keen on this going on?'

'You assume correct. It was the one thing he wouldn't tolerate. Punishment beatings were frequent in those days. I

remember hearing tales of decent folk, pub landlords and
shopkeepers being beaten because they wouldn't pay him
protection money.'

I was getting the picture. 'What do you think happened to
Bancroft?' I asked him.

'I wouldn't want to guess. It's not how I was taught to
think.'

'I think he was murdered by Salford,' I found myself
saying. 'A punishment beating which went too far.'

Branning didn't disagree with me.

I sat in my car, rolled the window down and took several
deep breaths of air. I needed to get the smell of the care
home out of my nose. I leaned back against the headrest and
closed my eyes. I had to proceed on the assumption that
Andrew Bancroft had been murdered by Frank Salford. I
opened my eyes. It was no time to lose focus. The clock was
ticking in respect of George Sutherland. I needed to know
about his role in all of this. I was sure it was going to be the
leverage I needed.

I took the jiffy bag Johnson's wife had given me out of the
glove compartment and stared at it. I had a pair of latex
gloves in the car. I'd laughed when Sarah had bought them
for me, but yet again, she was right. I couldn't resist looking.
I carefully tipped Bancroft's wallet into my hands. I held it
up to the light and stared. The wallet was made from black
leather, but it had faded over time. Someone, presumably
Andrew Bancroft, had scratched in the words Hull FC with a
pen-knife. It was an identifying feature. I placed the wallet
back in the jiffy bag and took the gloves off. I found my
mobile and called Gary Bancroft's number. I said I had
something I needed him to take a look at.

Bancroft was ready and waiting for me outside of a pub on
Hessle Road. He was back drinking on his home turf. It had
no doubt once been a central hub in the fishing community,
but like many similar places, the smoking ban was slowly
killing it.

I opened the passenger door for Bancroft. 'Get in,' I said.
'Couldn't this have waited?'
I pulled out into the traffic. 'Not really.'
'Couldn't my mum have sorted it for you?'
'Only if you're a right heartless bastard.'

We sat in silence as I drove us towards Witty Street. It ran parallel to Hessle Road, but was much quieter, the home to light engineering companies and sundry warehouses. I pulled into an unused car park and put the latex gloves back on. I told Bancroft not to look so worried. 'What do you think I'm going to do?'

He didn't answer. I shook the wallet out of the jiffy bag and showed it to him. 'Recognise this?' The look of surprise on his face was genuine. 'Your brother's?'

'Could be.' He shook his head. 'It's a fucking wallet.'

'Take another look,' I said. 'Andrew scratched the name of his favourite rugby team into the leather.'

Bancroft reluctantly did as he was told. 'Doesn't prove anything.'

'You reckon?' I wasn't so certain, either, not until the contents of the wallet had been examined. But Bancroft was on the back foot, so I wasn't going to say any different. 'I think your brother was murdered.'

He went to open the door. I stopped him.

'I don't have to listen to this shit,' he said.

'Why did you speak to Alan Palmer the other day, then? Why did you try and put the frighteners on him?'

He pushed me away, got out of the car and slammed the door shut behind him. His reaction had told me all I needed to know.

I needed some time to think about the Bancroft brothers and what my next move should be. I still had the DVD I'd taken from Sutherland's pub in my possession. It was time to use it. I called Roger Millfield's office and once I'd given my name, I was told he was in a meeting. I wasn't in the mood to be put off.

'Could you pass an urgent message on, please,' I said to his PA. 'I have a DVD I think might belong to him, or maybe a mutual client, George Sutherland. If he's too busy to deal with it, ask him if I should give it straight to Tiffany?'

'I don't follow, I'm afraid,' the receptionist said.

'If you just go and tell Mr Millfield. He'll want to hear this. I'll hold the line.'

I watched as Gary Bancroft walked away. I still couldn't weigh up his attitude. Millfield's receptionist came back to me a few minutes later. 'Mr Millfield said he'll be leaving shortly for a meeting. He apologises, but could you possibly meet him at the Humber Bridge car park? It's on the way to his next meeting.'

'That's absolutely fine.'

I parked up and waited. A lone dog walker passed by. I looked at the Bridge standing tall to the side of me. The last time I'd been here, I'd seen off an unpleasant criminal gang from London, even though I'd needed Don's help and contacts to make it happen. This time I was on my own. I watched as a BMW pulled in and headed over to me. It cut across the parking spaces and came to a stop next to me. The window lowered. Millfield stared out at me.

I pointed to the cafe. 'Drink?'

He shook his head and opened the passenger door. 'Jump in.'

I did as I was told and closed the cold air out. Millfield appeared to be ill to me, like he wasn't sleeping. I wasn't surprised. He turned the engine off and stared out of the windscreen. 'You said you had a DVD for me.'

'Want to tell me about it?'

Millfield said nothing for a moment. We both stared out at the Bridge. The more I thought about, the more impressed I was. I was constantly surprising myself with how little I knew about things. As a child, whenever I asked my dad a question, he knew the answer, and he never paused to think about it. He always knew.

'Why are doing this, Joe?' Millfield said. 'I informed you that the job was over.'

I told him what George Sutherland had done to Connor. 'It's not over for me.' I passed him the DVD.

He took it from me and placed it in his jacket pocket. He sighed. 'I was stupid and drunk. And she was there. That's all there was to it. A moment of weakness.'

I considered what Neil Farr had told me about his close friendship with Kath Millfield. It probably didn't leave much room for Roger Millfield in his own marriage. I took a chance. I'd been thinking about why a respectable businessman would be working with a criminal like George Sutherland. 'Are you money laundering for him?' I said.

'Absolutely not.'

'Tell me, then.'

Millfield drummed his fingers on the steering wheel. 'I shouldn't have dragged you into my problems, Joe, and you'd do well to not push me on this. Don's taking care of this for me, as you well know. Keep yourself out of it.'

I took another chance and told him why I needed a line into Sutherland. I gave him the basic outline about the cigarettes. He looked shocked. 'I'm trying to help my family,' I said.

'You don't know what you're getting into. My best advice to you is that you persuade your brother to go to the police. They'll investigate and arrest Sutherland.'

'That's not going to happen.' It wasn't an option. Niall was every bit as guilty as George Sutherland.

'I don't think I can help you any further, given the circumstances.'

'Whatever you've got to be so scared of, it's in your interests to tell me.' I shuffled around in my seat to face him and leaned in closer. 'We're on the same side here. I think we both want the same thing. I've told you the truth. I can't stop until I've brought Sutherland down.'

Millfield was uncomfortable. His voice was practically a whisper. 'You can't win against a man like him.'

'I haven't got a choice.'

'Take my advice. Leave me alone and call the police before things get any worse for you.'

'Can't do that.'

'You've no idea, have you, Joe?'

'Tell me, then.'

'Sutherland's blackmailing Don.' He made sure he had my full attention before he spoke again. 'Rebecca isn't my daughter. She's Don's.'

CHAPTER SIXTEEN

I sat in my car, trying to process what Millfield had told me. Don had a secret child. I needed time to think about it rationally before speaking to him. I needed to think about what I was going to say. There was also Sarah to think about. I had no idea what to do. I settled for calling Peter Hill. He needed to know about George Sutherland's plan. 'We need to talk,' I said to him.

'It's not a good time.'

'It's in your best interests.'

'My wife's at work and I'm trying to control the children.'

I cut him off. 'It's not a social call.' I said I'd go to him and put my mobile back into my pocket.

Hill was waiting for me at his front door. He'd received the same treatment as Niall. The bruises were starting to fade, but the damage was clearly visible. Hill told me to be quiet as I followed him into the kitchen. 'I've got the kids playing upstairs in their bedrooms. I don't want them knowing you're here.'

I pointed to his face. 'Want to tell me what happened?'

'I'm sure I don't need to.'

I looked at the large canvas print of his children on the wall and felt bad for bringing bad things into his house. It was the opposite of Gillespie's place. The clutter and mess signalled a busy family life, not a man who'd given up. Hill offered me a drink, but I waved his offer away.

'I've got something stronger if you prefer?' he said.

'Too early for me.'

I waited while he poured himself a drink. 'How's Niall doing?'

'He wants this sorting out.' I didn't need to look too hard at his face to see he was worried, too. I sat down at the table. 'I have to go across to Zeebrugge tomorrow night and bring some cigarettes back.'

Hill didn't say anything. He made himself a cup of tea and sat down opposite me. 'That's not a good idea.'

'You're telling me.'

'You've got to put a stop to it. I assume you know what will happen to you if you're caught?'

I said that I did. 'Someone called George Sutherland owned the cigarettes. I thought he was a small-time criminal and that I could handle him.' I paused for a moment. 'He's threatened people I care about.' I tapped the table with my right hand. 'I need to know how to make it work.'

Hill opened his mouth to say something, but couldn't find the words.

'How do I make sure no one stops me bringing the cigarettes into the country?' I asked him.

'You can't.'

'Sutherland did.'

Hill shrugged. 'Different situation altogether. It's not that simple.'

'It is from where I'm sitting.'

Hill shook his head. 'Even if it could be done, it's not something you decide to do overnight.'

I told him I needed his help.

Hill walked over to the sink. He ran the cold water tap and splashed his face before turning back to me. 'I can't take any more of this.'

I thought about telling him that he needed to keep a cool head for his family's sake, but it wouldn't help the situation. We both had our concerns, but we were also very different. He was scared, but I was determined. It scared me, too, but this was what I was good at. 'We've got one thing in common' I said.

'What's that?'

'We both want George Sutherland out of the picture.' Hill looked at me, his face full of hope. I had to burst his bubble. I wasn't a miracle worker. 'I need your help to do it.' Hill sat back down and said nothing. I outlined what was going to happen. 'You need to do what's best for your family. Get them out of this house to somewhere safe, send them on a holiday if you have to. Tell your neighbours you're going on holiday and then go and stay at a mate's house. Keep your head down.'

'How on earth can I tell my wife that? I've got no money to send her away with.'

'Sutherland will be coming for you soon,' I said. He started to panic. I told him to get a grip of himself. 'You've got to sort the situation out.'

He stared at me. 'What are you going to do?'

I was ready to leave. 'If you don't hear from me, you know what to do.'

Peter Hill hadn't been able to help me with what I needed to know about George Sutherland's cigarette smuggling. My only other option was Terry Gillespie. I stopped at an off-licence on the way to his house. When he answered the door, I held out the carrier bag to him. In it was a four-pack of bitter and a large bar of chocolate. His face was black and blue from the beating he'd taken from Sutherland and Palmer. It took him a moment to process the fact I was holding out a gift. He took it from me and stepped back into his house. 'Don't be thinking I didn't recognise you when you came here with Sutherland.'

I wasn't bothered about that. Not now. I cleared some space on his settee and sat down. I watched him struggle slowly across to his seat. He rummaged in the carrier bag and took out a can before offering one to me. I shook my head.

'Fuck knows why I'm offering you one,' he said. 'You hit me.'

'It's the least you deserved.' He didn't have an answer to that. I pointed to the can. 'I've brought you some drinks to take your mind off it.'

He snorted. 'You've got some nerve.'

'We've got something in common now.'

'Have we?'

'We've both definitely got a problem with George Sutherland.' The look on his face said he didn't want to hear what I was going to say, but I didn't care about that.

Gillespie had lied to me and dragged my brother into this mess. He was going to help me get us out of it.

'Let bygones be bygones?' he said.

'That's right.'

He drank back a mouthful of bitter. 'Never believed in any of that shit.'

It was the response I'd been expecting from him. 'Sutherland isn't going to go away. He'll come back.'

Gillespie drank his bitter. 'He can't get blood out of a stone. He can keep kicking the shit out of me if he likes, but it'll be the same result. I've got nothing to give him.'

Looking around the room, I believed him. His personal possessions weren't worth much. The television and stereo had seen better days. There was little else. He had nothing, either in terms of people or belongings.

He eyeballed me as he drank another mouthful. 'You're still on the hook for the cigarettes?'

'We've come to an agreement. I'm going across to Belgium with Niall.'

Gillespie laughed. 'Are you fucking mad?'

'I've got no choice.'

'You've always got a choice.'

'Not this time.'

I knew exactly what I was staring at if it went wrong. 'I want to know the mechanics of how the operation works.'

'And you think I would know that?'

'I'm asking for your help.'

He put his drink down. 'You think four cans of bitter makes up for you coming here and laying into me?'

'It was only one punch.'

'Fuck you, Geraghty.'

'If I hadn't hit you, Palmer would only have carried on. You lied about not recognising him when I showed you his photograph in the pub. Do you remember that?'

'I was never told how it worked. I was told to have the storage space available when the cigarettes arrived. That's all.'

'Why did Sutherland trust you to look after them?'

'Because I'm fucking worthless, aren't I? If something goes wrong, it doesn't matter all that much. Imagine the shit Sutherland would be in if they were found on his property?'

I knew he was right. Sutherland wasn't that stupid. People like Gillespie and Niall meant nothing to him. He could control them.

Gillespie helped himself to another can. 'You don't think I was doing this out of choice, do you? He set me up, letting me use his girls in the pub, saying it was all alright, that it could go on the tab. No pressure, he said, but he gave me the choice in the end. I could either pay up what I owed or I could work the debt off.'

I'd heard all I needed to know. Gillespie wasn't going to be able to help me, either. He was a mess, and it was only now I realised it, a lonely man. No wonder the extras Sutherland's pub offered appeared tempting to him. As much as he'd brought it all on himself, Sutherland had taken advantage of him. I told him to look after himself.

He smiled and drank a mouthful of bitter. 'You're the one smuggling cigarettes into the country.'

I called Neil Farr from my car. He didn't sound all that surprised to be hearing from me. I told him I needed a word. Urgently. He protested, but I told him he could help me. If he did that, I wouldn't need to bother him again.

'Do you know the driving range on National Avenue?' he said.

I knew it. It was in another area which had once been the home to heavy industry, but was now a mixture of small businesses and leisure facilities. The place wasn't busy. A small number of people were standing in separate booths, driving golf balls into the netting at the end of the field. Farr was working his way through a large bucket of balls. I watched him swing. The ball flew off to the side. 'You've shanked that,' I said.

Farr stared at me. 'I'm still learning. Christmas present from my wife.'

'Harder than it looks?'

'Aren't most things?' He walked across to me. 'You said your call was urgent.'

I didn't have time to mess about. I got straight to the point of my visit. I told him what Roger Millfield had said to me about his daughter. I asked him if it was true.

Farr put his driver down. I got the impression he'd been waiting for this day to come. We watched as the man in the neighbouring booth took aim. The ball sailed perfectly into the netting. Farr glanced at me. 'Not in here.' He led us out of the building, back to his car. I sat in the passenger seat and waited for him to speak.

'It was a mistake,' he eventually said. 'A one-off mistake Kath made. She told me about it one night when she was drunk, but Rebecca was always Roger's daughter.'

'Has Roger always known?'

'I'm sure he's always had his suspicions. It's probably why he doesn't like me all that much. Kath would rather talk to me than him.'

Farr was most likely right. How could Roger Millfield be happy about the closeness of his wife's friendship with another man? Their marriage certainly wasn't conventional. I asked Farr how Don had found out the truth.

'She wasn't so discreet in those days after having a drink. That's why she stopped and threw herself into the charity work. I think it gave her some purpose, helped her sort things out.'

'Who else knows?' I'd already worked it out.

Farr confirmed it for me. 'George Sutherland.'

I could see it now. 'Sutherland is trying to blackmail Don.' Farr fell silent. I pressed on. 'The man's unstable. You might want to wise Kath up.' I thought back to seeing him argue with Kath in her office. 'She knew this was coming, didn't she?'

Farr nodded. 'It was always going to come out some day.'

I'd got the confirmation I'd come for. Don was the father of Kath Millfield's child. My options were narrowing. Sutherland was in a position of strength. I had nothing to throw back at him.

Farr spoke. 'Don's got another daughter, hasn't he?'

'Sarah.'

'That's right. How do you think she'll take the news?'

Sarah was working when I walked into the bar, serving a group of customers. I was able to quickly move past her in the direction of the kitchen. I couldn't tell her what I'd learned about Don. I couldn't tell her I'd discovered she had a half-sister. It would tear her into pieces. I was being a coward, but so be it. Niall stopped what he was doing when I walked in.

I nodded. We stood there for a moment in awkward silence before we both went to speak. 'You first,' I said.

'I just wanted to say I'm sorry for what I said. I was out of order. I know you're not to blame for what happened to Connor.' He put the knife down. 'It was the shock of seeing him after the attack, I suppose. I flipped. I wanted someone to blame because I hadn't been there for him.'

I knew my brother. He meant what he said. He wasn't one for wasting words. It was the way we behaved, like when I'd been best man at his wedding, and how we'd come together to take care of our mum when we'd buried our dad. It went largely unspoken. I told him I was sorry, too.

I leaned against the table and turned to business. 'We're collecting a van from Sutherland's pub before boarding the ferry. That's the plan.' He didn't like it, but there wasn't much either of us could do about it. I was running out of other options. I told him the same I'd told Peter Hill. 'Can you send Ruth off to her sister's for a bit, just as a precaution?' He didn't look he was going to enjoy trying to persuade her. 'Just for one night. It's important.'

I went back into the bar and called Coleman to tell him I had the wallet. He answered and said he was at his flat.

'Bring food with you.' I hadn't eaten all day, so it sounded like a plan.

His flat looked like mine when I'd first moved in. The decoration was not only out of date, it was uncared for.

Wallpaper was peeling off at the nearest corner. The carpet was worn, and if it had been described as furnished to Coleman, he was paying over the odds. The only personal touch was a framed photograph of his daughter on top of the television.

'It's home for now,' he said, his eyes following mine around the room.

I put the pizzas down. 'It took me a while to sort my place out, too.'

'I've only signed a short-term lease.'

I hoped he was right for his own sake.

Coleman pointed to the food. 'Shall we eat as we work?'

I agreed and passed over the jiffy bag which contained the wallet.

Coleman had started to tear into a slice of pizza. He stopped and wiped his hands on the settee. 'Let's have a look.'

I pointed at the jiffy bag.

Coleman wiped his hands before carefully tipping it out. He didn't touch the wallet. 'Do you think it's genuine?' he said.

I told him I'd spoken to Bancroft's brother. I pointed to where Hull FC had been scratched into the leather. 'Doesn't prove anything, though, does it?' I bit into my pizza as he examined the wallet. Like me, he decided to use latex gloves.

'Looks convincing to me,' he eventually said. 'Not that we'll get anything from it.' He took the gloves off.

I waited until Coleman bit into another slice. 'Why did you stop Gerard Branning talking to me?'

Coleman struggled to control a long string of cheese. He chewed his way through it before answering. 'I needed you to work a bit harder.'

He could see I wasn't impressed with his explanation.

'Nothing personal, Joe. I needed you to buy into my theory.' He tore into another slice. 'Way of the world, that's all.'

'Like your promotion?'

He looked embarrassed. 'I need something. I've got nothing else.' He threw his half-eaten pizza slice back into the box. I did the same. He wanted to talk seriously.

'What else do you know?' he asked me.

I ignored the question. I wanted some answers myself. 'What happened when Andrew Bancroft was reported missing? I assume there was a proper investigation?'

Coleman shook his head. 'There wasn't much of one. Holborn was assigned it, but what can you do if a grown man disappears?'

'He didn't do a thorough job?'

'The file does the job. He asked the right people the right questions.'

'Or he said he did?'

Coleman agreed. 'That's exactly the point, isn't it? No way of knowing either way.'

'What about Don's involvement?'

'He was never on the record with it.'

That made sense to me. Like with Branning and Salford, I knew people took cases personally if they didn't think justice had been done.

We went back to our pizzas. It was Coleman who broke the silence. 'I spoke to Johnson again.'

I was surprised. 'Why?'

'He asked for another meeting.'

'Alone?'

'He wanted to make sure he could trust you.'

I couldn't believe what I was hearing. 'Is he taking the piss?'

'Far from it. He's deadly serious.'

I knew if I didn't help him, he wouldn't help me with George Sutherland. Catch-22. He was my only option.

Coleman tossed his empty pizza box on to the floor. 'I know the wallet doesn't prove anything on its own, so that's why I went back to him. It was his test to see if you were serious. He gave me a date for the killing of Andrew Bancroft. And an alibi.'

'And you want me to check it out?'

Coleman shook his head. 'Reckons he was at a City match. Never missed one. He's got his season pass collection at home and says there are people who can vouch for him.'

It wasn't the best alibi I'd ever heard. I asked Coleman if the date fitted.

'I Googled it. It ties in with the reporting of Bancroft's disappearance.'

We both knew it was worthless, but it would be hard to provide a solid alibi for something that happened so long ago. I did know that Salford and all his men were into football, though.

'Are you sure you want to do this?' Coleman said.

I nodded. I was justifying it by not thinking of it as helping Johnson. I wanted to make sure he was telling the truth. If he was taking us for fools, he had to stay behind bars. I could help ensure that happened.

Coleman walked over to where he'd put his coat. He took out a manila envelope and passed it to me. 'Johnson pointed me in the direction of these.'

I opened the envelope and let a handful of black and white photographs fall onto the table in front of me. The first one I picked up had been taken in a field at night. I could see a dirt track and some bushes and trees. There was nothing else in the scene. Coleman was staring at the wall, leaving me to take them in. I picked up the next photograph. I recognised Andrew Bancroft straight away. He was strapped to a chair in some sort of an outbuilding. He'd been beaten, his face covered in dry blood. 'Fucking hell.'

'Indeed.'

I put the photograph down. This had been where the trail was leading, but it was still a shock.

'Look at the other photo,' Coleman said, pointing to the last one left on the table. It had landed face down. Coleman stared at me as I turned it over. 'Recognise him?'

I picked up the photograph and nodded. Thirty years younger, but I recognised the face staring back at me.

CHAPTER SEVENTEEN

I knocked loudly on Don's front door. The curtains were drawn in the living room, but I could see light shining out at the top of them. I knocked again before bending down to open the letterbox.

'I know you're in there,' I shouted. I glanced down the hallway, but there was no movement. I shouted again. 'I know, Don. I know about Rebecca Millfield. I know she's your daughter.'

I took a step back and looked around. The neighbours' cars were parked up for the night. A cat walked slowly across the road. It stopped halfway and turned back to stare at me. The spell was broken by Don opening his front door. I followed him into the house.

'Wait in the living room,' he said.

I did as I was told. He'd reframed the family photographs on the mantelpiece, but I couldn't look at them. It was too much. Don walked into the room. He had a bottle of whiskey and two glasses with him. I told him I wasn't here for a drink. He shrugged and poured himself a generous measure.

I waited. It had taken countless questions, beatings and his house being violated to get us to this point. It was as if a weight had been lifted off his shoulders.

'Does Sarah have any idea?' I asked him.

'Of course not.'

'Want to tell me about it?'

'Seems like you already know.'

'Only what Roger Millfield told me.'

'There's probably not much more to tell.' He poured himself another drink. 'It's like I told you before. I had an affair with Kath. That was it. She had Rebecca and I didn't think anything of it until she turned up drunk one night. Lucky I was home alone. She told me how she couldn't live a lie any longer. She said I had a right to know I had a daughter. The next day, she changed her tune. I wasn't to tell anyone. I wasn't to mention it ever again. She didn't need me or my money. Rebecca was Roger's daughter and that was it. End of discussion.'

I let that sink in. I'd seen Rebecca Millfield's photograph on her father's desk. She was going to be following in his footsteps in the accountancy practice. 'Did you have a test?' I asked.

'Never going to happen.' He shrugged. 'I didn't need one to know the truth. I just knew I was her father.'

'And you followed Kath's demands?'

'To the letter. I've never said a word about it. I decided to live with the situation and keep my distance. I've got Sarah. She's all I need.'

'Kath Millfield told Sutherland, though.'

'I know she did.'

Rebecca was in her mid-twenties now, so Sutherland had held back the information for long enough, just waiting to use it. The time was now right for him. He was far more desperate than I imagined.

'Sutherland's getting nothing from me,' Don said. 'Not a penny.'

I was pleased he was facing up to the situation at long last. 'Why didn't you tell me he was blackmailing you? I had to get confirmation from Roger Millfield.'

'You hardly drop it into conversation, do you?'

'I would have helped.'

'You can't do anything for me.'

'Sutherland isn't going to let this go.'

'I'm done lying.'

I stared at Don. 'Do you want Rebecca to know about you?'

He shrugged. 'I'm tired of lying, Joe. That's the truth.'

'You should speak to Sarah.'

He sighed. 'A long time ago, I thought you two were made for each other.'

'Times change.'

'I was probably too hard on you.'

I smiled. 'I kicked back too much.'

'Hardly matters now. We're more alike than we'd care to admit.'

'How so?'

'Deep down, you're not a bad guy, Joe, I know that. I can even overlook the fact you played for the wrong club.'

Whether he meant it or not, I knew he was really asking me not to judge him for the things he'd done. I wasn't sure if I was able to do that. Don swallowed the last of his whiskey and stood up, swaying a little. 'You never could handle your drink,' I said. I thought about mentioning Andrew Bancroft's murder, but it could wait until he was sober. 'I'm going over to Belgium tomorrow with Sutherland.' I didn't need to explain what we were doing. 'It's the only way I can pay the debt back.'

Don shook his head. 'You should go to the police.'

'You know me better than that.' We both smiled. I walked to the door. 'I need you to keep an eye on Sarah and Lauren until I'm back.'

Don started to say something, but I cut him off. He wasn't stupid. He knew what the score was and he was in no position to dictate to me. I repeated the message of keeping an eye on them.

I wasn't ready to go home yet. I knew Alan Palmer had more he wanted to say about Andrew Bancroft's murder, that much was obvious. There were things I needed to know and I now had more information. Palmer had told me he spent his evenings in the pubs of the Old Town. I started at one end of High Street and worked my way down, avoiding the louder pubs which catered for the younger market. I found him sitting in a quiet corner of Ye Olde Black Boy. True to his word, he was nursing half a pint of orange juice.

I stood in front of him and waited for him to notice me. When he did, I spoke. 'I know Andrew Bancroft was killed. I've seen the photographs.'

He pushed his soft drink away. 'Best get me a proper drink, then.'

I hadn't expected it to be that easy. 'Sure?'

He nodded. 'Pint of lager.'

I headed for the bar.

'And a whiskey chaser,' he said to my back.

The barmaid poured our drinks, but not without suggesting I take Palmer somewhere else once we were done. She left the drinks on the bar and walked across to her stool, sat down and went back to her magazine.

I watched Palmer drink the whiskey, shaking as it went down. He then swallowed a mouthful of lager. I didn't touch mine. I didn't want it.

'I was involved in Bancroft's death,' he said. 'I was told to pick him up and drive him out to the pig farm.'

He wanted to talk. I had to ask the questions, even though I knew he was going to set something serious in motion with the answers. 'Who told you to go and get him?' I said.

'Frank Salford.'

'What happened?'

'I went to Bancroft's house and told him Frank wanted to give him a reward for the work he'd been doing. Like an idiot, he believed me. He swaggered into Frank's office thinking he was the business. It was only when the door shut behind him that he started to get the picture. Frank floored him with a punch and he was tied up and held until it went dark. Then we threw him into a van and drove out to the countryside.' He paused for a moment and composed himself. 'Bancroft knew what was coming, that was for sure. I can still hear him begging us to let him go, but all Frank did was laugh and turn the radio up.' Palmer picked up his lager before deciding he didn't want to drink it. He put it down and pushed it away. 'Frank hadn't been feeding the pigs, so they were starving. You could see it in their eyes. They were jostling around their pen, making these horrible squealing noises. Bancroft was begging, screaming really, like an animal, but Frank didn't care because no one would hear him. It was the middle of nowhere. I remember Frank pointing to the grave that'd been dug next to the pigs. He told Bancroft he could take his pick. He could either get in the pig pen or get in the grave. It was his choice.'

I stared at the wall behind his head, hoping the feeling of nausea would pass. Dave Johnson had once taken me out to a freshly dug grave in an attempt to frighten me. Maybe I'd had a lucky escape.

Palmer spoke. 'Bancroft lost it. He fell to the ground, shouting out for his mam. I couldn't look at the kid.' He lowered his voice. 'I've done some bad things in my life, and that's the truth, but I've never seen anything like that. Frank was possessed, shouting and laughing manically that Bancroft had to choose either the pigs or the grave. I can't tell you how horrible listening to someone beg for their life is.'

We sat in silence for a few moments. Unburdening the details had shaken Palmer. I waited until he pulled himself back together. I needed the time, too. My heart was beating a little faster. 'What had Bancroft done?'

'Skimming on the cash he was picking up.'

'That's it?'

'Frank wouldn't stand for it. If he let it go, others would do the same.'

The punishment wasn't in line with the crime, but Salford wasn't a rational man. It was genuinely shocking to me. 'Which did Bancroft choose?'

Palmer lowered his voice. 'The grave.'

There was a tear in the corner of his eye. I turned away, not wanting to embarrass him. I gave him a moment before pressing on. I didn't want to hear it, but I couldn't afford to let it go. 'Was Dave Johnson there?'

Palmer shook his head. 'Not that time.'

'Why not?'

'Couldn't tell you.'

'Was George Sutherland there?'

'He was definitely there.'

I thought about the photographs I'd seen. Sutherland must have taken them. And now Dave Johnson had them. There was another face in them that I recognised. 'Why was Roger Millfield there?'

Palmer looked puzzled. 'Who's he?'

'He's an accountant.'

Palmer thought about it before nodding. 'A warning I suppose. Frank worked that way.'

That was what I was thinking. It was the only thing that made sense. I had one more question, maybe the key one. 'Was Reg Holborn there?'

Palmer said he was. 'He was the one who authorised it.'

I closed my eyes and my stomach lurched again. Millfield would have known he couldn't go to the police. He had no option but to keep his mouth firmly shut.

'Not even Frank would do something like that without permission,' Palmer added.

It made sense. Salford wouldn't have been able to exercise such a grip on the city if he didn't have powerful allies.

Palmer stared at me. 'What do we do now?'

I didn't know what to say. All I could think of to say was that I knew Bancroft's mother.

I threw my coat on to the back of the settee and walked into the kitchen of my flat. I rinsed out a dirty glass and filled it with water before sitting down. If there had been anything stronger in the flat, I would have tried to blot the conversation with Alan Palamer out of my mind, even if it would only be a temporary fix.

'I've been thinking,' Connor said to me. 'I want to help.'

'What with?'

'The ferry.'

I cursed myself. I'd left the tickets in the flat. I put the glass down and shook my head. 'It's in hand. It's going to get sorted.'

'I should help.'

'Don't even go there.'

Connor continued. 'It's my mess. I should go on the ferry with you, Dad shouldn't have to.'

'I appreciate the thought, I really do, but it's not that simple.'

'I need to do it.'

I tried to explain. 'I have no idea what we're going to walk into over there. It might be dangerous. It's certainly stupid. There's every chance it could go wrong. I'm not putting you in that position.'

'I'm not scared of going to prison.'

'You should be.' We sat in silence until I spoke. 'Your dad wouldn't want you doing it. I know that much.' He was about to protest, so I continued. 'The way to put it right is to take your second chance. You made a mistake and that's fair enough. We've all made mistakes.' I thought about Alan Palmer. He'd made serious mistakes and they'd ruined his life. Connor wasn't going to do the same. He didn't really want to get on the ferry with me, I could tell that much. He was a boy. There was no way I could let him do it. I rubbed my face and swallowed the water. It was another complication I could do without.

Connor changed the subject. 'Milo's found us a nightclub we can put our night on at. We're going to check it out in a bit.'

'Reckon it's suitable?'

'Sounds it.'

'Good.'

We lapsed into silence and watched television together until he was ready to leave. I told him to take my bed tonight. I knew I was going to fall asleep on the settee again. I made myself comfortable and fumbled around for the hi-fi controller. I flicked to the radio and turned it down low, wanting the background noise. Aside from Palmer's confession, it was like I'd closed the book properly on something tonight and said goodbye to Don. And Don Ridley & Son. There was no going back now. Things had shifted and it wasn't reversible. I lifted the glass and offered a toast to my previous life.

It couldn't be avoided. I reached for a writing pad and started to make notes, hoping things would look clearer that way. Andrew Bancroft had been murdered. It had been a punishment so others would think twice before stealing from Frank Salford. Salford didn't need to explicitly say he'd killed him, either. Bancroft's disappearance and the building up of a myth would be enough.

I threw the writing pad to one side. It wasn't doing any good. The only fact that mattered to me was that George Sutherland wasn't going to loosen his grip on me. Knowing he was involved in Bancroft's death was one thing, proving it was another. Coleman would laugh me out of the room if I suggested arresting him in connection with Andrew Bancroft's murder. I was going to need more.

My eyes were drawn to the photograph of Debbie on the mantelpiece. I hoped she would understand why I was doing this. She'd always said you had to look forward, whatever happened. What was done was in the past. I hoped she'd agree that putting things right for Niall and Connor was a price worth paying, even if the price was Dave Johnson's freedom.

I found the envelope Coleman had given me and looked at the photographs again. Coleman had made copies for me to take away. Andrew Bancroft's scared eyes stared back at me. I turned it over, not wanting to look at it any more. I took out the photograph of Roger Millfield that Coleman had surprised me with and tapped it with a finger. Millfield was stood next to the pig pen, looking every bit as scared as Bancroft must have been. I wondered what Millfield had done, the decisions he'd made that had taken him to such a place.

My mobile started to ring. The display said it was Sarah calling me. I stared at it for a moment before deciding to answer.

'What's my dad doing in my house?' she said, her voice low.

'I asked him to.' The line went quiet and I listened as she walked through her house. I heard a door being opened. I could picture her standing in the back garden.

'You asked him to?' she said.

I took a breath. 'I'm getting on a ferry tomorrow night with Sutherland.'

'Why?'

'We're bringing some replacement cigarettes back with us.'

'Are you mad?'

'It's the only way of getting him off my family's back.'

'Are you out of your mind, Joe?'

I assured her I wasn't. 'I'm doing it so Connor doesn't have to.'

She went silent. I knew I was right. There was no other way unless I could come up with a plan. Sarah eventually broke the silence. 'It's still wrong.'

'It's got to be put right.' I told her it wasn't even the worst of it. 'I visited Dave Johnson today.'

I heard her draw breath. 'You went to the prison?'

'Coleman took me.'

'Why would you want to speak to him?'

'He knows about Andrew Bancroft.' I repeated what Alan Palmer had told me. 'Sutherland was involved.'

'Isn't that enough to have him arrested?'

I found myself shaking my head. 'There's not enough there yet.' I told Sarah I had to go and finished the call. I turned to the envelope Coleman had given me and looked again at the photographs of the murder scene. It was getting late, but I decided to call Roger Millfield. There was no answer. I left him a message, saying we needed to talk about Andrew Bancroft. I knew what had happened to him. I needed him to put George Sutherland in the frame for Bancroft's murder. Otherwise, I was getting on a ferry tomorrow night. Going back to Millfield was the only option I had left. He was my last roll of the dice. I put my mobile down and made myself comfortable. I switched the radio off and closed my eyes.

Hull, September 1990

The boxing hall was full of people talking and laughing. Don Ridley made his way back from the toilet and sat down at the table. The lights went down and two young boxers stepped into the ring. In one corner, the taller boxer stood in red shorts, the shorter man in the other wearing blue. Two young women in tight T-shirts and shorts circled the canvas with numbered boards held above their heads to signal the first round. The crowd roared their approval. The boxer in red took control of the fight, working his opponent into a corner with a succession of quick and accurate jabs. Ridley's seat was close enough to hear each blow land. The youngster in blue was showing enough courage to stay in the fight as the bell went to signal the end of the round. Ridley watched as the man sitting next to Holborn collected their empty glasses and made for the bar.

Ridley moved quickly across into the empty seat. 'Bet you didn't expect me to be here tonight?'

Holborn smiled, clearly pissed. 'Not really, Don.' *He leaned in so he could be heard above the crowd.* 'People enjoy my company. I'm a people person. You, on the other hand, are known for being a bit of a cunt.'

Ridley smiled. 'An honest cunt, maybe.'

'Truth be told, I won't miss you all that much.'

'Looking forward to a long and prosperous retirement?'

'Too fucking right I am.'

'You won't be looking over your shoulder at all?'

'I sleep like a baby.'

The bell sounded the start of the second round.

'No regrets?' *Ridley asked.*

Holborn shook his head. 'Not a single one.' *A pint of lager was placed in front of him. Ridley ignored the man standing over his shoulder. He wasn't ready to move yet.*

'You must have regrets, though, Don? Loads of them, I should think.'

'Just the one, really.'

Holborn lit a cigar and inhaled deeply. 'You shouldn't live that way, Don. No regrets. That's the only way to do it. I'm retiring as a DCI. You'll never hit the same heights.'

Ridley concentrated on the boxing. The boxer in red shorts carried on where he'd left off in the first round. He had his opponent in the corner and was peppering him with vicious blows to the head and the body. The crowd roared him on.

Holborn leaned in to speak to Ridley. 'You can go on about teamwork as much as like, and all that noble bullshit about a higher calling when you join up, but you have to make it happen for yourself. That's the bottom line.'

'At any cost?'

Holborn picked up his drink. 'At any fucking cost.'

'I'm surprised you didn't invite Frank Salford along tonight.'

Holborn offered a toast. 'You always had a sense of humour, Don. I'll give you that much.'

'I'll find him, you know.'

'Find who?'

'Andrew Bancroft.'

A roar from the crowd went up. Both men turned their attention back to the ring. Another powerful right hook from the fighter in red and it was all over. The referee stood over the boxer in blue and counted to ten before moving to the red corner and holding the boxer's arm in aloft. Holborn stood and led the applause.

Ridley waited for him to sit back down and repeated that he'd find Andrew Bancroft. 'I know Frank Salford had him killed, so that means you knew about it as well.'

Holborn drank a mouthful of lager before putting his glass down. 'You always get winners and losers in life, don't you? People like me and Frank are the winners. Now, if you don't mind, Don, do me a favour and fuck off.'

CHAPTER EIGHTEEN

My sleep was broken by the ringtone of my mobile. I fumbled around, finding it underneath a cushion. It was Coleman calling.

I sat up and answered. 'Bit early, isn't it?'

'Where are you?'

'Home.'

'You might want to get yourself to Roger Millfield's office.' It went quiet as he spoke to whoever was standing alongside him. I waited for him to return. 'Sorry about that,' he said when came back on the line. 'There's no easy way of saying this, Joe. Millfield's killed himself.'

Coleman finished the call, saying he had to go. I sat in shock on my settee for a moment. My head was filled with questions, but I had to focus. I needed to get myself into the city centre as soon as possible. It was only as I was about to leave that the thought struck me. I'd left Roger Millfield a message late last night, telling him I knew all about Andrew Bancroft's murder. I was to blame.

I joined the steady stream of cars and buses ferrying workers into the city centre. It was a slow drive down Princes Avenue and Spring Bank. Once I was in the city centre loop, I headed straight to Millfield's office on High Street. From the outside, there was no sign of activity. I called Coleman. He answered and told me to wait where I was. He eventually appeared and said we should go somewhere else to talk. He suggested the cafe in Hepworth Arcade on the other side of Lowgate.

The place was empty other than an old man in the far corner with a pot of tea. Coleman ordered two coffees and two bacon sandwiches.

'You can't have eaten, the time it took you to get here,' he said.

He wasn't wrong, but I had questions to ask first. Coleman explained that they'd received a call and he'd been alerted to it by someone at the station. I watched as he bit into his sandwich. I pushed mine away and wondered if I'd ever grow as immune to death as he had. I asked who'd found Millfield.

'The receptionist. She comes in early to open up and sort things out. She saw the light in his office was on and went in to ask if he wanted a coffee.'

'Poor woman.'

Coleman agreed with me.

'Did he leave a note?' I asked.

'I'm told there was one, but I haven't seen it.' Coleman pointed to my bacon sandwich. 'Don't you want that?'

I pushed the plate towards him. 'Go for it.'

He did, wiping away the grease from the side of his mouth.

'I left Millfield a message last night,' I said.

Coleman put what remained of the sandwich down. 'Why?'

'I wanted to speak to him about Andrew Bancroft.' I'd probably never know why Millfield had been forced to witness his death, or what he knew. It didn't feel so important now.

I watched as Coleman processed what I'd told him. He shook his head. 'You can't blame yourself.'

'Easier said than done.' I picked up my coffee and thought about the contents of the letter. I wondered if it mentioned his daughter. Or more accurately, Don's daughter.

Coleman leaned in closer to me, not that anyone was listening. 'He got involved in something way over his head. This thing goes back years. It was bound to be a difficult load for him to carry.'

But he'd done it when I'd been pushing him. I'd been willing to use him to get George Sutherland off my back. What made me think he would have been willing to help me? I'd asked him to open himself up to a world of trouble. My problems had blinkered me to the difficulties he had been facing. But another piece of the puzzle clicked into place. I suspected Roger Millfield hadn't been truthful when he'd hired me. It wasn't his wife's potential affair he was bothered about. He was worried about himself and what might come out and damage his own reputation.

Coleman finished the sandwich and wiped his hands on a serviette. 'So what do you know?'

'Nothing I can prove.'

'Still got your problem with Sutherland?'

'Without doubt.'

'Want to share?'

'Not at the moment.'

Coleman picked up his coffee and shrugged. 'Your call.'

We both knew something had changed, that there had been a shift. A man had died. A man with a family, however fragmented it appeared to be. I watched as Coleman took an envelope out of his pocket. He held it out to me.

'What is it?' I asked.

'One of Holborn's neighbours reckoned she saw a man hanging around the area just before the fire.'

I looked at the e-fit. It could be any number of men, but one name immediately came to mind.

'Recognise him?' Coleman asked me. 'I could have a good guess who it is.'

'Same here.'

Coleman nodded. 'The old guy's back from his holiday. Only just got in touch.'

I put it in my pocket. 'Why are you doing this?'

'Seems like we both need a result.' He put his mug down. 'And I can't be the one asking the questions.'

I put the envelope into my pocket, understanding the point he was making.

I left the cafe and walked back to Millfield's office. A handful of people were standing around outside. I assumed they were employees. Some of them were smoking, some were talking on their mobiles. I was on the opposite side of the road to them. I had no business being with them. I was about to leave when Neil Farr escorted Kath Millfield out of the front door. He stopped when he saw me. He said something to her and walked across to me, pointing. 'I thought you'd have the decency to stay away.'

I was about to say something, but he cut me off.

'I want you to leave Kath alone. Whatever you know means nothing now. Is that clear? It means nothing. The past stays in the past. Leave Kath and Rebecca alone.' His arm dropped as the anger left him.

I stared at Don's name in my mobile, trying to decide whether I should call him or not. How big a coward was I? I knew what I had to do. I pushed the button and called. He had a right to know about Roger Millfield's death. The media would pick the story up soon enough and it wouldn't be right if he heard about it that way. He didn't answer, so I left a message saying he should call me as soon as possible, that it was urgent.

I flicked through to Sarah's number. She answered and was shocked when I told her the news. 'Coleman called me first thing,' I said.

'Have you spoken to his family?'

I glanced at Millfield's office and told her I hadn't. Neil Farr had made his feelings very clear to me. I knew I had to be careful what I told her. I was feeling guilty about pushing Roger Millfield in respect of his involvement with George Sutherland, but long-hidden secrets about his family life were pushing their way to the surface and it was Sarah who was in the firing line. As I put my mobile away, I knew I'd avoided the real issue. I hadn't told her about her half-sister.

I drove east to the house of Reg Holborn's neighbour. Her front door was open before I'd finished locking my car. I walked down the drive to her. 'Can I trouble you for a word?'

She said she'd put the kettle on. I sat down in her living room. It was as neat and tidy as I expected it to be. Family photographs on the wall, a pile of weekly magazines next to a reading chair.

I accepted the mug of coffee and waited for her to sit down before getting straight to the point. The clock was ticking. 'I understand one of your neighbours noticed a man hanging around the area before the fire.'

Her eyes narrowed. 'How would you know that? You said you're a Private Investigator, Not a police officer.'

I told her she was correct. 'I've spoken to Acting Detective Inspector Coleman.'

She shook her head. 'I don't know the name.'

'We've been dealing with Reg's son.' It wasn't a lie, though I hoped she wouldn't be speaking to him in the near future. I told her to call Coleman if she had any concerns.

She let it go. 'You think this man might be responsible for the fire?'

I let her question hang there. She'd told me that Reg Holborn wasn't a smoker. She already had her own doubts about the situation.

She stood up. 'I best take you to see Harry, then.'

'You must be Jimmy's lad, then?' Harry said to me.

'That's right.'

He leaned forward. 'I remember your old man well. I was regular in his pub. I used to love a drink and a natter in the place.' He smiled. 'Your dad was a good bloke. Decent rugby player, too.'

I told him about the display we'd made in Niall's bar from his shirts.

Harry picked up a biscuit. His hand trembled slightly. 'If I was able to, I'd come and have a look. Walking to the old Craven Park from here on a Sunday afternoon used to be one of life's great pleasures for me. We'd all go. Me, the wife and the kids. We'd often stop for a quick drink in the pub on our way. Those were the days, alright.'

His face still had some life in it. I told him that my dad used to take me to games when he could. My memories were similar to his, despite the difference in our ages.

Harry shuffled back in his seat. 'You could have been a great player, I reckon.'

I thanked him for his kind words, but I wouldn't be the last player to have a career taken away by injury. It wasn't important now. I took the photograph of Carl Palmer that Sarah had taken at St Andrews Quay out of my pocket and passed it across to him. 'Was this the man you saw outside of Reg's house?'

He took a long look. 'Terrible business. I was lucky to be away when it happened. My daughter's got a caravan at Bridlington, so I like to get some fresh air when I can.' He passed it back and nodded. 'That's the one.'

I thanked them both for their time and left. I got back in my car and drove the short distance to my dad's pub. I parked up outside and stared at it. In many ways, it looked no different to me. Things were becoming clearer to me now. Reg Holborn's death was down to George Sutherland. Carl Palmer would have been acting on his orders. Sutherland had tried to blackmail him, like he had others who had something to lose if news about Andrew Bancroft's death came out. But something had gone wrong. Maybe Palmer was only meant to threaten Holborn, but Holborn was infirm. If Palmer dropped a cigarette and left, there was nothing Holborn could have done about it. It wasn't enough, though. I had nothing more than the fact Palmer had been seen close to the house. It was useful information and confirmed certain things, but it wasn't proof in itself. I opened my eyes, and taking one last look at my dad's pub, I put my car in gear and drove away.

I checked the time. I was due at George Sutherland's pub. There was no way of avoiding it now. I drove across the city towards his pub. The front door was slightly open. I pushed it open and walked in. There was a middle-aged woman cleaning the bar. Carl Palmer was sprawled across the seating, reading a newspaper.

'You won't find the latest economic news in there,' I said to him.

He put it to one side. 'Glad to see you've still got a sense of humour despite the shit you're in.' He picked up his mobile and made a call.

We waited in silence until Sutherland walked down the stairs and joined us. He stared at me. 'You didn't want a drink did you?'

'No.'

'Good. The till isn't set up yet.' He turned to Palmer and laughed. 'At least we don't need to tell the cunt where the toilet is.'

I let them have their joke. I stared at Palmer, thinking about his dad and what had happened to Andrew Bancroft. I thought about Reg Holborn, too.

'Are you listening, Geraghty?' Sutherland said.

I snapped back to the conversation. 'I'm listening.'

'Good.' Sutherland lit up a cigarette. 'This is the plan.' He outlined it to me. 'I'm getting a van sorted. You and your brother are going to drive it over. Me and Carl will be going over as foot passengers. Once we're in Belgium, you're going to drive to Bruges and pick us up from the train station. Get a map. It's not difficult to find. We'll go and see my supplier, load up the van and then you're driving it back over. He's not happy, so you're going to show your face and apologise if that's what he wants. You're going to tell him you want to put the situation right. I had to fucking beg to get this sorted at short notice, so it's the least you can do.'

'This clears the debt?' I said.

Sutherland laughed. 'Are you taking the piss? You're involved until this is all sorted out. I've got to make it up to my contact over here yet. They're testing me, Geraghty, and if I fail, the deal collapses.' He pointed at me. 'You can work it out. If that happens, I'll hold you responsible. If it gets sorted out, it's likely I'll have some other jobs for you to do, but I'll consider your brother out of the picture.'

I didn't have any choice but to accept the deal. I'd worry about myself later. I nodded my agreement.

Sutherland passed me an envelope with my documents in it.

'My catering contacts have provided the paperwork. You're going over to buy some supplies. It's as simple as that. So far as I can see, you're an unemployed no-mark looking for work. This company, which specialises in continental coffee and shit like that, is giving you a chance. And don't worry about the van. The number plates will check out. It's a piece of piss if you don't do anything stupid.'

'That's it?'

'Peter Hill seems to have fucked off on holiday, so that's it. Have some faith in your own abilities, Geraghty. We don't need him.'

I was no expert in how you went about smuggling cigarettes into the country, even if it was only a relatively small amount in a van, It went way beyond what I could bring into the country for personal usage. Although I was expendable in Sutherland's eyes, I was expecting a bit more of a plan than shutting your eyes, driving through and hoping for the best. He had financial difficulties and was rolling the dice. But there was no other choice.

Sutherland took a long drag on his cigarette and stared at me. He eventually shrugged. 'Plan sounds ok to me.' He stubbed the cigarette out and leaned forward. Palmer threw me a mobile phone.

Sutherland spoke. 'He bought it for cash yesterday. It's pay-as-you-go and unregistered.'

I turned it over in my hand and looked at it. It was basic and functional.

'I've got the same. There's only one number in it. It's under the name Lloyd. Mine says Hubbard.' He smiled at his own joke. They were the two kickers whose battle had been decisive in the all Hull Challenge Cup Final of 1980. Hubbard had kicked his attempts. Lloyd hadn't. Sutherland could obviously sense my reluctance. He passed another envelope over. 'Open that, Geraghty.'

I did as I was told and took out a photograph. I was looking at Lauren standing at the school gate, talking to one of her friends. It was the exact same trick he'd pulled with

Peter Hill. There was no point being angry. I didn't want to show any sign of weakness in front of him. I put it away and told him I'd do what he wanted.

'That's the spirit. You wouldn't want them hurt, would you?'

I leaned across the table, meeting him halfway, unable to check myself. 'You mean like you hurt Don?'

'Don made his choice.'

It confirmed what I knew. Palmer's description matched with what Don's neighbour had given me. It made sense now. I took another chance and stared at him. 'Is that what happened with Reg Holborn?'

Sutherland relaxed into his seat. I knew I'd scored a hit. He didn't take his eyes off me as he spoke to Palmer. 'Fuck off for a few minutes, Carl.'

Palmer stared at me, obvious hatred for me in his eyes. I winked at him, wanting to get under his skin. He eventually stood up and left.

Sutherland spoke. 'I suggest you watch your mouth, Geraghty, before it gets you into serious trouble.'

'I know all about you.'

He lit up another cigarette. 'You know fuck all.'

'You'd be surprised.'

'Can you prove what you think you know?'

I had no answer to that. Sutherland laughed. 'Didn't think so.'

'Did you know Roger Millfield killed himself last night?' I said.

His eyes narrowed before he eventually shrugged. He took another drag on his cigarette. 'Best find myself a new accountant, then.' He stubbed the cigarette out. 'Do you think Don's going to help you out this time?'

'Maybe when he's recovered the beating you had Palmer give him.'

Sutherland sighed. 'You're getting tiresome now, Geraghty.' He leaned forwards and put his hands together on the table. 'Shall I tell you about your precious Don? Don was always a self-righteous cunt when he was in the police. Nobody liked him.' He sat back. 'Especially your dad.'

I felt stuck to my seat, my throat dry. 'My dad?'

'Didn't you know they were acquainted?'

My head was spinning. I knew I was about to learn something unpleasant.

'Do you remember your dad being put in hospital? No doubt you were told it was a punter who got carried away, or some such shit?' He smiled. 'Of course you were.' He jabbed a finger at me. 'Your dad's pub was one of those looked after by Salford. Or it would have been had he just paid up, like he was told to.'

I found myself asking what had happened.

'Holborn would have a quiet word with people who wouldn't play ball, maybe threaten to take a look at their licence. It's not rocket science. Holborn would sometimes take a trusted side-kick with him, someone who could help him out if it got a bit unpleasant. It seems on this occasion, he took Don with him.'

I could barely speak. 'Don?'

'Your precious Don.'

I felt sick. Don had never given any indication that he'd met my dad. I tried to breathe normally.

Sutherland repeated the time he expected me to be back here for to collect the van. 'Don is fuck all help to you now.' He stood up. 'Don't be late.'

CHAPTER NINETEEN

I left Sutherland's pub in a daze. I was still shaking as I got into my car. I needed to stay in control of what was happening. For a start, I only had Sutherland's version of events. I couldn't trust him. Was he telling me the truth about Don and my dad? I punched the steering wheel and screamed before hunching over it, taking deep breaths. It was a waste of energy. I told myself this wasn't helping. I drove slowly across Hull, behind a stream of lorries and tankers heading for the motorway. There was an obvious place to head for.

Niall's bar was already busy. He was definitely going to make a go of it. I was proud of him for that. I was sure our dad would feel the same. He was sitting in the corner, working on his laptop. I walked over and told him I needed a word. We went through to his office. Niall sat down behind his desk. I perched on a corner of it. 'You're not getting on the ferry,' I said.

He looked at me. 'It's all sorted?'

I shook my head. 'I'm still going.'

'I should go as well.'

I walked over to the door and made sure it was shut before leaning against it. 'I need you to keep an eye on things here.'

'I'm not a kid, Joe. You don't need to patronise me with that type of shit.'

I stood my ground. 'I don't want you on that ferry. I've no idea who these people in Belgium are, or what Sutherland has in mind.'

'What are you going to do?'

It was a good question. I told him about the documents Sutherland had given me. I'd photocopied them and posted them to Niall. It was a precaution.

My brother was lost for words. 'It's too dangerous,' he eventually said. 'You can't do it.'

I moved back across the room and sat down. George Sutherland has said it would settle Niall's debt. That was reason enough for now. My own situation would wait.

'Why are you doing this, Joe? It's not your mess. I should be sorting it out.'

The reason was obvious to me. 'You're my family. You're all I've got.' I was prepared to trade off my past with Dave Johnson for their futures. It was as simple as that. 'I've got nothing to lose.'

'You've got Sarah?'

'I haven't got Sarah.'

'You could have if you wanted.'

I shook my head, telling him he was wrong.

'I don't think so.' He smiled. 'I'm your big brother. It's my job to know these things.'

It didn't matter whether he was right or wrong about Sarah, I knew of things that couldn't be spoken, things that would sit there like a cancer in me before inevitably rising to the surface. Some secrets always come out, like the one Kath Millfield and Don had been carrying for decades.

I changed the subject. 'Do you remember when dad was attacked at the pub?'

He was surprised by my question, but he said he did remember. 'Day after the Challenge Cup Final? That's why I remember it. Me and you out on the field behind the pub, replaying the game? Do you remember that?'

I did. George Sutherland had reminded me of it, but it wasn't a day I was going to forget in a hurry.

Niall continued. 'All I really remember is dad refusing to go to hospital. Mum had shouted at him, but he wouldn't budge.'

'Do you remember seeing people hanging around the pub?'

'There were always people hanging around.'

'Out of place people?'

He blew some air out and shook his head. 'I was only a kid, really. I wasn't really looking.'

It was what I expected him to say. He asked me why I was interested. I told him what Sutherland had told me.

'Protection money from dad's pub? I can't see it.'

I took my brother's point. The area was hardly a crime hot-spot, but it would have been easy pickings. 'It could be bullshit,' I said.

'But you don't think so?'

I shook my head. It all fitted. That was the bottom-line.

'I was always told it was a drunk with a grudge who did it, jealous of dad's success.' Niall paused for a moment. 'He changed after the attack, didn't he?'

'Definitely.'

'He was a shadow of himself.'

I didn't need to say I agreed. It was a fact.

'I know I've never said it, but dad would be proud of you. You know that?'

I hoped that was true. 'I need you to do one thing for me.'

'Name it.'

'I need you to keep an eye on Connor, too. He's going to make it, you know. He'll have that club night up and running before you know it. He just needs a bit of a support. That's all.'

He nodded to me as I left.

I'd missed three calls from Coleman. I returned to my car and called him back. He answered immediately. 'We need to talk,' he said. 'Do you know the pull-in on the road to Paull, down the side of BP?'

I told him I did. It wouldn't be hard to find.

'Can you come now?'

The traffic as I crossed Hull was light. I passed the prison and wondered what Johnson was doing. I wondered if he was counting down the days until he was released? I didn't want to think about it. The landscape thinned out. BP Saltend loomed large on the right hand side, a tangle of piping and cooling towers. I turned off the main road and looked for Coleman. He was easy to spot. I pulled my car in alongside his and stepped out. He was leaning against the bonnet, staring out across the patchwork of fields which led across to the village of Thorngumbald. It was desolate. A single car made its way towards us, coming from the direction of Paull.

Coleman lit a cigarette. 'I was waiting for you before I started another one.'

I smiled. 'You'll have a habit if you're not careful.'

'Least of my problems.' I watched him take another long drag on his cigarette. 'I've been talking to Johnson.' He jabbed it out in front of him at the field. 'Andrew Bancroft's out there somewhere.'

'I know.'

Coleman blew smoke in my face. 'You know?'

I qualified my comment. 'Not specifically, but I've spoken with someone. Buried alive, they said.'

Coleman winced. 'Poor bastard.' We stood in silence with our thoughts until he finished his cigarette and threw it to the floor. 'Johnson was suitably vague about what he knew. He can't pin-point it exactly, but he's out there somewhere between Paull and Thorngumbald. We know there was an outhouse of some sort. I'm sure someone cleverer than me can figure it out. Obviously Johnson wasn't there on the night in question. He's sticking to his alibi on that one.'

I looked out to the fields and thought about it. 'Five miles or so between the two villages?'

'Something like that.'

It wouldn't be too hard to find the right area. If there had once been a building, the details would have to be recorded somewhere. That said, I didn't envy the police the task of trying to find the body. 'What happens next?'

'It'll become official.'

I knew there was something I had to do before that happened. 'I need to speak to his mother.'

'You want to deliver the death message?'

'I made a promise.'

'You best do it straight away, then.'

I told him I would.

'And she best look surprised when I come knocking on her door.'

'I don't think it will be a surprise to her at all.'

Coleman shook his head. 'Probably not.'

I felt like asking him for a cigarette. The news about Andrew Bancroft's body wasn't surprising, but it still shocked me. 'Did you tell Johnson about Roger Millfield?' Coleman said he had. Millfield had been his best card to play. Millfield would have to back up his story and cut a deal of his own with the police. He obviously wouldn't be doing that. That only left Alan Palmer who knew the truth. Who would take the word of a man with a criminal record and a drink problem? Letting the police know about the body was Johnson's last move. I found myself pacing around in a small circle. I asked Coleman about Holborn's death.

'Nothing to report.'

I stopped pacing. 'Nothing?'

Coleman pushed himself off the bonnet of his car and told me to calm myself down. 'Give me something, Joe, and I'll make a noise with it.'

I had nothing. Holborn's neighbour wasn't able to say anything more than he'd seen Palmer hanging around the area. 'It was George Sutherland's handiwork.'

'Can you prove it?'

'No.'

Coleman took out his packet of cigarettes and toyed with it in his hands before putting it away again. 'I was hoping you would give me better news than that.'

'You need something else to pin on Sutherland so you've got the time to work on tying him up to Bancroft and Holborn?'

Coleman nodded. 'There's no chance of making what we've got stick.'

'How about cigarette smuggling?'

He shrugged. 'If he was caught red-handed.'

I told Coleman what I was doing. He looked at me like I was mad. 'You're prepared to sacrifice yourself for your brother and nephew like that?'

'They're all I've got.'

'You understand what telling me this means, don't you?'

I held his stare. 'You might want to talk to a guy called Peter Hill.'

Coleman took out his cigarettes again and lit one this time. He shook his head and turned away from me.

I headed for Bancroft's mother's house. As Coleman had said, no one wants to deliver a death message, but I'd made a promise. I was going to see it through. I pulled up outside and took a deep breath before knocking on her front door. When she opened it, she had a coat on, ready to go out. I told her I needed a word and followed her back into the house.

'Gary's been attacked,' she said. 'He's in hospital.'

I wasn't surprised by the news. I asked when it had happened.

'Last night. They've only just got a telephone number out of him.'

'What did the police say?'

'Not much. Only that Gary had been attacked outside of his house and found by a neighbour.' I made sympathetic noises. I was genuinely upset for her. Gary Bancroft was harder to feel sorry for. George Sutherland had caught up with him. Or more likely Carl Palmer. It had to be. They'd obviously found out that he'd been speaking to Alan Palmer. Her face gave nothing away. It was another incident in a long line of them for her.

'I know Andrew's dead.' She held my stare. 'I'm not stupid. All these years have taught me there's no point pretending otherwise.'

I told her to sit down and asked if I could get her anything.

She shook her head and continued. 'It's the fact you can't say goodbye which gets to you. The uncertainty of not knowing. Of not being able to hold a funeral and draw a line under it. That's what eats away at you. There's always a chance, that possibility of hope, but trying not to let yourself feel it.'

I sat down opposite her. Whatever had happened with my dad, whatever the truth of it, I knew I had to be grateful for not being in this woman's shoes.

'I've been told I should move on, but how can I? I've got Gary, but you've seen him. He's no son to me.' She paused for a moment. 'Have you got family?'

'A brother.'

'Do you get on?'

'Most of the time.'

'You should make it all of the time, then.'

I smiled. She wasn't wrong. 'Live with the living,' I said.

'Exactly.' She shuffled forward in her chair and told me to say whatever it was I'd come to say.

I left Bancroft's mother sitting in her chair. I knew she wanted to cry, but that she didn't want to do it in front of me. There was nothing more I could do for her. The police would contact her soon enough, and I assumed, start the search for the body of her son. I thought about what I'd said to her. You had to live with the living. Maybe that made some sense if you knew what had happened to the dead. I looked at her house one last time before driving away. I had a visit to make which I couldn't avoid any longer.

I stepped back when Don opened his door to me. He wasn't pleased to see me. He was dressed in his whites, ready to go to his bowls club. 'Your game will have to wait,' I said, pushing past him. We went through to his living room and sat down. He stared at me, saying nothing. My mouth went dry and I shuffled in my seat. The silence between us was uncomfortable.

'I assume you know about Roger Millfield?' I said as an opener.

He nodded. 'What happened?'

'He was found this morning in his office,' I said, making sure he was looking at me. I wanted to see his reaction. Don was visibly shaken by the news his friend had taken his own life. I didn't spare him the details. He walked across to his drinks cabinet.

'Bit early for that,' I said.

Don poured himself a drink regardless. He lifted his glass. 'To Roger.' He swallowed it and put his glass down. 'I assume you've got questions?'

I had plenty. 'You knew George Sutherland was blackmailing him? It was nothing to do with his wife having an affair.'

Don nodded. 'He wouldn't tell me why. I didn't want to know the details.'

'You knew though, didn't you? He was coming for him because he knew the truth about Rebecca.'

'I suppose I wanted a shot at George Sutherland, too. I knew what had happened to Andrew Bancroft, but I couldn't do a single thing about it. That's the kind of thing that stays with you, like a wound that refuses to scab over.'

Fine words, but they felt empty to me. 'Why didn't you do something about it? There must have been someone you could have spoken with?'

'I was dealing with powerful people. They were far more powerful than me. They would have squashed me.'

'You turned a blind eye?' I could feel the anger rising in me. 'You made a habit of that during your career, did you?'

Don stared at me. The look on his face said he wished he was twenty years younger so he could take me outside. The mood I was in, I would have accepted. I wanted nothing more than to hit him, but if I hit him once, I wouldn't be able to stop.

'I didn't turn a blind eye,' he said. 'I did what I could.'

'Are you sure you did all you could, Don?'

'Going to hit an old man, are you?'

My hands had bunched into fists. I took a deep breath and told myself to get a grip. What was I doing? I paced the room.

Don held out the bottle to me. 'You could use a drink.'

I shook my head. 'I thought we were friends?' It sounded pathetic as it left my mouth. I should I have said I thought we were family, that he was the one man I truly admired and looked up to. He was the man I thought had more integrity than any other I knew. He'd been a second father to me, which was ironic given the situation.

'Things change, Joe.' He poured himself a drink and sat down. 'People change.'

'I thought you were better than this.'

'I try to be.'

'You never mentioned you'd been in my dad's pub with Holborn.'

We stared at each in silence. It was out there now. The room felt much smaller and hotter. He was definitely shaken.

'You weren't meant to find out about that,' he eventually said.

I waved the comment away. 'What happened, Don? What the fuck happened?'

'I wasn't involved.'

'Don't lie to me.'

'I wasn't involved,' he repeated.

'You turned a blind eye.' I jabbed a finger at him. 'Again.'

'Who told you?'

'Sutherland.'

'You should have asked him for the full story.'

'Why don't you tell me it, then?'

Don sighed. 'Are you going to believe what I tell you?' I had no answer to that, so he continued. 'Reg Holborn took me to your dad's pub. I assume you know exactly what Holborn was?' I said I did. 'He was there to give your dad a warning. He owed protection money to Salford, but he'd refused to pay. Holborn was as corrupt as they come. He was on a percentage, so he went along to make sure your dad got the message the police wouldn't help him.'

I cut him off. 'But why were you there, Don? What possible reason did you have for being there?'

'Because Holborn had a little gang. You were either with him or against him. He wanted to see which side of the line I stood on.'

'And which side were you on, Don?'

It was Don's turn to point. He thrust a finger at me and told me to watch my step. 'I did my job properly. I wanted nothing to do with Holborn and his people.'

'So why didn't you report what you'd seen?'

'People like Holborn were too powerful around the station.'

I laughed. 'That's it? You threw in the towel, even though he was corrupt? What about people like my dad?' I found myself shouting. 'To all intents and purposes, the kicking he took killed him.'

'I'm ashamed, Joe. I was ashamed then and I'm ashamed now. That's the truth of the situation. I made an enemy of Holborn. I thought if I found out the truth about Andrew Bancroft, I could take him down, and that would go some way to making up for things. I did what I thought was best.'

'You did what you thought was best? It doesn't even touch the sides, Don.' There was nothing else to say. I stared at the man I'd once been close to. That was gone now. I headed for the door before stopping. 'What are you going to tell Sarah about Rebecca? She has a sister she doesn't know about.'

'I've told her,' he said, before turning away from me.

I returned to my car, trying to regulate my breathing. I had no idea what I'd expected Don to say, but the truth was that he hadn't done anything to help my dad. He'd stood there and watched as others had put the boot in. He'd said he'd done what he thought was best. I'd done exactly the same and seen it end badly as well. Did that make me as bad as him? I hadn't told Sarah what I knew and she would know exactly what that made me. I looked down. My hands were wet with tears.

I wiped the tears away on my sleeve and set off for the ferry terminal. I pulled up once I was clear of Don's street. I couldn't board the ferry without speaking to Sarah first. I called her number but it went straight to voicemail. By the time I'd reached the first set of traffic lights, she'd called back to say she would be in a cafe bar on Newland Avenue for the next hour. I was running late, but I knew I had to do it. I took the mobile Sutherland had given me out of my pocket and sent him a text message. I told him I had a family emergency to deal with and that I'd see him onboard the ferry. He wouldn't like it, but I couldn't see that he had any choice in the matter. He was under pressure to make the trip, so there was no chance of him cancelling it. I switched the mobile back off and put it away.

I found Sarah sitting in the far corner of the bar. The place wasn't busy. A handful of students were sitting around writing essays on their laptops. I sat down opposite Sarah. She didn't look at me.

'Why didn't you tell me the truth about Andrew Bancroft, Joe?'

'How could I?'

She eventually put her drink down and stared at me. 'Did you really think my dad was corrupt?'

I wanted to say I'd never given it a moment's thought, but I was done with lying. 'I didn't know what to think. Once I knew Bancroft had been murdered, I didn't know where it was going to lead, or who was going to be implicated.' I paused, trying to find the right words. 'My main concern was for you and Lauren.'

Sarah shook her head. 'I can't believe you even entertained the thought. There's no way he would be involved in anything like that.'

'Did he tell you what happened when he went with Reg Holborn to my dad's pub? Frank Salford was running a police-approved protection racket. My dad received a visit.' I explained how Holborn linked everything together. He was corrupt and had his own team working for him.

'You don't know my dad well at all if you doubted him even for a minute.'

'I had to be sure before I told you about it.' For all the anger I felt towards Don, I knew deep down that he wasn't corrupt. But it was a fine line. 'He was there when my dad was beaten. He didn't stop it.' I didn't need to say anything further. The beating may have been the cause of his death, but there was no way of knowing. Dwelling on it wasn't going to help me. 'I said some bad things to your dad.'

Sarah shuffled round in her chair to face me. 'Maybe you had a right to, but you still should have told me.'

She was right. I had no excuses other than my own cowardice. 'Coleman knows where Bancroft's body is.'

'It's all going to come out?'

'I hope so.' I ordered a coffee and sat in silence until it arrived.

Sarah spoke first. 'My dad didn't give you a job because of what happened in your dad's pub, you know? It wasn't some sort of secret he was using for his own redemption. He had nothing to feel guilty about.'

I held her stare. The thought had crossed my mind. Don must have known who I was as soon as I'd told him my name. I'd met him in a city centre pub and told him about my life. He'd told me my tenacity was impressive and then he'd made me the job offer, subsequently upgraded to a partnership offer, and my life had changed.

Sarah continued. 'My dad took you on because you were good at the job. You were good at finding the truth and giving it to people. You did what was right. He recognised himself in you.'

She didn't need to add anything to that, even though I now knew she was somewhat blinkered to her dad's shortcomings. 'I was trying to protect him, too.'

Sarah laughed quietly. 'From me?'

'From everything, I suppose. I needed to be sure.'

She picked her drink up and took a moment to compose herself. She drank a mouthful and placed it back in front of herself. 'Where did we go so wrong, Joe?'

Her question took me by surprise. 'I didn't realise we'd gone wrong.' My problems were with Don and what he'd done and what he hadn't done. 'If I marginalised you, I did it with good intentions.'

'You should have trusted me,' she said.

'I couldn't tell you what I knew.'

'I'm a big girl, Joe.'

'Even so.'

'Don't patronise me, Joe.'

'I'm not.' I started to explain that it hadn't been my place to tell her what I knew about her dad, that I'd tried to persuade him to do it. It sounded weak and worst of all, I knew it.

'You should have shown some faith in me, Joe, trusted me to help you. I would have done that, you know? I would have kept things separate.'

That was her final word on the situation. Having had her help me with countless investigations over the last couple of years, I knew I was making excuses. There was nothing more to be said. I told her I had a ferry to catch.

'I can't believe you're going through with it,' she said.

'I've got to. As it stands, I haven't got enough against George Sutherland. He'll keep coming back,' I said. 'If I have to make a sacrifice, I will.'

Sarah smiled. 'And that's you down to a tee, isn't it?'

'Maybe it is. What about you?'

'What about me?'

'What are you going to do about Rebecca? She's your sister.'

'And you knew about her before I did.'

She said it with anger. I was going to try and explain why I hadn't told her, but it would sound like more excuses. I knew this would mean things between us would never be the same again. When I started asking why Roger Millfield had wanted Don and not me working for him, I hadn't expected it to be for this reason.

Sarah looked up at me. 'I have no idea what I'm going to do about her, Joe. I have no idea if it's even fair to tell her.'

There was nothing more to be said. She certainly didn't need me to point out the irony of her keeping secrets because she thought it was for the best. I stood up, ready to go to the ferry terminal. 'Take care of your dad,' I said.

As I walked away, I heard her tell me to take care of myself.

CHAPTER TWENTY

I was travelling light. I had no luggage, only the mobile George Sutherland had given me and the Euros I'd quickly changed at the terminal. My problem was going to be boarding the ferry without being noticed. I'd dumped the van and was travelling as a foot passenger. I was expecting a welcoming committee. I bent down to tie my shoelace, but I was really waiting for the group of men behind me to walk past. They were my best bet to offer some cover. I stuck close to them as we walked onboard. To my right was the Information Desk. In front of me, Carl Palmer had his back to me, busy on his mobile. My heart pumped a little faster. I quickly moved to the left and entered a narrow corridor of cabins. I had the key for mine, but I stopped myself. I had to take every precaution I could. Sutherland could potentially convince a ferry employee to give him my details. I had no idea who he had access to. I didn't want to be found yet. I found the nearest toilets and locked myself into a cubicle. It wasn't ideal, but I was staying where I was until the ferry set sail.

I switched the mobile back on and chose to ignore the string of text messages and missed calls from Sutherland. I turned it back off and put it back in my pocket. There was little Sutherland could do about Niall not being on board, but I wanted to totally remove any options he had. Once we were out in the North Sea, I was banking on him being unable to get a mobile signal. I didn't want him communicating with people in Hull.

I waited until I judged it safe to make my move. I took a cap out of my pocket and put it on. It was the best I could do at short notice for a disguise. I walked back toward the Information Desk with a plan in mind. The ferry was congested with passengers. A loop of messages played over the tannoy, advising when the duty free would be opening. A large queue of people had already formed for the restaurant. It was easy to spot the lorry drivers who used the route regularly. Their eyes said they were bored and wanted the journey over with. The bright-eyed tourists chattered excitedly in a variety of languages.

The onboard cinema was open with a film due to start in fifteen minutes' time. I made my way across to the desk and bought myself a ticket. With Sutherland likely to be actively searching for me, this was my best bet. I went in and found an empty seat in the middle of the back row. I could see the door, but it would be difficult to spot me in the dark.

The film was never going to hold my attention, but more importantly, it finished with no disturbances. The ferry swayed slightly from side to side on occasion, reminding me we were now well out of port. It was time to go to work. I made my way to the bar, bought a pint of lager and found an empty table to sit at. A man with an electric guitar strummed over the top of backing-tapes, playing a mix of popular hits. A handful of people were dancing. I didn't touch the drink in front of me. I waited. Ten minutes later, Carl Palmer found me. 'You're here,' he said.

'I am.' I thought about telling him I was ready to be found, but kept my mouth shut.

Palmer picked up the beer mat and wrote a cabin number on it. 'Five minutes.'

I waited as instructed and then walked down the maze of corridors, finding the right deck and cabin. I knocked once on the door and stepped back. Palmer opened it and told me to come in. George Sutherland was sitting in the corner. I looked around the cabin. A small bathroom was next to the door with a bunk bed running against the rest of the length of the wall. Against the other wall there was a chair, desk and mirror. Palmer closed the door behind me.

'Where the fuck have you been?' Sutherland said to me.

'Doing my duty free shopping.'

He sighed and nodded in the direction of Palmer. I felt a blow to the back of my head. It sent me to the floor. Once it was clear it was a warning shot, I slowly stood back up.

Sutherland spoke again. 'Where's your brother?'

'Family emergency.'

I tensed myself for another attack. Sutherland was still processing what I'd told him.

'Did I not make myself clear enough?' he said.

'It couldn't be helped.' I kept the smile off my face. Sutherland was angry, but there was nothing he could do about Niall not being on the ferry.

'I'm not fucking happy about this,' Sutherland eventually said.

Palmer was smiling at me, like he was hoping I'd give him the excuse he needed to hit me again.

'We'll sort this out when we get back,' Sutherland said. We both knew he had no other option but to let it go. 'I suggest you fuck off, Geraghty. We've got an early start in the morning.'

My cabin was the mirror image of Sutherland's. I sat on the bottom bunk. The crossing became increasingly rough as the night wore on. I listened to the rain beating against the porthole and let my thoughts run to other matters. I was pleased I'd managed to speak to Sarah before leaving Hull, even though she wasn't happy with what I'd done. I was sure she understood why I was doing this, even if she didn't agree with my reasons. My relationship with Don was much more difficult to reconcile. I owed him a lot. He'd given purpose back to my life when I'd needed it, but I hated him for turning his back when my dad needed his help. More than anything, I was disappointed in him. Trying to make amends by linking Frank Salford and Reg Holborn to Andrew Bancroft's disappearance wasn't enough. I stood up and walked into the bathroom. I stared at my face in the mirror before running some water. I was still scared for myself and my brother. I was in the middle of the North Sea, heading to Belgium to collect some illegal goods. I wondered what Debbie would make of the situation. Was it justifiable? I washed my face and returned to my bunk, hoping sleep would come. What I was about to do was beginning to feel very real.

I hadn't been able to sleep. I had too much going on in my head. I gave in as the sun started to rise and looked out of the porthole at Belgium. All I could see was the faint outlines of cranes through the mist and half-light. The shower in my cabin was basic, but it freshened me up. There was no reason to hide, so I walked down to the restaurant and bought a coffee. I found an empty table and stared out of the window as I drank. The coffee was bitter and lukewarm, but it did the job. I stayed where I was as the tannoy made a series of announcements for people to return to their vehicles and assemble at various disembarking points. I finished my coffee and walked off the ferry as a foot passenger.

Because Palmer had taken the van onboard, I'd been told to get myself to Bruges and meet them at the station. I found the transfer bus and sat down at the back, well away from the tourists heading to the town for a day trip. Zeebrugge was very much like Hull, a working port with a landscape dominated by freight containers and cranes. As we left the place behind and picked up speed toward Bruges, the scenery changed. Houses lined the road and a steady stream of cars slowed our progress. The bus pulled up outside the station, and as arranged, Sutherland and Palmer were waiting for me. I watched the groups of tourists head in the direction of the town square and canal tours.

Sutherland walked to the back of the van and opened the door. 'Get in.'

'I'll travel in the front,' I said.

'Don't start, Geraghty.'

I did as I was told and got in the back. Sutherland closed the door behind me. He gave Palmer an address to put into the Sat-Nav. We waited for it to calculate the route before pulling away.

It was only a short drive. I wasn't going to see the sights the tourists were heading for. 'Who are we meeting?' I said.

'A business contact.'

'Who?'

'None of your business.'

'How dangerous are these people?

'It's a business deal, Geraghty. That's all.'

I wasn't reassured. Sutherland wanted me there in case a problem arose. I was the sacrifice he'd be more than willing to make. We drove in silence until we pulled up outside a row of industrial units. It was like countless similar ones I'd seen in Hull. The only differences were the language on the signs and the currency on the price lists.

He told me to get out and led the way over. The shutters were still down. There was a steel door to the left hand side of the property which had been reinforced with additional locks. A small buzzer was positioned in the middle of the door. I looked up and saw a CCTV camera staring straight back at me. The lock on the door was released. Sutherland told Palmer to go in first. I was next in line. We walked into an empty space. It was a basic warehouse. In the far corner, stairs led up to an office. The concrete walls were bare, the floor was completely empty. Our footsteps echoed around the room.

We stood in the middle of the floor and waited. Two men appeared from the office and walked down the stairs towards us. They were both around thirty and were wearing battered leather jackets. One was tall with a shaved head, the other one short with blond curls. Both were chewing gum. 'The boss in, then?' Sutherland said to them, confirming what I thought. They were muscle.

The shorter one took a step forward to Sutherland. 'Soon.'

Sutherland was surprised, but continued. 'We're all set?'

The two men spoke to each other, ignoring him.

Sutherland smiled and told them to stop. 'Just English. Don't be getting clever.'

They ignored him and continued talking between themselves. 'Where's the boss?' he repeated. 'I didn't come all this way to be fucked about by you two.'

'I am here.'

We all turned to see a man walk in through the same door we had. He wore the same leather jacket as the other two, but the way they immediately stopped talking and paid attention to him made it very clear he was in charge. He was slightly older than they were.

'I'm sick of being fucked about,' Sutherland said.

The man smiled. 'Shut your mouth.'

'Where are the cigarettes?'

He ignored the question and pointed at me. 'Who is this?'

'The man I told you about,' Sutherland said.

I held the man's stare. I wasn't going to show any fear. He was doing his best to remain nonchalant and in control. 'I do not know him,' he finally said.

Sutherland was flustered, but was cut off from speaking. The Belgian wasn't interested in hearing from him. He pulled a gun from the inside pocket of his leather jacket and pointed it at me.

I took a step back, unable to keep myself in check. It took all my courage to stare directly at it. If I had to die, I was going to face it head on and look it straight in the eye. I wasn't going to let the man know how I scared I felt. He smiled at me before turning the gun at Sutherland. 'I keep saying it, but I do not hear an answer. I do not know this man. Why would you bring this man here?'

'I thought you might want to speak to him.'

'My business is with you, not him.' He pointed the gun at me again. 'I do not know who you are, friend, so I ask you to politely fuck off somewhere else before I do have a problem with you.'

He was the man holding all the cards. Sutherland was going to do as he was told. I didn't need to be told twice to make myself scarce.

I leaned against the outside wall of the building and vomited. I spat the last of it out of my mouth and straightened myself back up. I composed myself and moved quickly towards the nearest road I could see. I walked in what I thought was the direction of Bruges centre before jumping on the first bus which was passing. It wasn't heading directly to the station, but that suited me fine. There was no way Sutherland and Palmer could find me if I had no idea where I was myself.

With the driver's help I eventually made my way back to the station. All I had was my cap as a makeshift disguise, but I made my way to the ticket desk by falling in with other travellers. I was certain I wasn't being watched.

I boarded the ferry in the same manner, huddling together with other travellers. I threw away the mobile Sutherland had given me and made sure the SIM card was in pieces before flushing it down the toilet. I bought a ticket for the cinema, and finding myself a seat in the dark, I kept an eye on the door. I had no idea what had happened in the lock-up after I'd left. Sutherland and Palmer weren't going to be so forgiving this time, not after having had a gun pointed at them. Once the film finished, I put the cap away and headed for the bar. I had to assume they'd settled their differences with the Belgians and the van was loaded with cigarettes. There was no way I was driving it off in the morning. As with the outward journey. I bought a pint of lager, found a table in the corner and waited. It didn't take Carl Palmer long to find me.

He leaned over the table, angry. 'Where the fuck did you go, Geraghty? Shit your pants when he got the gun out?'

'I was told to disappear.'

Palmer straightened himself back up and laughed. 'You pathetic cunt.'

'Just following his orders,' I said. 'I know you, Carl. I know what you are. I bet you were the one shitting himself.'

He shook his head. 'Follow me.'

I smiled at him. 'You can tell Sutherland where to find me. I'm not moving.' I pointed at the window. Night was falling. We'd left Belgium behind. 'I'm enjoying the view.'

'Don't make me lose my temper with you, cunt.'

I relaxed back into my seat. I knew there would be nothing he'd like more than to hit me. 'Be a good lad, Carl, and run along.' I watched as he struggled to control his temper. He left me sitting there and returned five minutes later with Sutherland. He looked as angry as Palmer. 'Why didn't you answer your mobile, Geraghty?'

'Flat battery.'

Sutherland leaned in closer and spoke. 'Don't think you're walking away from this. The Belgian cunts were taking the piss. You should have been a man about it. Carl had to take the van onboard, and that wasn't the plan, was it? You owe me and the debt's mounting after today.' He jabbed a finger at me. 'You're driving it off in the morning.' He straightened himself back up. 'It won't be the last you hear of this.'

I told him he was wrong. 'I did as you asked. I came across with you. They didn't want to talk to me, so fuck you.'

'What?'

I stood up to face him. 'I said, fuck you.'

'Who do you think you're talking to, Geraghty?'

'You might be able to push around people like Terry Gillespie and Peter Hill, but you're not doing it with me.'

Sutherland sneered. 'Those fuckwits? They got everything they deserved. Like you and your brother will.'

I pointed at him. 'Leave Niall out of it.'

'Not a chance. I own you two now.'

I laughed. 'Like you owned your wife? She saw sense and walked away, didn't she?'

'Watch your mouth, Geraghty.' Palmer took a step towards me, penning me in.

'Look at the pair of you' I said. 'You think you're hard men, but you can't organise a piss up in a brewery.' I pointed at Sutherland. 'You've spent your life in the shadow of others, hanging on to Frank Salford because you didn't have it in you to do it yourself.' Before Sutherland had chance to speak, I turned to Palmer. 'And look at you. You're this fucking idiot's sidekick. The way you're going, you'll be worse than your old man soon.'

Palmer launched himself at me, pushing the table to one side. I heard screams as he threw wild punches at me. I retaliated as best I could. As people shouted and tried to get out of our way, glasses smashed on the floor. Out of the corner of my eye, I saw Sutherland walking calmly away from the trouble. Palmer soon had the better of me. I kept wriggling and moving, so the blows glanced off me. I managed to throw a punch which caught him square on his jaw. He staggered back slightly, allowing me to throw another punch which connected with his nose. It was all I managed, as Palmer regained his balance and hit me with a punch so hard I snapped backwards into my chair. The room swam a little. Palmer landed another punch before a number of Security Wardens appeared and pinned us both down on the floor. I felt my arms being forced behind my back before I was roughly picked up and marched away, Palmer's threats fading into the distance.

CHAPTER TWENTY ONE

I walked away from the ferry terminal without looking back. A stream of cars and lorries disembarked and passed me. I put my head down, my face aching from the beating Carl Palmer had given me on the ferry. It especially hurt when I smiled, but it was a price worth paying. Around me, holidaying families were struggling to coaches and cars with suitcases. I heard a car horn sound. I looked around and saw the vehicle parked up outside of the terminal building.

Coleman got out and leaned against the door. He shouted across to me. 'You've got some balls, Geraghty.'

I walked over to him. 'No idea what you're talking about.'

Coleman laughed. 'I assume you need a lift?'

'I was going to get the bus.'

'Get in.'

There was no sign of a bus arriving and I was going to be at the back of the queue. I got in. Coleman pulled away from the ferry terminal building, took a left at the roundabout and joined Hedon Road.

'Where are you heading for?' Coleman said to me.

I thought about it for a moment. 'The office.' It was too early for Queens and I didn't want to go back to my flat. Not yet.

'Sure?'

I said I was. We fell into silence and I stared out of the window as it started to rain. I didn't look as we passed Hull Prison. I didn't want to think about Dave Johnson. I glanced at the docks, knowing the industry was dying, desperately needing the green technology investment to accelerate. The old and the new were rubbing up against each other. It was my Hull in a nutshell.

'It was a clever move, Joe. I'll give you that,' Coleman said. 'So far as I can tell from my colleagues, you took a day trip to Bruges as a foot passenger. There's no trace of anything untoward other than my lingering suspicion you're not really a city-break type of person. Sound about right?'

'No idea what you're talking about.'

Coleman indicated and pulled out to overtake a foreign lorry. 'Can you imagine my colleagues' surprise when they discovered the cigarettes in George Sutherland's van?'

'Must be pleasing to have shut off a supply line?'

'Without doubt. Sounds like they've got some people in Belgium in their sights now.'

'Seems like a result to me.'

We pulled up at the traffic lights on Myton Bridge. Coleman spoke. 'My bet, and correct me if I'm wrong, is that Sutherland put pressure on you to drive that van over, but you weren't so keen.' He paused for a moment. 'You engineered a fight and were escorted off the ferry by their security staff. That would, for argument's sake, mean you couldn't be anywhere near the van when it came to driving it off the ferry. You didn't drive it on, so you would simply deny any knowledge of it. You were a regular foot passenger travelling alone who got into a disagreement at the bar.'

I smiled. 'No comment.' I always knew Carl Palmer's temper was going to be his downfall. Starting a fight with him on the ferry and gambling on being held overnight by the authorities had been my only option.

The lights changed and Coleman headed into the city centre. 'Are you in trouble with the ferry people?' he said.

'I don't think I'll be welcome in the future.'

'I'd say that was a small price to pay. Turns out a guy with Customs received some intelligence and acted upon it. Imagine that?'

I was pleased Hill had sorted it out. If he and Terry Gillespie kept their cool, they'd be fine. 'Have you spoken with Sutherland yet?' I asked.

'I'll get my chance with him soon enough. He's safely under arrest.'

It was all over. 'Did you pick up Carl Palmer?' He'd also been escorted off the ferry when it had docked.

Coleman shook his head. 'We'll find him when we're ready. He won't be far away. I've spoken with Reg Holborn's neighbour. I reckon he'll pick him out of a line-up.'

If Palmer had any sense, he'd talk. He didn't really owe Sutherland anything. He was in deep trouble otherwise. Coleman would soon have enough to bring charges for Holborn's murder. There was no point in Palmer taking the full blame for it. It would probably be enough for Coleman to seal his promotion, too.

Coleman spoke. 'I'll have to ring Holborn's son, too.'

I agreed. I hadn't enjoyed speaking with him, but he was going to have to be prepared for what was coming. It would be embarrassing for him on a professional level, but that would be the least of his considerations.

'What about Dave Johnson?' I asked him.

'He's continuing to help us with our inquiries, but don't be thinking I like it any more than you do.'

There was nothing I could say to that. The man responsible for my wife's death would no doubt be leaving prison earlier than he expected in return for the co-operation he'd given. And I'd helped to make it happen. But Niall and Connor were going to be ok. That was the main thing.

Coleman interrupted my thinking. 'Alan Palmer walked into the station earlier this morning and confessed to his part in Andrew Bancroft's murder.'

'Poor bastard,' I found myself saying. 'It ruined his life.'

'Working for people like Salford often does.'

I said nothing. I knew that was the essential difference between us. Years of police work had hardened Coleman. I was trying to see the good in a man who'd spent his life working as an enforcer for an organised criminal.

'Palmer reckons it was Salford who carried out the murder. All he did was drive Bancroft to the site.'

I asked Coleman if he'd spoken to Andrew Bancroft's mother yet.

He nodded. 'She didn't take it particularly well.'

'She wants to bury her son. That's all.'

'I know she does.'

We pulled up outside the office on High Street. Coleman switched the engine off. We both stared at the building.

'What about Don and Sarah, then?' he said.

'It's history.' It was the way it had to be. I'd had plenty of time to think about it during the ferry crossings. I could try to forgive and forget with Don, but I knew I'd fail. Our friendship, or whatever it had been, was over. Everything about him had been exposed and there was nothing I could do about that. It was for Sarah to decide what happened next between them. We couldn't be as close as we'd once been. Too much had happened.

'You should go into business for yourself,' Coleman said. 'Apart from being too clever for your own good, it's what you do.' He smiled. 'I suppose that's meant to be a compliment.'

I opened the car door, ready to leave. 'I put the photos of Andrew Bancroft in the post to you. I don't want them.' I had no need for them. Roger Millfield, Alan Palmer, George Sutherland. They'd all been complicit in some way. Even Don had. Bancroft's brother had known all along and left his mother with the false hope that her other son might walk back in through the door one day. It broke my heart.

Coleman was right, though. I was good at my job, but it scared me, too. Trouble had a way of finding me and I seemed to welcome it with open arms. It was what I did and I was unable to fight it. It was me and I had to carry the weight of my own bad decisions and culpability with me. Coleman had said I was a lone wolf. He was probably right. I closed the car door behind me and stared at what had once been my place of work. Truth was, I had no idea what was next.

Lightning Source UK Ltd.
Milton Keynes UK
UKOW04f0626081113

220622UK00001B/16/P